Operation
Blackbird

By Ellen Butler

A Companion Novel to *The Brass Compass*

Inspired by true events

Power to the Pen

A Power to the Pen Imprint
PowertothePen@ellenbutler.net

Digital ISBN: 978-1-7343650-3-0
Print ISBN: 978-1-7343650-4-7
Categories: Fiction, Historical Fiction, Spy Thriller

Cover Art by: Power to the Pen

Dedication

To my parents Bill and Marilyn.

I couldn't have finished this book without your help during this insanely busy year.

Chapter One
The Recoleta

Argentina, October 1952

It was merely a glimpse, but, in that moment, memories from almost a decade ago flooded back as if it had happened only yesterday. The pungent scent of gasoline, crackling wood, and black clouds billowing in the air. Screams of terror from women and children trapped inside—only women and children, for the men had already been rounded up and marched off to a camp, the old and infirm shot on sight. Black uniforms of the SS surrounding the burning chapel. Finally, the peppering spray of gunshots, which, at that point, was merciful to those inside. I—on a ridge, too far away to do anything— watching in horror. I could smell the acrid smoke, tasting its bitterness on my tongue. The day's hot breeze only sought to enhance the jagged memory.

The wail of a small child crying for his mother distracted me, pulling me back to the present and away from the terrible memory. The mother snatched the toddler, who was dressed in a sailor suit, by the hand and chastised him for running away from her.

When I looked back, the man had disappeared. My heartbeat slowed and the memory faded. Perhaps it wasn't him. My vantage point was about fifteen yards away. His features had been in profile to me, and he'd been speaking to another person who had been out of my line of sight.

Of course, I followed him. Luckily, I was wearing the new pair of espadrilles I'd purchased at the market yesterday. The rope-soled shoes made little sound as I darted past the extravagant sculptures and marbled mausoleums in the Recoleta Cemetery. He'd been wearing an ocher suit, and I heard dress Oxfords tapping along the tile flag way ahead of me. At the next lane, I turned right and hurried forward, catching sight of a man's brown shoe rounding the far corner. Barely dodging a mourner placing flowers in front of a mausoleum, I received a well-deserved frown and excused myself for disturbing her lamentations. Around the bend, I followed my quarry, only to be caught up short as I practically plowed into a bespectacled, elderly gentleman in a tan linen suit innocently reading the scripture on a particularly ornate angel statue.

"Un millón de perdones!" I gasped.

He mistook my anxiety. *"Con permiso, estás perdido? Puedo ayudarle?"* he asked kindly in a soft Argentinian accent.

With effort, I lightened my features. No, I assured him, I didn't need help; I was not lost. I glanced down, observed his brown Oxfords, and realized I'd been chasing the wrong footsteps. Pardoning myself again, I retraced my path.

I put an ear out for the telltale sound of men's dress shoes. Unfortunately, it was Sunday and the Recoleta was full of sightseeing tourists, and families who had come to place flowers for their dead. Similar to the famous above-ground cemeteries of New Orleans, the mausoleums at the Recoleta were packed tightly together and it was easy to lose sight of someone amongst the ten- to fifteen-foot-high burial vaults. Moreover, many of the visitors had come from church and wore their best dress shoes, which clicked and tapped along the tile avenues.

After twenty minutes of traversing the labyrinth of alleyways, with not another sign of the man, I gave up and asked an elderly nun dressed in full habit if she could point me in the direction of the closest exit. Taking the map from my hand, she used her gnarled finger and drew an easy path for me to follow.

I found myself on a different road from where I'd entered at the busy main gate. A car zipped down the street, but there was little pedestrian traffic. The sun, at its zenith, beat down upon my head and shoulders, and the concrete sidewalk seemed to throw the heat back up at me. My hair prickled with sweat beneath my straw hat, and the cotton of my checked mint green-and-black dress stuck to my back. Parched and desperate for a drink, I spotted a handful of outdoor tables indicating a restaurant and headed straight for it.

Three French doors across the front of the building were open, to allow the breeze to enter. Inside, along the right, a dark walnut bar seated half a dozen diners, and tables were lined up symmetrically from front to back. The open windows, white tablecloths, walnut-paneled walls, and general hum of conversation from the patrons created an open and inviting atmosphere. I chose a small exterior bistro table, beneath a Jacaranda tree, and took the menu from beneath the salt and pepper shakers. A waitress in her mid-forties wearing a chambray dress and a yellow scarf around her neck arrived to take my order. I chose empanadas and iced tea.

The feathery leaves of the Jacaranda fluttered in the breeze, and a purple blossom dropped at my feet. I removed my hat and gently fanned myself with it. Closing my eyes, I allowed the murmur of Spanish conversations to wash over me. I'd been in Argentina for two days, and my ear was now attuned to the language.

The tea arrived, and, using the tiny tongs, I transferred the four cubes of ice from the metal cup into the warm tea along with a twist of lemon. The combined earthy-lemon flavor quenched my thirst, and I reflected upon what I'd seen.

The man must have simply borne a resemblance to the Waffen SS platoon officer who'd helped to carry out the destruction of the tiny farming town outside of Lyon, France, in 1944. The town had been destroyed in retaliation for a successful French Resistance mission which blew up a rail line and killed a dozen soldiers, including an SS-*Sturmbannführer*. Eighty-six people were murdered. I'd been a courier for the team that destroyed the rail line.

Perhaps he had merely been a ghostly vision conjured by my own imagination. After all, I *had* been roaming one of the most famous cemeteries in Buenos Aires. Why my subconscious would have conjured up such a horrible man, I had no idea.

A different waiter—a young man in his mid-twenties wearing black pants and a white shirt—placed a plate in front of me. "*Su empanada, Señora.*"

I thanked him and ordered another iced tea. The outer

shell of the empanada had been cooked to a perfect golden color. I poked a hole in the flaky crust of the crescent-shaped meat pie to allow the steam to escape and to cool down the pie before eating it.

Laughter erupted at the bar area, drawing my attention.

My breath caught.

The fork slipped from my fingers and clattered onto the plate. The noise was overshadowed by the boisterous merriment. Now, instead of fifteen yards, the man stood only fifteen feet away—behind the bar. A shaft of sunlight clearly lit his chuckling features, and recognition instantly flooded my senses. His hair was longer and bushier—steely locks mixed with the dark curls—and ten years of age lined his features. An extra twenty pounds made his frame stockier, but not outright fat; after all, he'd been on the thin side during the war, as were we all. He'd removed the suit jacket, rolled up the sleeves of his dress shirt, and wiped down the bar with a white rag. I supposed he would have been considered rather attractive for a middle-aged man. Knowing the atrocities he'd committed, though, I could see nothing but the monster, even when he smiled in response to a patron's comment.

My tea arrived, brought again by the young waiter.

"Who is that man behind the bar?" I inquired in Spanish.

The waiter barely glanced over his shoulder before answering. "That is Señor Cabrera, the owner."

"He is popular with the customers," I remarked as another round of laughter burst forth. "Has he always owned the café?"

"No." The young man shook his head and put a hand on his hip. "He bought it in 1946. I grew up nearby and remember it was a rubbish street café. Señor Cabrera has made many physical improvements to the place. Now it is a true restaurant. He hired a Swiss chef and expanded the menu to include European dishes, such as the *schnitzel* and *croute au fromage* . . . my favorite," the young man said with pride. "Europeans living in Buenos Aires come often to enjoy a taste of their own food." He placed my empty ice cup on his tray.

The boy seemed quite proud to work at the establishment, and I needed him to continue talking. "It is quite an inviting place. Is Señor Cabrera from Spain?" I peeped at the waiter from beneath my lashes, delivering a tentative smile.

Not immune to my charm, the young man reddened. "No, he grew up on a farm in Mendoza and only came to Buenos Aires in 1945."

"I see. But he speaks other European languages?"

"Oh, yes, French and German, some English. He spent time traveling the continent . . . when he was younger," he said with pride.

Yes, I remember just how well he spoke French as he ordered the women and children into the village chapel before his men set it ablaze.

A patron flicked his wrist at my waiter, indicating he wanted the check.

"You have other customers; I mustn't keep you any longer."

He bowed and retreated.

The perspiration on my neck had dried. I replaced my hat, pulling it down onto my forehead, and shifted my chair further behind the Jacaranda tree trunk, out of the bar's line of sight.

There were a few things I knew — first, Señor Cabrera did *not* grow up on a farm in Mendoza, Argentina. Second, German was his first language, not the adopted Spanish which he spoke fluently. Third, his real name was Helmut von Schweiger, and he was from Reinsberg, Germany — a small farming village west of Dresden. Finally, Helmut von Schweiger looked mighty sprightly for a supposed corpse.

Chapter Two
Unexpected Visitor

The Canon S-II Rangefinder shutter clicked once, twice, and a third time, for good measure. I'd purchased the handy little camera, a gift to myself, before heading out on this trip. Helmut finished his conversation with the barman, picked up a package, and walked to the rear of the restaurant, toward the kitchen. Two days had passed since I'd first witnessed him in the Recoleta. I'd held plenty of mental debates, trying to decide what to do about him. After the first day, I thought perhaps I'd been mistaken, that I was seeing something not there. So, I returned to the café and watched from a bench across the street for almost an hour before Helmut arrived with his wife—the middle-aged waitress—and I knew I wasn't wrong.

I'd contemplated sending another telegram to the office. However, considering I was a bit AWOL and not quite prepared to reveal my location, which would lead to uncomfortable conversations about why I had not returned on the date I'd originally specified, I dismissed the idea. The fact that Helmut might have been put there by my own people also occurred to me. By the end of the war, the Office of Strategic Services was making all sorts of deals with Nazis who were willing to provide intelligence, and, in exchange, agreed to work for the US in other parts of the world. After all, the one thing the

United States and the Nazi party had in common was a fear of the spread of Communism. While Stalin might have been our ally during the war, the Soviets were decidedly our enemy now.

On the other hand, Juan Peron had been sympathetic to the Nazi cause. He allowed many Germans to emigrate before, during, and after the war through Spanish and Italian ports via his "rat lines," established by Argentinian intelligence officers and diplomats. Even if America had not helped Helmut to South America and was interested in having him stand trial, we had no extradition treaties with Argentina. Getting Helmut to a trial outside of the country might be a near impossibility. If Peron had a hand in getting Helmut to Argentina, there was no way he'd allow the extradition.

It would have been easy enough for me to forget I'd ever seen him and continue my travels. I could simply report what I'd seen when I eventually returned home. That avenue was a tough pill to swallow. The following day, I still didn't have an answer but determined some visual evidence might come in handy. Which is why I returned to take photos of the restaurant's name, Helmut, his wife, and the closest cross street.

The espresso was too hot, so I pulled a cigarette out of the pack to have a smoke while it cooled. A lighter flared in front of my face.

The lit cigarette dropped from my mouth.

He caught it before it hit the pristine white tablecloth, perching it in the ashtray.

"Jacob Devlin, as I live and breathe."

"Miriam. Good to see you. Mind if I sit?" He didn't

wait for an answer before sliding onto the metal chair across from me.

It'd been more than half a dozen years since I'd seen him. He pushed a hank of hickory hair that had gained a smattering of silver off his forehead. Newer and deeper lines marred his handsome features, including a pair between his thick brows and around his mouth, drawing it downward.

"It's been a while." Even though every fiber in my body was on high alert, I infused nonchalance into my next question. "What are you doing here in Buenos Aires?"

"I came to see you," he replied with similar insouciance.

"Why?" I didn't bother to ask the obvious question— *how did you find me?* He worked for the same people I did. They probably knew where I was as soon as my feet hit Argentinian soil. After all, I hadn't traveled under an alias. There was no cover identity or disguise. I found it a bit surprising they'd given me five days before sending someone.

Sending Jake was . . . unexpected.

"You've been gone a while." He unbuttoned his suit jacket, crossed one leg over the other, and leaned back in his chair as if there was nothing unusual about his turning up out of the blue. "You were expected back last week."

Not for an instant did I believe his relaxed stance. If I bolted from the table, he'd be on me in seconds. Picking up the cigarette, I drew in a breath, and allowed the smoke to penetrate deep into my lungs. A sense of calm filled me. "I sent a telegram, to explain I'd been delayed," I replied, blowing directly in his face.

He didn't flinch. "You didn't used to smoke. When did you pick it up?"

I shrugged and glanced away from that penetrating gaze. "I found it a useful habit. Did the company send you?"

He grinned. "No, I volunteered."

"And why would you do that?" I asked, sipping my coffee.

"I have a car. Why don't we go for a drive?" He rose, pulled out a money clip, and dropped a wad of pesos onto the table.

I squinted up at him, deciding whether or not to refuse.

"We should speak in private," he explained.

In the end, I acquiesced. Taking my sweet time, I finished the strong espresso, placed the camera in my handbag, and drew in one last drag on the cigarette before stubbing it out. "Lead the way."

He clutched my elbow in a firm grip, as though he expected me to take a runner. I had no interest in running. Like Alice down the rabbit hole, my curiosity only increased as he held the Mercedes door open for me. The leather barely squeaked as I settled the straw purse in my lap, clasping my fingers over it.

"Very nice," I commented. My hand brushed over the supple gray interior.

He didn't respond to my comment.

Once he nosed the heavy black car onto the main street, I asked, "Did the company send you to retrieve me? Is this an abduction? Are we heading to a safe house where I'll be drilled for hours?"

With one hand loosely curved around the wheel, he had the temerity to laugh. "No. I have a job and requested to work with you."

"That's funny," I said without humor. "I specifically asked *never* to work with you."

Chapter Three
Shutdown

Washington, D.C. September 1945

The moment Lily's driver opened the door of the maroon Cadillac, a sick feeling crawled up my throat. Something was wrong. It wasn't the first time my instincts warned of danger or bad news. However, on the previous incidents, I'd been placing explosives along rail lines while dodging German patrols or passing messages under the noses of SS troops. I followed Lily up the stone steps and through the white columns of the Navy Hill building which housed the Office of Strategic Services — headed by General "Wild Bill" Donovan.

Employees walked past us at fast clips. Packing boxes lined the hallways, and the sound of ripping tape blended with the cacophony of voices echoing off the walls. Large bins labeled *BURN* were scattered everywhere. I watched a sergeant stack three more cartons onto a growing pile.

A thin, fiftyish woman named Edna marked a document on her clipboard. "Sergeant, they need more in room 205," she barked.

"What is going on?" Lily asked the question uppermost in my mind.

Edna glanced our way. "Where have you two been?"

"We've just returned from a meeting at the Pentagon," I replied crisply. It's not as though we'd slept late and decided to stroll in at eleven in the morning.

Edna tapped the pencil against her clipboard. "You had better report to your supervisor. Change is in the wind." With that, she disappeared through an open door.

Lily and I hustled toward our offices under General Magruder, Deputy Director for Intelligence. Our clacking heels against the marble floors only added to the overall din.

"Get those files boxed and labeled ASAP!" a young Army lieutenant hollered at a corporal as we strode past another open door.

I noted plenty of open doors, an abnormal sight to see in a building filled with secrets. Lily stepped aside to allow two women, each carrying a carton, to pass by. My thoughts mirrored her concerned expression, and the tautness between my shoulders only increased as we arrived at our office to find a litter of boxes surrounding the three desks that made a U-shape in the middle of the room. Jane, our colleague, crouched on the floor in front of a filing cabinet with the bottom drawer open, practically throwing classified folders into an open box. She had a pencil tucked behind her ear, and her pixie hairstyle was decidedly ruffled—an unusual happenstance for our lithe and always tidy coworker.

"Janie! What on earth is going on?" Lily cried.

Jane stood, straightening her black skirt and pulling down her polka dot blouse. "Truman is shutting us down."

"What?" My brows furrowed. "What do you mean?"

"Orders came down from on high. Donovan is out, and we have ten days to transfer files, shut down, and clear out."

"Everyone? The entire intelligence division?" Lily gasped in disbelief.

Jane shook her head. "Not just the division, the entire kit and caboodle. OSS will be shuttered as of October first. Magruder wants me to remain and help with the transition. You two need to file all your correspondence by close of business Friday and pack up in case they decide to lock us out earlier." Jane slapped a smaller carton onto her desk and placed a dying fern and her coffee mug inside. "There's a memo on your desks explaining what to burn and how to label your files. All boxes must be double taped."

"What does that mean? Are we . . . out of a job?" I asked.

"I can see if Magruder will keep the two of you on for the next few weeks. I don't think it will be difficult, considering everything that needs to be done." She glanced around the walls of jam-packed file cabinets and bursting bookcases. "However, once everything is packed . . . well, ladies, I hate to say it, but it looks like the unemployment lines." She frowned.

"Just like the factory girls losing their jobs to the men returning from war," Lily said faintly, drumming red lacquered nails against her own neatly organized desk.

"I don't understand. Why the rush? What happened?" I stared at the pile of correspondence on my desk, not as neatly organized as Lily's, and wondered if I could finish it all by Friday.

Jane flopped onto her chair and swiveled to stare at the row of filing cabinets along the back wall. "Close the door."

With flick of her wrist, Lily slammed the door shut, leaned against it, and crossed her arms.

Jane rotated to face us. "Rumor has it, the War Department did a whack job on the entire OSS in a report that made its way to the top brass. Moreover, President Truman never trusted Donovan because he was one of Roosevelt's cronies. And you have to admit, Wild Bill did not endear himself to the man while he was Vice President. His brash ways and daring ops either worked spectacularly or became utter flops."

Lily bit her lip. "Oh dear, I was one of those failed ops."

Jane jumped up from her chair. "That's poppycock, and you know it!"

Those of us who'd done time in the field all had horror stories we didn't like to discuss. I'd only participated in half a dozen missions before being pulled out of France after British intelligence identified a double agent. Even though their people eliminated the agent, OSS feared the entire ring had been compromised and shut us down. Afterward, I spent several months in Britain, perfecting other agents' French accents and requesting further missions which never came to fruition. The tides turned in favor of the Allies, and at the beginning of March 1945, I was shipped back to Washington, where I ended up working with Jane. Lily joined us a few months later.

Lily smiled wanly at her friend's outburst. "Just tell me what to do."

Jane glanced at the mess of boxes on the floor and

pressed a pair of fingers to her temple.

I empathized with the action. I had my own headache brewing right between my creased brows. "But . . . I still don't understand. Where will all the intelligence go? Who will run intelligence for the country?"

Jane sighed. "I'm not sure. Magruder's hot-footed off to some of his contacts in the War Department to see what he can do."

Lily sighed, picked up a box, and began clearing out her desk. My personal items were limited to a fountain pen given to me by my grandmother, my handbag, coffee mug, and a small, black, metal desk fan which lazily blew the humid Washington air around. It wouldn't take but a moment to toss them in a carton. Instead, I drew the cover off my typewriter and got to work on the pile of papers.

"Janie, what will you do? Where will you go?" Lily paused her packing and scrutinized her friend.

They'd once shared a tiny apartment on Capitol Hill, where Jane still lived with a charming southern belle named Evelyn. After returning from France, Lily moved into her father's Georgetown home instead of returning to their flat. Lucky for me, because a month ago, my own shared apartment situation became untenable. The growing mice population was bad enough, but when my roommate moved her gentlemen friend, his parakeet, and a rather aggressive German shepherd who liked to chase the mice into the mix, I'd had it. Lily was kind enough to offer me a room.

"I could talk to my stepfather about getting you a job at the State Department," Lily suggested.

Jane closed the bottom file cabinet drawer and

plopped the lid onto the full box. "Perhaps I'll take you up on that offer." She pulled a length of tape across the box top. "Right now, I'll wait to see where Magruder ends up."

He was General Magruder or just "the General" to the rest of us. Jane was the only person in the entire division that called him Magruder or Mac. She'd been with him for the past nine months, and Magruder had developed a soft spot for Jane. He treated her as a favored daughter and likely realized he couldn't do without her calm efficiency. Her manner was cool, but friendly, and her tiny frame was always dressed neat as a pin.

In contrast, Lily was a striking beauty. She could have graced the silver screens of Hollywood. I rounded out our trio. The only blonde in the group, taller than my coworkers, I was often referred to as statuesque. Jane was pretty in a plain sort of way, allowing her to fade into the background at will. She would have made a magnificent spy, and I knew from her manner that she had the nerves to handle it. However, I doubted Magruder would have ever allowed her to leave his office. Undoubtedly, wherever the general ended up, Jane would be right by his side, keeping him organized and in line.

"What will you do, Lily?" I asked, pulling the paper from the typewriter and placing it in a file folder.

"I don't know. I suspect I'll spend time planning the wedding. What about you, Miriam? Do you need a job, or will you return home?"

Mentally, I shuddered at the thought of returning to my family home. "No," I quickly replied, "I'll need to find another job and would be grateful if your stepfather can help."

My mother was the only one still living in the drafty, old Victorian homestead—though she had a girl to cook and clean three times a week. My father died of a heart attack when I was four. He and his brother ran a real estate business, and after he died, my mother went to work for Uncle Joe as a secretary and eventually became the firm's office manager. My maternal grandmother came to live with us, to help raise Fred, my older brother, and me.

Cancer stole my precious Gra-mere the year I turned fifteen. Three months later, Fred, Mother's favored child, headed to Penn State. The emptiness had been quite an adjustment for the Becker household. My mother's feelings toward me could best be described as tolerant. She was never outright cruel, but neither was she warm and affectionate the way she'd been with my brother. *He* was *her* cherished pet, while *I'd* been Gra-mere's pampered child.

When Mother wasn't working at the real estate office, her favorite hobby seemed to be pointing out all my imperfections. She thought she was being "helpful." I wasn't an unruly child, but I'd certainly bucked against her "kind" suggestions, from clothing, to hair, to the way I ate my roast beef. I, in turn, began nitpicking at everything she did "wrong" or different from Gra-mere, because I knew it would hurt her to be compared to her genial and loving mother who'd spent more time with me than she did. Without my grandmother playing interference, or Fred around for Mother to fawn over, our communication turned aloof, bordering on stilted.

Though we'd had a contentious childhood, in later years our relationship matured, and I'd longed for my brother, desperately looking forward to the holidays when he returned for visits. His junior year, he left college to join the Army. I finished high school and followed his lead by joining the WACs. When I'd told my mother what I'd done, a stricken look crossed her face, and, for an instant, I thought she might try to talk me out of it. Instead, she simply smiled and told me I was old enough to make up my own mind and to "enjoy myself." As if I'd announced I was going to summer camp. My fluent French, thanks to Gra-mere, and my fearlessness during training brought me to the attention of the Office of Strategic Services.

I didn't know what I would do once OSS was shut down, but I knew returning to the frigid bosom of my mother's arms was not in the cards.

Chapter Four
Wedding Dresses & Fiancés

Washington, D.C., October 1945

"Oh, Lily, it's simply stunning," I murmured in awe.

The wedding dress had been cut into a flattering sheath which highlighted and hugged Lily's hourglass figure. The deep V in the neck stopped just above what would be considered cheap or tasteless. Crystals accentuated the collar, narrow sleeves, and the hemline, which dusted the floor and flared into a small sweep-length train—sheer elegance.

I circled my friend, admiring the feel of the material along her arm. "Where did you find the fabric?" Even though the war ended, materials like silk were still difficult to come by.

Lily grinned, adjusting the sleeve. "They came from my mother's two wedding gowns. The crystals and satin sleeves were from her first marriage to my real father. The silk came from her second dress when she married my stepfather. Edward dug them out of the attic the day I returned from Europe and told him I was engaged to Charlie." She glanced lovingly at the ruby engagement ring.

Like me, Lily had lost family. Her real father, Martin St. James, died when she was a baby, and Lily claimed she had no memory of him. Her mother, Maria, passed before the war. Her stepfather, Edward Jolivet, was an undersecretary at the State Department.

Finished pinning the hem, the seamstress rose from her squat position. "That should be fine." She ran her calloused fingers along the waistline. There wasn't an inch to spare. "You must keep your figure trim. There is very little material to let out," she admonished.

Lily laid her hand in the seamstress's outstretched one and stepped off the platform. "Genevieve, you have worked a miracle! What would I do without you?"

"Gone naked, I assume!" Genevieve jested.

We chuckled, and I resumed my seat as the seamstress swept the changing room curtain closed.

"What are you wearing for your wedding to Hugh?" Lily asked.

I flipped through one of the many fashion magazines scattered across Madame Genevieve's coffee table. "Oh, one of my suits, I suppose."

"Not a suit!" Lily cried. "Oh, you mustn't wear a boring suit."

"Well, my mother has not-so-subtly offered up *her* wedding gown. Satin with lace overlay from head to toe. She's even got a dreadful lace cap." I shuddered at the thought of the waistless sack so popular in the twenties.

Lily's arms went up and her voice became muffled as the seamstress drew the dress over her head. "Have her post it. I'm sure Genevieve can work her magic with your mother's gown and what's left from my mother's. Can't you, Genevieve?"

"But of course. When is the wedding?" Genevieve asked.

"We haven't set a date. I am waiting until Hugh

returns from Europe. We'll make plans after that," I replied, flipping the page.

"I've forgotten, where is your home?" Lily asked.

"Lancaster, Pennsylvania." I tossed the magazine aside and picked up another. "In his last letter, Hugh wrote that he expects to be home in a month or two. Before New Year's Eve." Even though I spoke with casualness, I got a secret thrill thinking about his return. I couldn't wait until the holiday season when the city buildings would be decked with garlands and Hugh would be at my side. Perhaps we would go ice skating.

My friend stepped out from behind the curtain, buttoning the sleeve of her cream blouse. "Same with Charlie. He's promised October, but I wouldn't be surprised if it's November. Wouldn't a Christmas wedding be lovely?" Her eyes sparkled as she pulled on a peplum jacket that matched her cerulean blue skirt. She plopped into the chair next to me and grabbed my hand. "I can't wait to meet your Hugh."

I gave her hand a squeeze. "Me too."

Three weeks had passed since news of the closing had been delivered. True to his word, the president shuttered the OSS, lock, stock, and barrel on October first. General Magruder had friends in the War Department and stayed on to preserve the Secret Intelligence division, which was absorbed by Defense and was now called the Strategic Services Unit. We got the story from Jane, who, as I predicted, moved with Magruder across the river into the sprawling concrete walls of the newly built Pentagon building.

After October first, Lily turned the wedding planning

into a priority. However, even though Lily's marriage plans were of utmost importance to her, she couldn't seem to give up the job . . . yet. Her stepfather found positions for the two of us at the State Department. We had three more days before our new jobs began. Lily took full advantage of the few free moments left.

A crisp October breeze dislodged my hat, and I held onto it as we walked two blocks up M Street to our favorite French bistro. I'd fallen in love with the *Croque Monsieur*, prepared exactly the way Gra-mere used to make it.

"I'll have the *Croque Monsieur* as well." Lily handed the menu back to the waiter. "You haven't told me much about your beau."

A soft smile spread across my face. "I've known Hugh since I was in pinafores. He and my brother were thick as thieves growing up. They were roommates at Penn State. Hugh had always been friendly enough, but he simply thought of me as Fred's silly little sister. The year I turned fifteen, my grandmother passed."

"I'm so sorry," Lily murmured with sympathy.

"After the funeral, Hugh found me crying behind the old oak tree in our backyard. He drew me close, whispered soothing words, and gave me his handkerchief. When I ceased my impression of a watering pot and dried my tears, I found him staring at me as though he was seeing a completely different person. I remember he said, '*Why, Miriam Becker, when did you get so grown up?*' Hugh stole his first kiss from me behind that tree." I gently touched my lips, remembering the moment Hugh Whitman finally returned the affection I'd felt for him since the age of twelve.

I paused my story as the waiter cautiously placed our full-to-the-brim martinis on the table.

"Do go on." Lily plucked out an olive-loaded toothpick and bit down.

"Hugh came home from college during the holidays, and we'd spend as much time as possible together. When he was away, we wrote letters. I still have all of them packed neatly in a wooden box he made for my birthday. We talked about getting married after he finished college. Then the war came. Two days before shipping out, he proposed, and I promised to wait for him." I fingered the filigree ring with a round-cut aquamarine. "This was his grandmother's."

Lily sat back, sipping her cocktail, and glanced at me with an impish grin. "So, you've been waiting for Hugh since you were a schoolgirl."

I shrugged. "There was nothing to do *but* wait. Sometimes it feels as though I've been waiting for Hugh all my life."

"And I thought my situation was tough, waiting for Charlie." She lifted her drink in salute. "To women who wait for their men."

"I'll drink to that." I tapped her glass with mine, spilling some over the rim.

"What did you tell him about your work during the war?" Lily blotted the table with her linen napkin.

"He knew I joined the WACs, and he believes I worked as a translator for Supreme Allied Command in London."

"Do you think you'll ever tell him the truth?"

Surprised by her question, I studied the red lipstick mark on her martini glass. We'd made oaths to keep our government's secrets. If the OSS hadn't just shut down, and, if it hadn't been Lily, I would have wondered about her motivation for asking the question. I would have wondered if she was trying to entrap me into admitting something that could be used against me. I didn't like to think about the horrors I'd witnessed during my time in France, but they occasionally woke me in the middle of the night—drenched in sweat, my heart hammering, mindless fear coursing through my veins.

Do I lie or tell the truth? I opted for honesty.

"Maybe one day." I sighed, watching a young mother cross the street, holding her toddler's hand in a tight grip. "But not for a long, long time. When the war is but a distant memory, a speck of time in our lives. When the secrets we keep are too old to matter."

A few hours later, we arrived back at Lily's home.

"I'm tuckered out." Lily removed her hat, tossing it next to the handbags we'd placed on the foyer table. "How about a game of gin rummy?"

"A penny a point?" I wiggled my brows in a coaxing manner, knowing Lily's competitive spirit and my own card-playing prowess.

"You're on."

"I've got a new deck of cards." I mounted the curved staircase. "I'll go up and fetch it."

"Bring them to the parlor. I'll make us spritzers."

Doris, the white-haired housekeeper, chugged out from the green baize door at the far end of the foyer, wiping flour-dusted hands on her apron. "There you are, miss. You've got company. A handsome Army gent." She winked and smiled. "I put him in the parlor."

Doris's announcement halted my upward motion.

Lily put a hand to her heart, drew in a breath, and her eyes rounded with excitement.

I knew the moment the dark-haired Army officer stepped out of the parlor that this man was *not* Lily's fiancé, Charlie McNair. I froze on the stairs as a sickly sinking feeling, once again, came over me.

"Jake!" she exclaimed. "What on earth are you doing here?"

The soldier took her hands. Lily kissed his cheeks and looked anxiously past his shoulder.

He shook his head. "He's not with me. He got stuck in New Brunswick, but he will be here in four days' time. He asked me to give you this." Jake pulled an envelope from his pocket.

Lily snatched the letter from him, and he chuckled at her enthusiasm. A step creaked as my weight shifted.

The pair glanced up as one and Lily's animated gaze shone upon me. "Miriam, come and meet a good friend—"

"Jacob Devlin." I took the stairs one tread at a time as my heart pounded and my breathing shallowed. "It's been a long time."

The smile slid from his face and his bearing stiffened. "Miriam, you're looking well."

I couldn't return the compliment. He looked thin. Without the smile, his cheeks were sunken and his face drawn with fatigue. And there was something else in his expression that I couldn't put my finger on.

"You two know each other?" Lily asked with a brow

raised in curiosity.

"Jacob was a friend to my brother ... and Hugh, growing up," I explained.

"I was sorry to hear about Fred." His tone matched the solemnity of his demeanor. "I understand it was at the Battle of Chambois."

I swallowed the rising panic and nodded.

"Jake," Lily said in a quiet tone, her earlier excitement gone, "what are you doing here?"

He glanced between the two of us and rubbed the back of his neck. "Maybe we should sit down."

Lily took in Jake's pensive expression. "Yes, I think maybe we should. I'll pour us drinks. Why don't we all retire to the parlor?"

I wasn't having it.

I needed to know now.

Right now.

"Hugh?" My voice trembled.

"Miriam ..." Jacob stared down at his shiny black shoes; his shoulders slumped forward. "I'm sorry."

"Oh, Jake, no ..." Lily fiddled with her letter, a pitying expression on her face.

"How?" I whispered. *The war is over! How can this happen?*

His sympathetic gaze returned to mine. "Hit by a troop transport. The corporal behind the wheel was drunk."

My body felt detached, as if I was floating. I didn't seem in control of my own limbs. "I think ... I'll have that drink now," I spoke in a silly, high-pitched voice.

"Yes, of course." Lily reached out to take my elbow,

to guide me into the parlor.

I didn't make it.

Jake was fast enough to catch me, as I collapsed into a sobbing heap at the base of the stairs.

Chapter Five
Bittersweet Resolutions

Argentina, October 1952

"That's funny. I specifically asked *never* to work with you."

Jake drew in a breath, and the only thing I could hear was the rumble of the powerful engine. He pulled off the main road and wound his way into the suburbs. Brick and stucco walls surrounded homes of upper middle-class residents. The walls reminded me of those I'd built around myself after Hugh's death. Walls that had held me intact and allowed me to continue to wake up in the morning. To continue to do my job. Some days ... to breathe.

Jake remained silent, and the guilt set it.

"I'm sorry. That was unkind . . . and many years ago." I stared at my ringless left hand. "You see, I was angry with you."

Jake's jaw flexed and his Adam's apple bobbed as if swallowing a retort.

"No." I shook my head. "Not for his death. I know you were nowhere near him when it happened. It may be difficult for you to understand . . ." I paused, trying to decide how to explain the utter devastation I'd felt when he'd given me the news that the man I'd loved since the age of twelve was dead, and I would not be planning our wedding, but rather his funeral. "You know my grandmother died at the beginning of the war?"

He grunted an acknowledgement.

"Then we lost Fred. But Hugh . . . Hugh made it through the war." I stared out the windshield, watching a little boy in dungarees play jump rope on the sidewalk. "We both did. I thought it was providence. All the pain and loss in my life would be righted because Hugh made it through the war unscathed, and we were to be married. And then . . . on that fateful day in October . . . after the end of the war . . . in the foyer of Lily's home . . . there you stood, all in one piece, delivering the worst news of my life." I stared at his profile. "I was angry at both of us . . . for being the ones to live."

Jake's fingers clenched tight around the steering wheel. He pulled the car to the side of the road and jammed the gear into park. "I can assure you," he ground out, "I asked that question often during the war. Why that corporal or this lieutenant? Why not me?"

I nodded with understanding. "Yes. There were times I felt the same way." Staring blindly out the windshield, I continued, "I have often thought about that day. Why couldn't it have been a stranger—like it was for Fred? Some faceless man from the War Department . . . or a boy from the telegram office? A person who didn't know Hugh. Didn't know me. A nameless stranger I could despise for giving me the worst news of my life. Why you? The last of the three musketeers?" I tried to keep the bitterness out of my voice when I spoke.

He turned to face me. "I did it because I thought it was what Hugh would have wanted."

"Yes. Of course." My head ducked in shame. "I know

that now. I know the resentment I felt was baseless—merely a tool of my grief. It was dreadfully unfair of me. I do apologize. I stopped being angry over Hugh's death a long time ago." My fingers shook only slightly, as I pulled out a cigarette and lighter from my purse. "I didn't think we should work together because . . . well . . . because I thought it would be too painful. The memories . . ."

"Miriam, I'm sorry." His voice wavered, and he cleared his throat before continuing, "Hugh . . . Fred . . . they were like brothers. You . . . were family."

Me? Family? Really? How can he say that?

After the funeral, I didn't recall seeing Jake again, except at Lily's wedding, where he stood at the altar as Charlie's best man. Something I'd buried deep inside bubbled to the surface, my face burned, and a brittle laugh escaped. "Do you know what happened to me . . . after the funeral?"

He shook his head; a look of confusion crossed his features.

"No? You got on with your life? Didn't you?" I lit the cigarette.

Jake's jaw hardened and his sea-glass green eyes narrowed in a penetrating gaze. "In a manner of speaking."

Ignoring this telling comment, I continued, "For the first month, I could barely get out of bed to eat or bathe. Lily begged me to leave the house. She said I walked around like a somnambulist—never initiating conversation, only answering when spoken to. Finally, she begged, or bullied, a gentleman friend of hers to take me out—Jerry or John was his name, I think." I tapped a finger to my temple, trying to remember. "It doesn't matter; we'll call him Jerry. We went to Jerry's tennis club for lunch, and he offered to teach me how to play. It felt so good to whack that ball with all my might. I joined the club and started playing every day." The tobacco's calming powers kicked in with the first lung-filling draw. "The tennis pro thought I was a natural. I didn't bother to tell him it was pent-up rage."

I cracked the window to allow the smoke to escape. "I slept with him, and we were a couple for a while. Well . . . as much of a couple as you can be, when one person is in love with your tennis capabilities and the other has gone numb inside."

Jake made a sound at the back of his throat, but I didn't allow him to interrupt me.

"Soon my life became tennis and parties. Did I mention the booze? Pots and pots of booze." I let out a hard laugh that held no amusement. "First, it started as a couple of nights a week. After Lily married Charlie, she moved out of the Georgetown house, of course. Then it was just me, Lily's father Edward, and the housekeeper. A couple nights a week turned into four or five . . . six. Every night, a new club. A new party. Lily knew something was wrong, but she was busy with married life. Charlie got a job at the Pentagon, and Lily continued working at the State Department." I took a drag and tapped the ash outside the window.

"Meanwhile, I took advantage of Edward's kindness. I became the girl everyone knew. Everyone wanted to be with me. A socialite, if you will. I was charming with my brittle smile, yet remote and mysterious. All the boys enjoyed my witticisms. I drank gin and tonics like water. On occasion, I'd mix it up with whiskey, but not before five." I wiggled a finger in front of his face. "That was my rule, no drinking before five. After all, I wasn't a cheap drunk. Eventually, the tennis pro moved on to another woman, and I had my pick of the men surrounding me. Up by noon, tennis, or golf, or a swim. Home at five—in time for a bath and to dress for the evening. Then, cocktails with Budgie, or Harry, or Frank, or, or, or . . . the latest gentleman who was willing to take me to dinner, the theater, a party, until the wee hours of the morning, and then to bed. Sometimes alone. Sometimes not." I turned to meet Jake's scrutiny and delivered the last line. "All to forget."

His mouth flattened, and he held an apologetic palm upward. "I didn't . . . understand. The parties and tennis club, I thought . . ."

I took a drag and let it out as I spoke. "Why should you?"

He shifted to face me and delivered in a matter-of-fact manner, "After the wedding, I phoned and came by the townhouse . . . a few times. You were always 'out' with one of your beaus. I thought . . . I thought . . . you were moving on with your life. I figured being around would only remind you of Hugh and Fred. When you never phoned . . ." He gave a half shrug.

Phoned? Had he? I didn't remember seeing any messages from the housekeeper. On the other hand, there was a time period when I simply crumpled up the notes awaiting me in the foyer. I couldn't be bothered to return phone calls. My new "friends" got used to locating me at the tennis club or knew to phone the house between five and seven. I shook away those thoughts and carried on with my story.

"One night we were drinking champagne, celebrating something . . . I don't recall. I offered to get us another bottle. Approaching the bar, I thought I saw Hugh. From the back"—I pulled at a lock of my hair—"he had the same hair color and stance that Hugh had. You know . . . that lanky slouch with one shoulder dropped lower than the other." I demonstrated. "For a moment, I thought . . . *maybe* it had been a mistake. The military had identified the wrong soldier and Hugh had survived. I touched his shoulder. As soon as the man turned, I realized the mistake was mine."

"Oh, Miriam," Jake whispered with pity in his eyes.

I turned away from his pity. "I don't know how much champagne I drank that night, but I remember the mortification of Edward finding me curled up by the front stoop . . . crying and covered in my own vomit. The following day, when he came to check on me, I asked him why he didn't kick me out of the house, send me home. I'd become a useless human being. He sat next to me and said, '*I was once in your situation. My wife, the love of my life, passed away in '38. I've been where you are.*' Did you climb into a bottle? I asked him. '*No,*' he told me, '*but I almost ruined the relationship I have with my only daughter.*'"

The forgotten cigarette burned low, and, after one last drag, I tossed it out the window. "Then he asked the one question that I'd not bothered to ask myself. He said, '*What would your fiancé think? Is this the life he would have wanted for you?'"* My gaze met Jake's sympathetic one. "I stopped drinking, and a week later, I started work at the State Department."

He digested my soliloquy and allowed the silence to linger. I'd said enough and didn't deign to break it.

He rubbed his chin. "I wish I'd known. Understood the situation better. Maybe I could have helped."

A young couple holding hands crossed the street in front of the car. I breathed deep and counted to ten. It wasn't actually painful now, only a memory of the pain lingered. I exhaled. "Even if you'd tried harder, it probably wouldn't have mattered. I wouldn't have seen through the red mist of anger I directed at you." I sniffed. "Hell, if I'd returned one of your calls, it's likely I would have screamed all my grief at you."

"Would it have helped?"

I bit my lip and shrugged.

Jake drummed his fingers on the steering wheel. "Do you—I mean . . . he's been gone for years . . . are you still . . ."

My brows rose as I watched Jake trying to put his thoughts into words. Finally, I put him out of his misery. "Am I still pining for Hugh?"

He gestured with his hand.

I shook my head and sighed with a tinge of regret for what might have been. "That time in my life is past. Frankly, I wonder if Hugh saw me now . . . would he even recognize me? Much less love me?"

Jake's forehead furrowed as he raked me up and down with his gaze.

"Not physically." I looked in the mirror every day

and recognized the maturation of womanhood on my face, but my body was still fit and slim. Not much different from the young girl Hugh proposed to. "Psychologically. Emotionally. I am not the girl he fell in love with."

"The war changed us all," Jake stated.

My fingers clenched around my handbag, and I stared down at my lap. "It's more than the war. Agency life changed me."

His gaze narrowed. Finally, he said, "I thought when the OSS dissolved, you were out. Why did you get back in?"

"My old officemate, Jane, came to me. Said she needed a socialite." I bit out a hard, ironic bark of laughter. "Little did I know my carousing habits would create the perfect cover. With the spread of Communism, I had an 'in' with people the new CIA needed to keep an eye on around Washington. Doors opened to me. I started as Jane's source, and eventually, she talked me into becoming a full-time officer. Jane can be persuasive like that."

He allowed my response to hang in silence for a moment before finally asking the million-dollar question. "Why didn't you return home last week?"

I fidgeted with my gold lighter, flicking the cover open and closed. "Did you know we assisted Nazis at the end of the war? Sent them right here to South America. They provide intelligence. Secret agents against Communism," I commented offhand.

He didn't respond.

"Men you and I—*and Hugh, and Fred*—fought against

roam free."

He removed the lighter from my hand.

I went on, "I'm not talking about army officers, I'm talking SS and Gestapo. The worst of the worst."

Laying the gold lighter on the dash, he probed, "Is that why you came here and stayed? You're on some sort of quest to—to what? Reveal former SS officers?"

Was that a note of incredulity I heard in his tone? My chin went up, and I countered with asperity, "Not at all. I came down here because I met a Swiss banker in Rio. He enjoys having attractive women on his yacht. He invited half a dozen of us. It just so happens the yacht was cruising down to Buenos Aires."

Jake's brow rose as if to say, *I don't believe you.* "And that is the *only* reason you didn't return? You wanted to take a cruise on Florian's yacht?"

Of course he knew exactly who I'd sailed with. I was tempted to tell him where he could shove his disbelief. After a moment of reflection, my annoyance deflated, and I opted for the bald truth. "I needed more time. My last assignment . . ." I winced and my glance skated away from that penetrating stare.

"I read the file."

"Oh?" My back stiffened and that edge of irritation reflooded my system. *You read a file and think you know?* "And did you see the pictures?"

"No." He shrugged as if the photos held no importance.

My jaw clenched at his insouciance, the pretense that he understood *anything* I'd experienced. My eyes narrowed to slits. "Have you ever had the breath choked out of you?"

His Adam's apple bobbed but otherwise his expression didn't change.

Placing a protective hand to my throat, I continued, enunciating each syllable as if in elocution class, "The bruises have faded, but I will never forget those thumbs pushing deep into my windpipe . . . choking the life out of me. My ears ringing. Lights dimming."

He didn't flinch. "I understand there was an icepick."

I licked my dry lips. "He'd requested a bottle of Campari and club soda from room service. I guess he'd planned to have a nice aperitif after throttling me." Removing the lighter from the dash, I placed it in my purse and said with forced calm, "I really should send a thank you note to the hotel. It was very sharp. It slid into his eye like slicing into Jell-O." My gaze swept up to his as I delivered the last, "I had to apply more pressure to push it into his heart."

Jake winced, and his face paled as he hissed, "Christ almighty."

Finally, I got the human reaction I'd been waiting for since we started this farcical conversation.

"Perhaps *now* you'll understand why I wasn't ready to return." I flipped a lock of hair away from my face.

He examined me with both respect and compassion, but there was also something else in that studied gaze. "Have you lost your nerve?"

Have I lost my nerve? Am I ready to get back into the field?

"You don't need to answer. Not yet, anyway." Jake started the car and drove me back to the hotel — he didn't have to ask where I was staying. Monuments and buildings—defined by their neoclassical architecture—passed by the window. I saw none of them as I stared sightlessly, masticating over Jake's question. Really, the *only* question that needed answering.

I broke the silence as we turned onto the avenue where my hotel was located. "When do you need to know for the operation?"

"In two days."

"Where is it?"

"Berlin."

I knew he wouldn't give me any more information until I agreed to the job, so I didn't bother to ask for details. "My German is a little rusty. I haven't worked there since forty-eight."

"One of the reasons I want you on the op." The car slid to a halt beneath the hotel's portico and a uniformed valet opened my door.

"Come by tomorrow at five. Buy me a drink. I'll give you my decision." I did not wait for his response or look back as I allowed the valet to help me exit the Mercedes. I already knew what my answer would be. It was either time for me to get back to work . . . or quit the agency.

Chapter Six
The Plan

West Berlin, Germany, Three Days Later

"Ladies and gentlemen, this is Operation Blackbird," Jake announced.

A Berlin map rolled open across the circular oak dining table. Jake dropped a set of files, a pad of paper, and handful of pencils on top of it. I placed an ashtray on one side of the map to keep it from rolling back up.

Beside me, four operatives sat around that table— Jake, whose non-official cover was Heinrich Wagner on this operation, Roy Schliemann, Bernard Conant, and Eva Dresseur. I believed I was the only operative who knew Jake's true identity, and he mine. Although, as the team leader, he likely knew the true identities of the rest. For safety purposes, we would all use our cover identities throughout the mission and while we remained in country. My own cover ID for this mission was Claudia Fischer, and Jake introduced me as such.

To my left sat Bernard. He had curly salt-and-pepper hair and small wire-rimmed glasses perched on his snub nose. With his tweed blazer, he looked like a university math professor. Sitting across the table was Roy. He had bushy eyebrows, a crooked nose, receding hairline, and a gap between his front teeth that he showed regularly with his easy smile. A stocky, six-foot-two man, he reminded me of a brawler from the twenties.

Elegant and remote were the best words to describe Eva. Sitting to my right, Eva wore her black hair in a low chignon. She had an aquiline nose, and the stark black turtleneck contrasted beautifully with her pale skin. I surmised she must have been in her late forties by the fine lines around her eyes and the age spots appearing on her veined hands.

Jake and Eva had been the first to arrive in the modern but sparsely furnished three-bedroom apartment. Bernard arrived a day later; Roy and I only a few hours ago. The building was so new the scent of paint still lingered in the air. It was one of the many blocky brick-and-steel structures popping up all over the city. Both East and West Berlin were going through a housing boom. Commercial real estate owners were buying up land and building as quickly as possible. The minimalist structures sought to fill a need rather than present attractive architectural designs to delight the eye like those destroyed during the war. Though the modern conveniences of the apartments couldn't be beat, I secretly longed for the creak of old wooden floors, tall ceilings, and casement windows that once defined this old city.

"We received intelligence that Soviet physicist Oleg Ivanov wishes to defect." Jake opened the top file and laid out a set of papers for us to peruse as he spoke. "A Ukrainian by birth, Ivanov and his family moved to Saint Petersburg when he was five. He studied at the Zhukovsky Air Force Engineering Academy and flew bombing raids over Leningrad during the war. He spent his post-war years as an academic at the Moscow

Engineering Institute, conducting research on rocket propulsion systems. At the end of 1947, he became a party representative."

"His file says he was sent to Berlin to serve on the Soviet Control Commission three months ago," Eva said, passing the file on to me. "I assume he has access to top-secret communications between the Kremlin and SCC staff."

"He does," Jake replied. "A month ago, he sent intelligence through an American agricultural scientist."

Ivanov's black-and-white photo revealed a man in his mid-forties wearing a suit and tie. His hair was slicked back on the sides, and he had a narrow nose. "We're sure this isn't a Soviet ploy to place an operative in our system?" I asked as I passed the materials on to Bernard.

"I assure you, Oleg is in earnest," Bernard said. He didn't bother looking at the materials, instead he passed them along to Roy.

"Our agricultural scientist, folks." Jake indicated our mild-mannered-looking professor, and all eyes turned to Bernard.

"What isn't enumerated in those materials—during the war, Oleg secretly joined an opposition party. He'd become disillusioned by the Communist party and sought to remove Stalin from power through political means. When he found out a faction within the party planned to assassinate Stalin and a handful of top-level government staff, he left the group," Bernard explained.

Roy leaned back in his chair with his hands shoved in his pants pockets. "The KGB never found out?"

"Not yet." Bernard removed his glasses and began

cleaning them with a handkerchief. "A month ago, he received an anonymous package. It contained a grainy photograph of Oleg at one of the opposition group meetings. His face was circled."

Roy let out a whistle between his teeth.

"This followed a week ago." Jake pulled a mimeograph of a typed letter from the file and laid it on the table.

I picked it up. It was written in Russian.

"The message requests ten thousand Rubles. Ivanov has been given until the end of the month to gather the funds, in cash. Instructions for delivering the money will be forthcoming," Bernard explained, replacing his glasses. He must have assumed I couldn't read Russian.

I didn't correct Bernard's assumption. Though I wasn't proficient enough to be a native speaker, I'd been learning the language over the past year, and the letter was rather simplistic. I dropped the paper on the pile. "This photograph is a ticking timebomb for Ivanov."

"Indeed." Bernard nodded. "Oleg is concerned that even if he pays the money, the blackmailer will reveal him to the KGB."

"Or continue to ask for more money," Eva added.

"Why didn't he walk across the border and request asylum after he got the photograph?" Roy asked, leaning his chair back on its rear legs. "While the rest of East Germany is walled off up and down the border, the Berlin borders are still porous as a sieve. We've got thousands of East Germans defecting ever year."

"Three reasons," Jake answered, holding up three fingers. "Reasons one and two—Oleg's wife, Yelena, and eight-year-old daughter, Katya, have not been allowed to move to East Berlin with him." He pushed a pair of files across the table. "They remain in Moscow, and he travels home twice a month to see them. They finally received tourist papers to visit Berlin and arrive today."

"In other words—" A pack of cigarettes lay by my elbow; I pulled one out and offered the pack to the rest of the crew as I spoke. Roy took one; the rest shook their heads. "We aren't just retrieving one person, we're pulling out three."

"Correct." Bernard sparked a match and lit my cigarette.

Eva perused Yelena's dossier. "I assume we're talking KGB protective services."

"Exactly. That's the third reason Ivanov hasn't simply trotted across the border," Jake explained. "The Soviets like to keep an eye on their scientists, especially those participating in their rocketry program. Oleg is under constant surveillance."

"The Ivanovs will not be allowed to visit West Berlin. His wife and child will be escorted everywhere by KGB protective services while they are here," Bernard stated softly.

None of this information surprised me. The KGB devoted an entire division to surveilling their own people. In Berlin, it was easier for defectors to travel out of the Eastern sector, as Ulbricht's Communist regime had not yet created a wall through the city in the manner that they'd done earlier this year. Up and down the 880-mile border between East and West Germany, from the Baltic Sea to Czechoslovakia, the East Germans had built a concrete-and-barbed wire fortified wall, replete with watchtowers and guard dogs. The East Germans claimed it was to keep out Western spies and criminals. In reality, it was to stop the continued flow of brainpower and laborers from leaving the East and depleting its workforce.

I blew a cloud of smoke toward the ceiling. "Thus, the reason the Ivanovs need our help to defect."

Bernard nodded. "Precisely."

If our team was caught helping Ivanov and his family escape, we would be accused of being exactly what we were—spies—or worse, perverse capitalist kidnappers trying to abscond with one of their top scientists. We would likely be tortured and shot, or, the alternative, kept barely alive in the squalor of a Soviet gulag in case we became useful enough to be used as collateral in a trade between nations. Before going in, we would each be given a cyanide ampule. It would be hidden, perhaps in a glasses frame, pen cap, or piece of jewelry.

Roy's chair banged back onto all four legs. "What's the plan?"

The map had gotten buried beneath the files and assorted papers. Jake pushed them aside. "On Wednesday, Oleg will be speaking at a symposium at the Hotel Adlon. The girls are planning to go shopping at the market on Eisenbahn Strasse. KGB secret service will be driving them. After lunch, Yelena has been directed to request a visit to a children's clothing shop, here." He pointed to the Markthalle IX, a shopping area that dated back to the 1890s. "She will choose some clothes and take Katya to the dressing rooms to try them on. Eva, you will be waiting for them. There is a rear exit into the alley. Roy, you will be driving a blue Wartburg."

Roy wrinkled his nose in disgust.

"Don't worry," Jake assured him, "the intake system has been modified, and a reed valve has been added which will supply plenty of power and speed should you need it. The trunk has been fitted to house Yelena and her daughter. If it is a clean exit, Roy will bring them into West Germany via the Reinickendorfer Strasse. Eva, you will leave via the U-Bahn. Turn south and walk two blocks to the Waldemar Strasse bus stop. Get off at the Spittelmarkt stop to take the subway back to the apartment."

"And if we don't get out clean?" Eva asked.

"If you can't get out clean, join Roy and the Ivanovs in the vehicle. If the escape routes via the roads aren't available, try the Berlin Ostbahnhof. It's a busy station; blend in with the crowd." The three of them discussed different plans for eluding the Ivanovs' KGB escort should it become necessary.

I picked up Yelena's file. The photograph showed a round face with a pointed chin, apple cheeks, and deep-set eyes. She wasn't traditionally pretty, rather, she had a wholesome look about her. Yelena taught history, but during the war she became a radio operator for a tank unit in the Red Army. Throughout the war, Yelena participated in half a dozen different battles until she received a shrapnel injury to the leg in 1943. She met Oleg during her recovery. The pair married at the beginning of 1944, and their daughter was born later that same year.

Katya had her mother's round face and pointy chin,

but her dark hair was worn loose with curls, as opposed to her mother's, which was cropped as short as a man's. Yelena would have been more attractive with longer hair like her daughter. The pictures were replicas of their passport photos, and neither one of them was smiling.

"Claudia." Jake turned his attention to me, and I closed the dossier. "You and Bernard will work together to retrieve Oleg."

I nodded.

"He has an eye for the ladies," Jake said. "He's known for it."

My brows rose. "Even with his wife in town?"

"He will this time," Bernard interjected.

Jake continued, "You'll take up a position in the hotel's lounge. In your room, there is a green dress and red wig. After you—"

"Red wig?" I tapped a length of ash into the ashtray. "Isn't that rather conspicuous?"

"Oleg likes the redheads. KGB knows this," Bernard explained.

"Charming," I drawled.

Ignoring my sarcasm, Jake resumed his directions. "After sharing a drink, you'll invite him to your room. Make sure his KGB escort does not make it onto the elevator with you. Get off on the fourth floor, turn right, and go to the end of the hall. You'll find a freight elevator used by the staff. Bernard will be waiting in the elevator with a change of clothes for you and Ivanov. You'll take the freight elevator to the basement."

Jake rolled out a blueprint of the hotel's basement. "Go down the hall and through laundry services. Here," he pointed as he explained. "Walk out through the western door of the laundry room. Turn right and down this hallway. There is an exit at the end of it. You will come out onto an alleyway. I'll be waiting at the end of the alley to transport Ivanov and Claudia. Bernard, as you requested to maintain your cover, you will return to the lobby."

"Sounds easy," Roy put in and grinned at us.

Eva and Jake ignored Roy's comment. Bernard shook his head like an irritated parent of a disrespectful teen, and I gave him a dead stare while stubbing out my cigarette. Operations always sounded easy when you were sitting in a lovely, warm apartment having a smoke and assuming the other players would react the way you planned. Having had ops take a turn for the worse, I knew any overlooked detail or unexpected actions by the KGB could put all of us in serious jeopardy.

"This must be accomplished with precision timing. Eva, you need to leave with Yelena and Katya by 1300. We expect KGB to notice their absence first. Claudia, you have to get Oleg on that elevator by no later than 1305," Jake wrote the numbers in a column on one of the pads of paper. "Once KGB realizes they've lost the mother and daughter, the hunt will be on. We rendezvous at the apartment at 1400. The Ivanovs will be outfitted with new identities and on a flight to Paris along with Eva and Claudia at 1600. Embassy staff members will be waiting at the airport with a military escort to take the Ivanovs to America. Any questions?"

"How many KGB are we expecting?" Roy asked.

"We know two that will be escorting Yelena and her

daughter during the day. We're working on getting photographs. We've identified two agents for Ivanov." He pulled out a photograph from the bottom of Oleg's file—a pair of men in dark suits, one wearing a fedora and the other a bushy mustache. "However, we suspect at least two more are working undercover. Be aware Stasi will be all over the Hotel Adlon. We have two days to memorize the materials, surveille, and run the escape routes."

"Are we visiting the hotel?" I asked.

Jake shook his head. "KGB and Stasi are already camped out at the hotel. I don't want any of our faces on their radar. We'll do a drive-by. You'll have to memorize the floor plans from the paperwork. Any other questions?" One at a time, Jake looked at each of us.

Each person gave a head shake.

"Remember, once you're in East Berlin, eyes and ears of the state will be on you at all times. Assume anyone you meet is either KGB or a Stasi agent. The government will use any citizen to garner information." Jake pointed at me. "Watch yourself, Claudia. KGB hires lip readers and will be watching Oleg in particular.

"Thanks for the reminder." I stubbed out my cigarette.

"One last thing." Jake held up a finger. "It is my duty to inform you—if you are captured, the CIA will deny any knowledge of your actions."

For the next hour, the five of us reviewed the plans, the Ivanov files, the street map of East Berlin, and all the avenues that flowed across the Western side. A haze of smoke clouded above our heads as we worked.

Finally, the meeting broke up. Eva offered to make us spaghetti à la Bolognese for dinner, and I helped Jake sort the materials into piles. Upon rising, Eva allowed her fingers to drift gently across Jake's shoulder up to his ear. If I hadn't glanced up at that moment, I would have missed the movement. The caress of a lover, and it was followed by the ever-so-slight rise of Jake's lips. They didn't share a look or make any other comment, and if I hadn't seen it, I never would have guessed. Eva left to pick up the ingredients, and Bernard offered to go with her to choose the wine. Roy said he needed to pick up more cigarettes and soon followed the pair.

I retired to the room Eva and I shared. Twin beds were set up along the walls opposite each other with a short dresser between them, in front of the window. I stared at Eva's bed, wondering if she would be sleeping it in tonight. Roy and Bernard shared a room, and Jake had the large bedroom to himself. I mentally shook off those musings and got down to business.

A faceless mannequin head with a red wig sat atop the dresser. In the closet hung a slim cut, moss green, satin dress, matching heels, and a black trench coat. I pulled open my train case and perused the makeup bottles and compacts. I'd been a redhead in the past. My fair skin and blue eyes made for good coloring with wine and apple-red hair color. The wig supplied by the company held more coppery tones, so I'd have to change my normal color palette a bit. I was debating which eyebrow liner to use when Jake walked in.

"Which color do you think will be best with the wig?" I held up one in each hand.

"That one." Jake pointed at the lighter brown and sat on Eva's bed.

"Tell me about our team." I laid the pencil next to the wig.

"I've only worked with Eva. Two years ago, on a mission in Poland. Originally, she was recruited to work for the Research and Development division of the OSS."

"Does she speak Russian?" I asked.

He rubbed his chin. "Yes. Better than you."

I picked up the wig and began brushing out the tangles. "Want to tell me why Bernard assumed I didn't?"

"You were the last to join the mission. I may have been . . . brief telling them about your background."

"What about Roy and Bernard?"

"Roy's file defined him as a close combat specialist skilled at killing silently with a knife. Like myself, he was an intelligence officer during the war with the 758th Tank Battalion. Afterward, he worked on Special Projects at the Pentagon. Two years ago, the agency recruited him. The station chief assigned everyone on this op. You were the only person I was allowed to choose."

"And Bernard?" I prompted.

Jake's mouth turned down and he placed his elbows on his knees. "Bernard's file is . . . thin. He worked the X-2 division during the war."

X-2 was the counter espionage division of the OSS; they were often skilled at developing informants. "What's he been doing since the war?"

Jake shook his head, his palms turned up toward the ceiling.

My brows rose and I took a moment to comb through a tricky tangle before responding. "That's all?"

"All I was privy to."

"Obviously, he's been Oleg's contact. I assume he's deep cover."

"I assume so, and it's our job to do our best to keep his cover intact." He stared at me, concern marring his handsome features, which had filled out in the years since he stood in Lily's foyer.

Surprised by my thoughts, I stopped brushing. When Jake didn't speak, I prodded, "What?"

His mouth worked as if struggling to find the words to express whatever notions were causing his anxiety.

"Just spit it out," I said with a huff.

"If something doesn't feel right . . . abort the op."

Putting the wig down, I sat on the bed opposite Jake. "You can't be serious."

"I'm afraid Bernard will do whatever he needs in order to maintain his cover. That could mean hanging you out to dry."

I pursed my lips together. "Mousey little Bernard?"

Jake squinted and pressed his palms together. "Don't be deceived by his demeanor. I have a feeling, when up against the wall, Bernard is deadly and will do what's best for Bernard."

I swallowed. This wasn't the best news. One thing an operative needed was the knowledge that your colleagues had your back. "Is there something specific you're not telling me?"

He rose and began pacing between the beds. "No. It's just a feeling. As long as everything goes to plan, I'm sure

Bernard will do his part."

An agent's instincts were nothing to joke about. That tingling feeling when the hairs on the back of your neck rose could often be the only indicator that something was wrong. A good agent learned to listen to that feeling.

"If things take a turn for the worse, I'm on my own?"

He ran a hand through his hair. "No. I'll be there backing you up. With or without Oleg, I'll make sure you get out." He stopped in front of me, bent over, and in a firm grip, took hold of my wrist. "If your gut tells you to get out, do it. Walk out the front door. Don't look back. Understand?"

Standing this close to me, I could smell the coffee on his breath. When I didn't answer immediately, his hand squeezed tighter, and his dark gaze speared me. "You're hurting me," I stated calmly. The pressure released immediately.

"Promise me," he breathed.

Slowly, my head bobbed. "If it doesn't feel right, I'll abort."

He didn't retreat. His face remained so close to mine, I noticed the ring of gold circling the edge of his pupils, and my stomach quivered. Not in fear or apprehension, but in a manner I hadn't felt in a long time—desire. I licked my lips. Jake gripped my shoulders, and his kiss came in quick and hard. The flutter exploded into fire, and I allowed it to continue. He tasted of coffee and cream, and the desire flowed outward from my belly to my fingers and toes. I'd been kissed by many men. None had ever electrified my body in the way Jake's kiss did. Not even Hugh.

The front door slammed, and we broke apart. Jake remained frozen, hovering above me.

"Hello?" Roy called. "I'm making Whiskey Sours. Who wants one?"

Releasing the breath I'd been holding, I shuttered my gaze and turned to my train case, mindlessly picking up a lipstick. My jerky movements brought Jake out of his trance.

"I'll take one." He jammed his hands in his pockets and loped out the door.

"Me too," I warbled. Clearing my throat to steady my voice, I added, "Join you in a jiffy." *Just as soon as I figure out what in the sweet hell Jake is playing at.*

Chapter Seven
The Operation

The Hotel Adlon was built during the turn of the century as a luxury hotel to rival New York's Waldorf Astoria and the Paris Ritz. While the hotel made it through the bombing of WWII, Soviet soldiers caused a fire in May 1945 that burned half the building. The portion that didn't burn was still a sight to see and continued to cater to upscale clientele of the Eastern Bloc. Lavishness and elegance were its main draw, and it was one of the few hotels in the Soviet sector of Berlin that met the expectations of Westerners—unlike so many of the barren, blocky concrete apartment buildings the Communist party built for its people.

Beautiful arched and frescoed ceilings greeted guests in the main lobby, and a central staircase, made of marble, swept visitors up to the mezzanine in grand style. The lobby lounge nestled guests into velvet chairs, assembling them in small groups to allow for private conversations, a shared drink, or to read the newspapers. Royal guests from the past included Tsar Nicholas II of Russia and Maharaja Bhupinder Singh of Patiala, along with wealthy industrialist John D. Rockefeller, and Hollywood stars such as Greta Garbo and Charlie Chaplin.

A stone's throw from the Brandenburg gate should have made it easy enough for Oleg to trot over into West

Berlin . . . had it not been for his KGB escorts and the risk to his family.

The green dress tightly hugged my curves. Too tightly, if you'd asked me. However, considering the appreciative, almost to the point of leering, glances I'd been receiving in the past hour, I supposed it was doing the job.

At the far end of the hall, the doors opened, belching out its occupants of scientists, physicists, and engineers. East German Communist leadership was using this symposium to prove they had as many brilliant minds working on advanced rocket technology as the West. The symposium was a relative Who's Who of Eastern Bloc scientists—all of whom were being watched by at least one or two of their own country's security agents and who-knew-how-many Stasi agents.

The low hum of male voices speaking a variety of languages reached my ears, and I swiveled to face the bartender. Symposium participants had an hour break before the next session began at one thirty. I had thirty minutes to flirt with Oleg, put his KGB minders at ease, and get him onto the elevator.

Ivanov, wearing a poorly cut dark gray suit and black tie, climbed into the chair beside me. *"Guten tag, Fraulein."* He continued in German, "A fine day we're having."

"I understand it's supposed to rain tomorrow," I responded, giving the required response identifying myself as Ivanov's contact.

"May I buy you a drink?" he offered, flagging down the bartender.

"Another champagne," I said to the bow-tied bartender, passing him my empty glass.

Ivanov ordered a gin and tonic, and, like those surrounding us, we fell into quiet conversation. He asked what I was doing at the Hotel Adlon, and I gave him my cover identity. Claudia was an East German secretary for a lawyer in town to negotiate the sale of land holdings. From the corner of my eye, I saw Ivanov's KGB escorts take up residence in chairs across the lounge and pretend to read the *Berliner Zeitung* newspaper — an East German publication filled with Communist propaganda.

Ivanov and I flirted. He complimented my face and figure. I smiled and gave him coquettish looks beneath my lashes while laying a hand on his forearm. We spoke only in German. His was quite good, and I had no trouble understanding it through his Russian accent.

Bernard sat at the opposite end of the bar. At ten to one, he waved to the bartender and quietly ordered a pair of beers to be delivered to the KGB agents in the lounge. Five minutes later, a tuxedo-clad waiter delivered the drinks.

"It's time," I whispered in Ivanov's ear.

He smiled, and we strolled casually but quickly to the elevator. Bernard, half a dozen steps ahead of us, pushed the call button and walked away. The elevators opened as Ivanov and I arrived. I pressed the fourth-floor button and witnessed our dark-suited Russians hurrying toward us. Ivanov gripped my jaw, and his lips were suddenly upon mine.

It was the second time in so many days a kiss had been forced upon me. The strong scent of citrus and pine from the gin overwhelmed me, and it took every bone in my body to remain loose and control my revulsion. I gripped his shoulder to sell the illusion. The elevator doors closed before our enemies reached us. With the slightest pressure from my hand, Ivanov pulled away immediately.

"Apologies. I thought . . . it would be safer . . ." he stammered.

"Yes, I understand." I took a handkerchief from my handbag and wiped away the bright lipstick, then handed it to Ivanov so he could do the same. "The stairs are on the opposite side of the lobby. It will take time for them to make it up the four flights. Do you think they will run?"

"Not through the public parts of the hotel . . . but on the stairs?" Ivanov shrugged. "My family . . ."

I glanced at my watch, five after one on the dot. "They should be on their way out of East Berlin as we speak."

"What should I call you?"

"Claudia Fischer," I said.

"What happens next?" he asked.

The elevator arrived at the fourth floor. I took Ivanov's hand. "Follow me."

Turning right, I hastened down the long hallway, pulling a reluctant Ivanov along. Thankfully, the worn oriental carpet runner muffled the sound of my high heels against the hardwood. Sconces threw eerie shadows against the dark, paneled walls, obscuring the visibility from one end of the hall to the other. A guest room door opened and Ivanov's hand jerked with unease. I squeezed tighter and didn't allow our steps to falter.

"Hurry, we haven't much time," I hissed.

Brightness flooded the end of the dim hall as the freight elevator doors opened. Bernard's curly gray head peeked out, and, seeing a face he knew, Ivanov scurried ahead of me. We gained the entrance, squeezing past one of the hotel maids' wheeled laundry bins. The doors slid shut, but there was no time to rest.

"Change into these." Bernard handed Ivanov a chestnut-colored pin-striped suit from the bin.

As the elevator began its downward descent, the wig came off, and I ran fingers through my hair to loosen the locks, allowing them to fall to my shoulders. I slipped a fresh blue shirtwaist dress over my head and shoved the green dress to the floor. A pair of flats, a wide-brimmed hat, and my black trench coat finished the transformation.

Meanwhile, Ivanov changed out of his pants and pulled on the new pair. I helped him into the suit jacket while Bernard scooped up the wig and our discarded clothes and buried them in the cart beneath the dirty sheets and towels. The only evidence of our quick-change was the pointy toe of my pump. I quickly shoved it down the side. As we arrived at the bottom level, Bernard plopped a brown fedora on Ivanov's head.

The doors opened, and we were met with a blast of sticky, humid air. After checking side-to-side, I waved the men forward. The wide industrial hallways were whitewashed, much like the interior of the elevator. Scratches marred the finish, and Bernard added another one. Shoving the laundry cart out of the way, he abandoned it in the middle of the elevator threshold to keep the doors from closing.

Our footsteps could barely be heard over the washing and drying machines, and we quickly walked past the workers, sometimes receiving surprised looks. I tensed, waiting for someone to call out. I needn't have worried. The German people had spent far too long under the thumb of first the Nazis, then the Soviets, and now their own crushing East German Communist government. They'd become conditioned to turning a blind eye to happenings that didn't interfere with their own lives. Though, I knew, when asked, they wouldn't hesitate to tell officials what they'd witnessed.

Laundry services were grouped into two different rooms. In the first, two dozen washing machines lined the walls, with drying machines stacked, two high, back-to-back down the center of the room. It reminded me of the laundromat I'd used while living in Washington. The second room was filled with tables for folding stations and lines for drying. Laundry carts were everywhere, filled with white linens in different stages of cleaning. We made it through the folding room, and the door to the hall, which would take us out the back entrance, closed behind us with a solid *whump*, effectively cutting off the noise. Unfortunately, the humidity from the washers still hung heavy in the air. The sign on the door at the end of the hall read *AUSGANG*, and I headed toward it with the men following.

"*Was ist lost?*" Ivanov's anxious tone reached my ears.

Whipping my head around, I found Bernard holding a Walther PPK with a silencer pointed at Ivanov's heart.

"Bernard?"

He said something in Russian so low that I didn't hear it. Ivanov's panicked face told me he had heard and understood Bernard's comment, and he held up his hands in a defensive manner.

I grabbed Bernard's gun arm and shoved the sight away from Ivanov.

"Run!" I cried.

Ivanov darted past the two of us. I paid no more attention to where he went, because I was now locked in a struggle for my life with Bernard. I had no doubts that Bernard planned to take care of me with that weapon after he'd done-in his "pal" Oleg. Belied by his age, he was stronger than I'd expected. My hat fell off as I bit down hard on the gun hand. His salty flesh compacted between my teeth, and I felt a crunch. He yelled incoherently, and the gun dropped, skittering across the floor. Bernard backhanded me with his uninjured hand.

I cried out as pain exploded across my cheek and jaw. Stumbling, I slammed hard up against the wall. Bernard searched for the gun. With one hand pressed against my face, I too scoured the cement floor. We both spotted the black weapon at the same time. Bernard reached for it, and I knew he'd get to it before I could. With a sweeping movement, I was able to kick it far down the hall, out of his grasp. The sweeping motion had an added benefit—I was able to trip him. Bernard went down hard to one knee, although he was able to catch himself with his hands before his face hit the cement floor.

While Bernard recovered, I liberated the frisk knife strapped to my thigh, a little piece of insurance I'd taken to carrying on all my ops. He dodged my stab. It merely grazed his bicep, leaving a slice along his suit jacket and dress shirt. Bernard lashed out, aiming a kick at my knees that I was able to sidestep. Unfortunately, I miscalculated his next move. He spun, and, the next thing I knew, he clamped both hands onto my knife wrist in a painful, numbing grip. I grimaced as he banged my hand against the wall. The knife fell from my grasp.

Drawing up a knee, I made contact with his marriage prospects. He released me, doubling over in pain with a curse, and backed away. I hugged my bruised hand to my chest while my heart hammered, and my mind spun in different directions. Should I flee or remain to fight? Where did my knife go? Could I get to it before Bernard recovered?

A muffled shot rent the air.

I gasped.

Bernard collapsed to the ground. Blood fanned out in a mothlike pattern across his chest like a Rorschach test. My head rotated and I found Ivanov holding Bernard's weapon.

The exit door flung open, banging against the wall, and a silhouette filled the doorway.

Ivanov swung around, his weapon at the ready.

"*Was ist los?*" Jake's voice echoed with concern. The door closed. He wore a black pin-striped suit, and I saw the glint of his silver pistol.

"*Nein! Wait!*" I shouted in German.

Scooping up my frisk knife, I scooted past Ivanov toward Jake. The two men pointed their guns at each other. "Put it away," I murmured in English. "Bernard tried to kill us. Ivanov saved my life."

Jake hesitated a moment before slowly tucking the weapon away.

I turned to Ivanov, whose hand shook. His eyes darted back and forth, fearful and unsure.

"Oleg," I said quietly in German, "it is alright. We need to go before the KGB catches up to us."

By increments, Ivanov lowered the weapon until it hung at his side. I waved him forward, and we caught up to Jake, who held the exit door for us. Ivanov went first, but my steps stuttered at a shout from behind me.

The doorframe next to my head splintered as the sound of a gunshot reverberated off the stark walls and floor. I ducked. Jake gave me a shove and wildly returned fire while pushing me outside. The heavy wooden door slammed shut behind him. Ivanov had taken refuge against the exterior stone wall and held his weapon at the ready.

"Go! *Schnell!*" Jake barked, pointing to his left.

I tore off down the alley with Ivanov on my heels. He stumbled and cursed. A quick glance gave me to know he wasn't injured, and I continued onward. Popping out between the two buildings, I searched left and right for the mud-brown Skoda Jake had acquired this morning. Thankfully, the foot traffic on this street was nonexistent, although I could see people crossing the intersection at the far end of the block.

"On the right!" Jake called.

Finally, I spotted the car parallel parked between a large box van and a black coupe. Whipping open the rear passenger door, I waved Ivanov into the back seat.

Stone chips shattered off the building as Jake darted around the corner. A hand went to his cheek.

Steps from the car, Ivanov slammed to a stop, pivoted, and backtracked.

"What are you doing?" Jake cried as Ivanov passed him, going the opposite direction.

The Russian plastered himself against the building, crouched, and peered around the corner. With quick, precise movements, he aimed and took two shots.

An injured cry echoed from the alley.

Jake reached the car, opened the front passenger door, slid across the bench seat, and scrambled to put the keys in the ignition. "*Get in!*"

I hopped in, and, via the side mirror, watched Ivanov race to the car, his arms and legs pumping like an Olympic sprinter. He dove into the back seat. We jerked away from the curb, scraping the bumper in front of us. Ivanov's door slammed shut with a resounding *whap!*

"Did you kill him?" I asked.

"*Nein*," Ivanov panted, staring out the back window. "The pistol throws right. It was merely a flesh wound."

"At least it will slow him down," Jake replied, cruising around a corner.

"I shouldn't have left him alive," the Russian chastised himself. "If he hasn't already, he will be able to radio his comrades. They will set up roadblocks."

Sure enough, Jake braked to a halt at the Unter den Linden stoplight, and an East German police vehicle, with lights flashing, blew past the hotel. It turned to block the traffic heading into West Berlin. A military transport wasn't far behind. Motorists blared their horns in disapproval.

Jake turned right, away from the Brandenburg Gate and our easy escape. As soon as he could, he got off the main boulevard and weaved his way through the potholed neighborhood streets at normal speed, making an effort to obey the road rules. There was very little vehicular traffic, and I felt conspicuous driving through abandoned streets.

During the war, Berlin had been heavily damaged, and its population decimated by death or departure. While both sides of Berlin still showed signs of the war—bombed and burnt buildings, uneven cobblestone walks, and rubble piles—West Berlin had been cash infused and empowered by its Western occupiers to rebuild. The Soviets had no interest in seeing the emergence of a strong Germany and did their best to keep both the people and her economy down. The oppressive government pillaged the country and spent the initial years of occupation imposing its Communist ideals on the population, thus leading to a mass exodus of both intellectual and manual labor talent. East Berlin's rebuilding was slower, and the city continued to look bleak.

Chapter Eight
On the Run

"I need you to get down out of sight," Jake mumbled to Ivanov.

Our passenger scooched down in his seat. "My wife and daughter?"

"The package should be safely out of East Berlin," Jake said.

"You're bleeding." I spoke in English and blotted the cut on Jake's cheek with my handkerchief. The blood matched the crimson lipstick stains.

He took the fabric from me and pressed hard to staunch the bleeding. "Stone fragment from the building."

"Is that the worst of it?" I asked.

"I certainly hope so." He glanced at my face. "What about you? I assume that's Bernard's handiwork."

Gingerly, I touched my tender, swollen cheek. "I've had worse."

Now that we'd escaped the immediate danger, spots of pain flared across my body. My left shoulder ached where Bernard had slammed me against the wall. Also, the knuckles on my right hand and wrist were already mottled and purpling with bruises.

Glancing out the back window, I spoke in Russian to Ivanov, "What did Bernard say when he pulled his gun on you?"

Ivanov gave me a funny look. "'Dmitri Sidorov sends his compliments.'"

I was familiar with many members of the politburo and KGB leadership. Sidorov was not one of them. "Who is Sidorov?"

"Head of the Kazakhstan SSR state security services. He recently joined the politburo as the first secretary of the Central Committee."

"Who is he to you?" I asked.

Ivanov sighed and began unscrewing the gun's silencer. "He attended meetings . . . during the war."

I raised a shoulder in confusion.

"The committee to remove Stalin from power," he clarified.

Ah. My head tilted. "And he knows you can identify him?"

"Just as he can identify me," Ivanov confirmed.

"I wonder if he received a blackmail letter, too," I mused, "and assumed you were the sender."

"Perhaps." He scrutinized me. "Your Russian is rather good."

I shrugged. "I'm still learning." Switching to German, I asked our driver, "Want to tell me how we missed a double agent in our midst?" I recalled his warnings in my room at the apartment. "Or did you know?"

"Your man was probably paid off," Ivanov interjected. "Sidorov is well connected and comes from money. His family owns half a dozen industrial factories, and he's got plenty of political connections. I doubt Sidorov planned to leave your man alive once he completed his mission."

Ivanov's explanation certainly sounded plausible; however, it still didn't explain Jake's nebulous warning two days ago.

"We've got a problem." Jake interrupted our conversation. "I think we've got a tail. Three cars back. Black sedan. It's followed me through the past two turns."

Ivanov moved to look, but I put a hand on his head. "No, stay down." I spotted the car Jake indicated.

We drove through a green light. The red coupe directly behind us turned, and the black car pulled closer. Now there was only a beige car separating us and our tail. The light at the end of the block turned yellow. Jake gunned the engine and sped through as the light turned red. The black car sped around the beige car, which was pulling to a stop, and blasted through the red light.

The chase was on.

"I was hoping to get you to the U-Bahn station, but they're too close, and the longer this goes on, the less likely you'll be able to get out." Jake downshifted and wheeled around the corner. "Three kilometers away, we'll come to the Oberbaumbrucke Bridge that crosses the Spree into the American zone."

"Then that's how we'll get across," I stated.

"If it's not already blocked." Jake shook his head. "If it is, I'm going to take the lower *Allee* along the Spree and drop you north of the Elsen Bridge. There's a place where you can get out unseen."

"Then what?"

He gave me a sidelong glance. "You know how to swim?"

I swallowed and nodded. Ivanov wouldn't be the first defector to flee via the Spree River.

"Swim across the river. The current will take you to the first canal on your left. It's the Landwehr Canal. It empties into the Spree, so you'll have to swim up the canal. Up the canal, you're in West Berlin. Climb out at one of the docks. Flag down the first car you see. There are a five hundred Deutsch Marks in my wallet. Right side coat pocket. Take it. Use it to get Ivanov to the safehouse. Eva will help you get them to Paris."

I dug out the money and shoved it in a secret pocket inside my trench coat. In exchange, I pulled out all the East German Ostmarks I had on my person and shoved them into Jake's wallet. "What about you?"

"I'll draw off the dogs."

I didn't like it. I didn't like any of it. It was October, and the river would be dreadfully cold, but what I liked least of all was Jake's part in the plan. The papers in Jake's wallet identified him as a salesman for a commercial window merchant. However, if any of the KGB agents could identify Jake as the man with Ivanov at the Adlon hotel, and they got ahold of him . . . it would not end well. *If* they kept him alive, after torturing and interrogating him, we *might* be able to make a trade. As long as he didn't use the deadly capsule first.

"Why don't you ditch the car and take a swim with us?" I suggested.

"If I thought we could all make it, I would do so. The only way to be sure you two get away is to lead our pursuers further into East Berlin."

"No. There's got to be another way. Just . . . let me

think." I pressed a finger to my temple. *Think! Think!* "Why don't we try the Ost Bahnhof? We're not that far away."

He was shaking his head before I could finish. "We'll never make it. KGB and Stasi will be looking for us. If we were lucky enough to catch a train heading west, there *will* be agents searching them."

I chewed my lip, my brain darting in all directions.

His erratic driving had put distance between us and our pursuer, but not enough, especially if there was a roadblock set up on the bridge.

There was.

I could see the flashing lights ahead. Jake popped the car over a curb, down a grassy knoll, and onto the lower Allee that hugged the river. Our pursuer crashed into a police car pulling out to follow our lead.

"We're out of time. A kilometer ahead is a tree-covered area where I can pull in and drop you off. Stay low. There's a brick bulkhead and the water will be about four feet deep near the edges before it drops deeper than twelve. No diving. Feet first."

Our conversation had been in English, and I turned to translate our new plan to Ivanov.

"I svim very vell," he said in heavily accented English.

I shouldn't have been surprised it was one of the languages he spoke. We'd been constantly underestimating one another. My attention returned to Jake, and involuntarily, these last moments of him imprinted on my mind—his eyes fixed and focused, the planes of his tightly clamped jawbone, the blood from the scratch on his cheek already clotting, those strong fingers gripping the wheel and shifter, and the pin-striped suit, with its red pocket square still intact, conformed around his muscular shoulders. I noticed a thin scar below his earlobe, which he'd obtained falling from his bike at the age of ten. It occurred to me, I could still see traces of the boy who'd once played in my yard with Fred and Hugh, and I knew this moment would remain in my memory for the rest of my life.

"Get ready," Jake said, snapping my attention to the road ahead. He slowed to a few miles per hour as he approached a large bush that jutted into the roadway. Jake swerved around it and pulled up on the low curb. "NOW!"

I dove out before the car came to a halt and rolled along the ground. "Oof!" One more bruise to add to the collection.

Ivanov followed with much more grace. He jumped up and pulled me to my feet. "Come. We go."

I couldn't help glancing at the brown beast as Jake put his foot to the floor and roared away. Sirens screamed up the Allee. Ivanov and I ducked behind a screen of brush. The Skoda dodged around slower-moving traffic. A young mother with a baby stroller turned to watch the police cars fly by. Ivanov and I took the distraction to get to the waterfront. Flat-bottomed boats and barges used for moving sand, bricks, and even beer intermittently lined docks on either side.

With trepidation, I stared down into the murky, greenish-brown water, which smelled of dirt and boat fuel.

"*Eins, zwei—*" Ivanov counted

"*Drei!*" We jumped in together.

Holy macaroni! That water was bloody cold! It came up to my neck before my feet hit the muddy bottom. Still, my head went under. I surfaced and took a moment to push the hair off my face and orient myself before kicking into a horizontal position to catch up with Ivanov, who was already a body length ahead of me.

Ivanov's hat fell off and floated by like a tiny brown island. My own hat never made it out of the hotel. I lost my cute little flats after the first dozen kicks. The trench coat billowed around me, making it more difficult to swim, but I dared not remove it. I feared the water would soak my dress, which would become practically transparent, and I would need the trench for modesty's sake once I got out of this disgusting water. Jake had dropped us at a narrower neck of the Spree, about twenty-five meters wide. We crossed the river at a diagonal, using the current to move us closer to the canal.

A barge passed by, going upriver, and I heard a shout but ignored the call. I caught up and motioned to Ivanov to keep swimming. I did not want to find help until we made it to the canal. My teeth were chattering by the time we reached it. Following Ivanov's lead, I began kicking. The canal's water flowed at a relatively slow pace. It was easy enough for a boat to motor up it. It should have been a relatively easy swim.

However, another vessel in the Spree created a wake. As I was about to tell the Russian to head for the nearest dock, a wave washed over him. He took an unintended swallow of the brackish water, which left him coughing and retching, and then his head disappeared beneath the water. I double-timed my strokes and swam back to where he'd gone under. The water was so dark, I couldn't see anything below. Diving down, I blindly splayed my hands and kicked my feet in hopes knocking into him.

No luck.

I came up for air and heard a sputter from behind. Spinning around, I gripped his coat collar to keep him above water.

"I've got you. Calm down. Take a breath." I spotted a dock up ahead and towed him toward it. I was swimming against the current, and we didn't make much progress until he was able to catch his breath.

"I can do it," he gasped, pulling out of my grip to resume swimming.

Together we stroked over to a shabby white dinghy tied to the dock. My arms were rubbery with fatigue. With one last burst of energy, I gave Ivanov a shove, toppling him into the boat. He, in turn, dragged me aboard, dumping me unceremoniously onto the hard bottom. It smelled of fish guts and swamp water. A stench which, no doubt, attached itself to my wet coat. I didn't care, as Ivanov and I panted to catch our breath.

"I lost the gun." He stared moodily into the murky waters.

"No matter. We should be fine without it." I tried to sound reassuring.

"Should we go find help?" Ivanov asked, indicating the little staircase that would take us to the top of the canal wall.

I glanced around, taking in the stone bulkhead

spattered with green moss. A dilapidated brick warehouse across the waterway stood in direct contrast to the beauty of the autumn red-gold leaves clinging to the tree limbs as if desperate to maintain the warmer weather.

Suddenly, I realized I knew this canal. "Not yet. Do you think you can get this started?" I pointed at the little two-stroke motor.

Ivanov tugged on the starter cord. Once. Twice. Three times. Nothing.

"Forget it, we'll use the oars." I sighed, staring dismally at the wooden paddles lying on the bottom of the boat.

"Not yet," Ivanov grumbled. Ever the engineer, he messed with the choke, wiped something with his soaking handkerchief, fiddled with a gauge, and gave it another go.

The little motor buzzed to life. I unhooked us from the dock, and we puttered up the canal.

I can't imagine the bedraggled picture we made. My locks hung in dripping ropes, while my clammy clothes clung unpleasantly to my body. I squeezed some of the water from my dress. It joined the inch of murky water sloshing around on the bottom of the dinghy. I wasn't sure if it was worse to leave the trench coat on or take it off. The air breezed past, and I hunched down, pulling it closer.

Ivanov, too, looked worse for wear. He'd removed his suit jacket, and the light wind plastered the wet shirt against his chest. His wool pants dripped at his ankles and made a squishy puddle where he sat. We certainly received some odd glances from pedestrians and passing boats. I didn't care. I was simply relieved to be out of the water.

Chapter Nine
The Houseboat

Twenty minutes later, I spotted the small houseboat moored to the side of the canal. It was one of a dozen, some more ramshackle than others. The door was freshly painted white, and one side of the chipped peacock-blue paint had been stripped down to bare boards, but otherwise not much had changed since the last time I'd visited in 1948. Shafts of afternoon sunlight sparkled on the water, and ripples from our dinghy disturbed the stillness.

Ivanov cut the engine, silencing the only noise in the waterfront community. We tied up to the splintered and careworn dock, and I gingerly stepped out, trying to avoid the worst of the rotted wood.

It was likely Petrus would be at work, however, I remembered where he kept a spare key. Letting myself in would be a rather brazen move, but I required time to dry off and regroup.

I needn't have worried. He answered the third time I knocked.

His thinning sandy hair stood on end, and he wore a maroon robe with no shoes. He blinked and shook his head as if to clear the cobwebs. "Buttercup?"

I was relieved he used my codename in front of Ivanov, because it could easily be mistaken for a term of endearment.

"*Was bist—?*"

"*Guten tag*, Petrus. Sorry to have awakened you." I clamped my teeth to keep them from chattering.

He yawned. "What time is it?"

My watch face was too foggy for me to make out the time. "Afternoon." I got to the point. "We need your help."

His gaze went past me, taking in my disheveled companion. Realization that this was *not* a normal visit crossed his features, and he invited us in.

I did not miss his cringe as I wafted past with my eau de swamp fragrance. It clashed with the scent of burnt coffee and stale smoke that hung heavy in the air. Dishes stacked high in the tiny sink. Old newspapers and a handful of glasses littered the coffee table. A wadded-up blanket lay at the end of the threadbare, velvet sofa. Ever the bachelor, the only feminine touch—white eyelet curtains hanging in the front window—were likely a gift from a female relative. Petrus's green uniform jacket hung on the coatrack, along with his duty belt and holstered service weapon, a Walther P38.

"Please excuse the mess. I had an all-night shift . . ."

I waved away Petrus's apologies; after all, we were the interlopers. "This is Oleg. Oleg, my friend Petrus. He's a detective for the *Kriminalpolizei*." Ivanov took a step backwards, and I realized I shouldn't have told him about Petrus's day job. "He is also a liaison to West German Intelligence. He is well connected, and we need him," I explained in Russian.

Hesitantly, the men greeted each other and shook hands. Petrus briefly raised his brow at Ivanov's accented

German but showed no other emotion beyond that.

"Have you some clothes Oleg can borrow?" I asked.

Petrus sized up my companion, who was at least two heads shorter and forty pounds smaller in comparison to the detective's broad, rugby player-like form. Even though he'd gained a bit of a pooch around his belly, Petrus was still in good shape for a man in his fifties. "I'll find something."

Soon, Ivanov was bundled into the bathroom with a change of clothes and a fresh towel. Petrus returned to the kitchen to find a fresh pot of coffee percolating on one of the kerosene burners, and me hovering over the other burner, trying to warm my freezing hands. The only good thing I can say about our little dip in the cold water—it had taken out some of the sting and swelling from my injured face and hand.

Apparently not enough to escape Petrus's notice. He lifted a swath of hair away from my face. "Want to tell me why you showed up looking like a drowned rat that went a few rounds with the family cat, while towing a Russian in your wake?"

I grinned. "Ah, Petrus, you always did have a way with words." During the war, Petrus worked the Underground Railroad helping downed pilots get out of Austria into Allied-occupied Italy. In '48, I was working an op that needed a German to gather information at the Bulgarian Embassy in East Berlin. Petrus fit the bill.

He poured a cup of coffee and leaned against the cabinetry.

I took a moment to determine what I would, and would not, reveal. "Ivanov and his family are defecting to the west," I explained. "One of our team was working for the Reds, and things got a little . . . dicey." Petrus's brows rose at my explanation, but he didn't interrupt. "His wife and daughter were being escorted by another team. I need to get back to the safehouse and assess the situation. I can't be sure he was the only double agent among our crew."

Silently, I cursed Jake for not abandoning the car and coming with us. He knew the team members better than I. As far as I could tell, Eva was the only person he trusted, leaving Roy as a wild card. Petrus waved a hand in front of my face, and I came back to Earth.

"In the meantime, I need you to keep Oleg with you, until I know he's safe. Also, call me Claudia. Claudia Fischer."

For a time, he sipped his coffee, contemplating my presence as I shivered over his stove. Finally, he replied, "Well, you can't go out there soaking wet and without shoes."

"I need you to get me some clothes. I have money. Go to a shop, or buy them off your neighbor, I don't care which. I just need something clean and dry."

"I'll get dressed and see what I can find." He poured another cup and retreated to the single bedroom at the rear of the boathouse. Ten minutes later, Petrus left with twenty-five D-marks from Jake's stash.

Ivanov came out of the bathroom wearing trousers and a plaid shirt that were at least two sizes too large for him. The trousers were held up with a pair of black suspenders, and he'd rolled the bottom of the pants up so they didn't drag along the floor. Dry towels flapped on the outdoor laundry line. I removed them so Ivanov could hang up his wet suit, then I poured him a cup of coffee and explained Petrus's mission to obtain clothing for me.

"What about my family?" Ivanov's face remained drawn with concern, and his fingers drummed anxiously against the arm of the couch.

I couldn't blame him for his worries, because I too shared them. However, I tried my best to reassure him. "No doubt, they are at the safe house. As soon as I bathe and change, I'm going to go over there and confirm it. Then we will arrange to get you on a flight out of Germany. In the meantime, I'll get my own bath."

"Can't we phone?"

I didn't want to forewarn possible enemies. A phone call would do just that. "The safe house doesn't have a phone," I lied.

Our original plan to have the Ivanovs on the four o'clock flight to Paris was a bust. The clock hanging in the kitchen read half past three already. Moreover, it was entirely possible Bernard had compromised the entire mission. If so, the new identities for the Ivanovs could get them killed. Just because we were out of the East Berlin didn't mean they were safe.

West Berlin was surrounded by East Germany, and a government ruled by the Soviet Union. While the East Germans claimed autonomy, we all knew—what the Soviets wanted, they got. Spies and agents from both sides flowed in and out of East and West Berlin as easily as the waters of the Spree.

Once the Soviets realized Oleg had made it into West

Berlin, they would enlist Stasi and send their own agents to the train stations and airports. A poison dart. Silenced gun shot. A knife to the lungs. These were only a few of the ways KGB could take out the Russian. I revealed none of this to Oleg. Either he'd already realized it, or he was blissfully ignorant, and I saw no reason to disillusion him. My gut told me the former rather than the latter as he jumped up to stare out the dirty window.

"Try not to worry. Everything will be fine." I reckoned the platitude fell on deaf ears. I couldn't blame him. I'd be mad with worry if I was in his place. Jake was still in enemy territory, and my own anxieties were held on a short leash.

The edges of the old clawfoot tub were worn, the enamel chipped from decades of use, and the faucet was rusted around the lip. No matter, it felt like bliss removing my sopping clothes and climbing into the steaming bath. Petrus's soap smelled of sandalwood and his shampoo of sage. After finishing my bath, I washed my clothes in the tub. The cotton shirtwaist wouldn't be dry for a few hours, but the Dacron trench coat would dry quickly on the line in the breezy sun. Petrus's sage shampoo did wonders to get out the smell of the Spree.

I borrowed Petrus's robe and laid my wet leather dagger sheath on the little hallway heater. Thankfully, I hadn't lost the knife during the swim. When Petrus finally returned, almost an hour later, it was with a brown sack and a triumphant grin.

Silently, I thanked the heavens for his return. Ivanov had drunk three cups of coffee and had taken to agitatedly pacing room. I feared he would soon strangle me with the lamp cord and demand the location of the safe house.

"Got these from my seventy-year-old neighbor." Petrus plopped down a pea-green calico housedress that must have been at least thirty years old. A pair of clunky brown brogues matched the ensemble. The bundle smelled like mothballs and liniment. "Here are some pins for your hair, and makeup"—he tapped his cheek—"for your face."

"Thank you," I murmured, taking the items into the bathroom.

My nylon underthings had already dried. The dress was enormous, and I used the belt on Petrus's dressing gown to tie it at my waist. The shoes were scuffed and well worn, but a relatively good fit. I was sure I'd be able to run in them should the need arise. Pulling my damp hair into a French twist, I pinned it in place. The creme foundation was too dark for my skin, but it did a good job covering the bruising. I patted it with some talcum powder I found above the medicine cabinet to lighten the tone. The mascara had seen better days; it was dried and clumpy. Unusable. I screwed the wand back in place and moved on to the lipstick. Mauve was not my normal shade, but it did give some color and moisture to my dry lips.

Ivanov and Petrus were smoking and playing cards when I returned. Ivanov didn't make a comment, but Petrus let out a guffaw. "I'm not sure it's an improvement."

"At least it's dry," I muttered.

The Russian rose, as if to go with me. I quickly

disabused him of that notion. "I'll go alone."

Petrus frowned, but it was Ivanov who objected first. "This is not a good idea. I need to see my family." He changed tactics as I shook my head. "You need my help. Remember, back at the hotel?"

My head stopped shaking. I couldn't argue with him about that. His quick thinking and military skills had come in handy. However, I wasn't ready to walk Ivanov into a trap. Jake had made it clear to the team that the Russian was a highly valued source for the US. Beyond the Soviet political intelligence he could provide, the knowledge he brought regarding the Soviet's rocket science program would be invaluable. There was another reason I didn't want to take him to the safe house — I wasn't sure what we'd find. His wife and daughter shot through the head? I shuddered at the thought.

"I'll be fine," I insisted.

"Can you ring the safe house?" Petrus suggested.

"It doesn't have a telephone." I repeated my lie.

Petrus's brows rose in disbelief, because he knew agency protocol would have placed some sort of communication device at the apartment.

To keep him from revealing that to Ivanov, I rushed on, "Besides, I wish to retain the element of surprise." I really needed to gauge the reaction of my arrival *if* anyone was at the apartment.

"Oleg is right. It's not safe for you to go alone," Petrus said. I opened my mouth to protest, but Petrus cut me off. "I will drive you over. Oleg will come with us. I will park nearby, but out of sight. If you don't come out in fifteen minutes, I'm coming in to get you."

"Me too," Ivanov stated.

I nodded. "Fair enough."

Petrus's Volkswagen Käfer was a nondescript gray with beige interior. I rode in front, directing him to the apartment complex, while Ivanov, again, played least-in-sight by lying across the back seat. While the car itself was just one of many in Berlin, it buzzed along with a telltale high-pitched *whistle-whuffle* common in Volkswagens. To keep from noisily announcing our arrival, I had Petrus park two blocks away.

Before I got out of the car, he laid a Mauser HSc—a small 7.65 mm German pistol made popular during the war—onto my lap. I glanced up to meet his bloodshot gaze.

"Don't get caught with this."

I nodded, tucking it in my right pocket. "I'll be back in fifteen."

Chapter Ten
The Ivanovs

I tested the door handle.

Locked.

Damn.

I'd been hoping for a surprise entrance. I rapped twice. Counted five. Rapped twice. Counted five and knocked three more times. If anyone from our crew was inside, they would recognize the code Jake had directed us to use. The rattle of the locks let me know, indeed, one of our members was on the other side. Unsure of what might greet me, I kept my hand hidden in my pocket, clutching Petrus's pistol in a tight grip.

"*Lieber Gott*, is it you? Where have you been? Where is Oleg? Did he make it out with you?"

Honestly, I hadn't been expecting Eva to answer the door. I'd had a nagging feeling that Roy had taken care of her, much like Bernard tried to take care of me. My body filled with relief upon seeing her.

Her lipstick had been chewed off, but her hair was still pulled back into the sleek chignon I'd watched her pin up this morning. She'd changed into a pair of slim ankle pants and a white turtleneck.

Still . . . while her tone exuded surprise, there was something else, undefinable, underlying her expression—a tautness around her eyes. Was it nerves? Excitement? Fear? I became watchful.

"We got split up. I expect him to arrive any minute," I replied to her question.

Rather than heading down the hall to the living room, Eva drew me directly into the kitchen, closing the door behind her.

Everything looked normal, but I found it to be an odd move. The remnants of a loaf of bread lay on the cutting board, along with half a block of cheese and a utility knife. A mug and pair of empty drinking glasses sat next to the sink, and a burning cigarette balanced on the edge of a saucer. Eva picked it up and took a drag.

"What happened? And what on earth are you wearing?" she whispered, indicating the ugly shoes with her cigarette.

"KGB got on to us. We had to improvise." Eva's brow furrowed, and I continued, "Ivanov and I ended up swimming the canals while Heinrich led them away."

"Bernard?"

I shook my head, carefully watching her reaction.

Her eyes narrowed in a calculating manner, but otherwise her face showed little expression. "Heinrich?"

"I don't know. I was hoping he'd be back here," I said with honesty. The longer Jake remained out of touch . . .

"No." She waved a cloud of smoke away from her face. "He hasn't returned."

"What about Ivanov's wife and daughter?"

"They're in the other room." Eva made a jerking motion with her head. "I've had a tricky time of it keeping them calm, especially when I hadn't heard from you."

"The flight plans to get the family out are ruined."

"I can contact the station chief to get new tickets issued." She tapped off the ashes, took another drag, and blew the smoke toward the ceiling. "When do you think Oleg will get here?"

Was that unease in her tone?

"Soon, I hope." I checked my foggy watch as if it revealed the time.

She sighed with acceptance. "You might as well come and meet Yelena and her daughter. They don't speak any English, so I'll do the talking."

I kept my face neutral, realizing that even Eva didn't know I spoke Russian. "Do they speak German?"

She stubbed out the cigarette. "Yelena, some. Not Katya. Come on."

Yelena and Katya sat next to each other on the sofa. Yelena wore a severely cut black suit with a white blouse—the outfit matched her short hair and serious mien. Katya wore a checked dress and black oxfords, and her curly hair had been tamed into a pair of braids. She held a grubby, well-loved doll in her hand.

The little girl jumped up when she saw us and cried out in Russian, "Where is Papa?"

Yelena, too, rose to her feet, shushing Katya. "Oleg?" The anxiety she was experiencing came through in that single word.

Eva replied in Russian, "He is on his way and will be here shortly. This is Claudia. She is helping your husband."

"*Guten tag, Frau Ivanov.*" I held out my hand.

"*Guten tag,*" she responded, shaking my hand. "Sorry, my German not good." She stuttered to get out the simple sentence.

"Don't worry." I smiled and bent to greet the little girl. "*Guten tag, Katya.*"

Her mother directed her to say hello, but Katya sheepishly hid behind her mother's skirts. Yelena tried to pull her away while apologizing profusely in both Russian and broken German.

"*Nein, nein.* It's fine," I reassured her.

Eva let out a tinkling laugh and told Yelena and Katya not to worry about it.

I turned to her and blurted in English, "Where is Roy?"

Yelena fell silent.

"I beg your pardon," Eva said, taken aback at my abruptness.

"Roy? Big, burly man with a crooked nose. Didn't he come back with you?"

Katya whispered to her mother, who stiffened, curling her lips inward.

"Y-yes. He went out for supplies since we weren't sure how much longer we'd be here." Eva's gaze darted to Yelena as she spoke, but I was fairly certain she hadn't heard Katya's comment. "Didn't I mention that?"

No. She hadn't. "I hope he brings back a bottle of booze. I could use a drink," I said lightly.

"I expect so." Eva chuckled and her shoulders relaxed. "I need to report to the station chief with our change in plans, and get the new tickets started. Keep an eye on the Ivanovs, would you?" She headed back through the kitchen door. Where the only telephone in the apartment was located.

Yelena sank down onto the sofa, fear plainly written across her face. She whispered agitatedly to Katya, who hugged her doll tight and buried her face in her mother's bosom. I put a finger to my lips. Yelena's eyes widened even more, if that was possible.

I caught her mid-dial. "Put the phone down, Eva."

She swung around, and, catching sight of the pistol in my hand, she slowly lowered the handset onto the cradle. "What are you doing?" she hissed.

"Apparently, Katya and her mother understand English better than you think. And, while my Russian isn't as good as yours, I get along rather well. Katya saw you shoot Roy. The poor man probably never saw it coming. Did he?"

"So, Bernard . . ." She backed up against the counter.

"Ivanov shot him . . . with Bernard's own gun," I relished delivering the last piece of information.

"Where is he?" Her eyes darted around the kitchen, as if searching for a way past me and the weapon I held.

"Not far. I wasn't lying about that. How long, Eva?" I stepped to the side, further cornering her while staying just out of reach, should she choose to lunge at me. "How long has Sidorov been paying you?"

Her gaze narrowed, and she replied with hauteur, "I don't know who Sidorov is. A man named Boris recruited me."

That didn't mean Sidorov wasn't behind her actions today.

Staring at her, I remembered her lover's touch, and I had to know. "And Heinrich?"

"You mean our friend, Flynn? At least that's the name

I knew him by." Her brows rose, and her chin went up. "Did you sleep with him?"

Ever so slightly, my head rotated back and forth.

"It is his signature move. He likes to sleep with the women he works with. He believes he can get into a woman's psyche by sleeping with her. He thinks he can read us like a book. That we can't lie to him . . . once he's been inside." Her gaze narrowed again. "But—I think you're too much like me."

"I'm *nothing* like you," I spat out.

"Oh, I believe you are," she said silkily. "Skilled at screwing while remaining completely detached here." She tapped her chest. "CIA calls us 'honey pots' while the Soviets call us 'swallows.'" An elegant shrug lifted her shoulders. "It's one and the same."

Defensive anger sluiced through me. Eva wasn't far off base, and, indeed, we did share similarities. "Is Heinrich/Flynn one of yours?" I ground out, wagging the gun at her.

"Ha! Not our true red, white, and blue Flynn. He's as patriotic as they come," she jeered.

I drew in a relieved breath.

A slight smirk crossed her features. "But they know who he is. If he's caught . . ." The smirk drew into a malevolent, self-satisfied smile.

It took every inch of restraint not to pull the trigger. "Why did you do it?"

She shifted. The smile disappeared. "My sister— she's . . . slow. They put her in a private institution so she'd be treated respectfully. My mother got cancer. A caregiver had to be hired. My father couldn't handle it.

He turned to the bottle, eventually lost his job. The bills piled up. They would have lost the house."

"Why did you leave the pair"—I tilted my head toward the living room—"alive?"

She hesitated only a moment. "KGB wants them. My orders are to wait here and eliminate Oleg if he should arrive."

"Otherwise, they'll use his family to bring him to heel?" I whispered.

"Was ist lost?" Petrus burst through the kitchen door, holding his service weapon at his side. In the living room, I heard Oleg reunite with his family

"That was more than fifteen minutes," I grunted in German.

The momentary distraction allowed Eva to acquire the knife on the cutting board.

"Don't be a fool. You can't stab us both before getting shot. Put the knife down," I coaxed.

She licked her lips; her eyes darted back and forth between the two of us.

The calm I exuded was nothing but a farce, my muscles were stretched as tight as a bowstring. The pistol practically vibrated in my hand, which was tense with anticipation. Eva's own hand began to shake as she slowly turned the knife downward.

I realized her intention. *"Nein!* Eva! Don't!"

A tear ran down her cheek. "They're coming," she whispered.

She'd been trained by the best and knew exactly where to cut. A quick flick and enough pressure sliced through the silky pants and deep into the femoral artery.

I stumbled backward, bumping into Petrus, as blood spurted from her leg, and Eva slid to the floor with a gentle sigh. Petrus cursed. The fluid continued to course from the wound, staining the new black-and-white tile; and a metallic tang scented the air.

A childish squeal from the other room roused me from my shocked stupor. "Katya mustn't see this," I uttered.

"Go. Get them ready to leave," Petrus said in clipped tones and unbuckled his belt. "I'll stop the bleeding."

"Can you stop it?" She'd cut rather high up inside the right groin muscle. The stain grew larger as every second ticked by. She'd be dead in minutes, and I struggled to gather the appropriate regret over her demise.

He scrutinized me for a moment, as if seeing a different person. "Just get them ready."

I firmly closed the kitchen door, leaving Petrus and the gruesome scene behind.

Oleg and Yelena were on their knees with Katya in between. Oleg's arms were wrapped around his family in a tight hug, and he whispered in fervent, loving tones. Their relieved faces focused on me.

I hated to break up the reunion, but I had no choice. "We haven't much time. Quick, follow me." My hand flapped, urging them to come along to the back bedrooms, where we pillaged clothes and hats for Yelena and Oleg from Jake's and Eva's things. We didn't have any children's clothes in the apartment. New clothes would have to be purchased for Katya.

I stuffed as much of my own clothing as would fit into the smaller of the two suitcases I'd brought. Then I headed into the room shared by Roy and Bernard. There was an old Army rucksack amongst Roy's things, and I crammed it full of items I found. Inveterate spies that they were, between them they had a switchblade, a set of lockpicks, a box of stamps for falsifying documents, and a fake mustache, all of which I packed in the duffle. Tucked away in one of Bernard's suit pockets was a cigar. I tossed that in, too. Figuring I'd probably need it, I also tossed in the Canon Rangefinder. Then, I directed the Ivanovs to cram everything they could into the two suitcases brought by Bernard and Jake. I would have happily filled up the larger suitcase I'd brought, but I knew there was no way we could all fit into Petrus's tiny car with it.

Petrus found me dropping last minute items—hairbrush, comb, lipstick—into my train case, while Yelena and Katya were in Jake's bedroom with Oleg finishing up their scavenging.

"Eva?" I asked without pausing my packing.

He shook his head, wiping his bloodied hands on a kitchen towel. "I need to call this in."

My mouth dropped in shock, and my hands froze. "What on earth are you going to tell them?"

"I'm an investigator." He shambled to the window and stared down at the street. "It's my job. I can't simply leave and say nothing."

My gut clenched with guilt for putting him in this position. *Damn Eva!* "What if we called an anonymous tip?" I assumed Eva and Bernard had already told the Russians the location of the apartment, meaning the safehouse was compromised. Sending in the police couldn't create further harm.

"I think the building is being watched," Petrus mumbled.

I sucked in a breath and joined him at the window.

"Black sedan." He pushed the curtain aside for me to see and pointed.

Eva had warned us that they were coming. She hadn't been lying. "We'll go out the fire escape. You've got to come with us. You can't stay here alone. If they come in—"

All four of the car doors opened at once, and four men in dark suits and dark hats exited.

"We're leaving now!" I trilled.

The Ivanovs must have heard the panic in my voice, for they came rushing out of the master bedroom, suitcases in hand, and Yelena carrying Katya.

"Nein! Not the front door!" I redirected them back into the large bedroom they'd just exited, through to the en suite bathroom, and opened the window. *"Out!"*

As Oleg led the way onto the fire escape, I gripped Petrus's sleeve. "Help me bar the door."

We ran to the foyer and threw the bolts, but I knew it wouldn't take them long to get through the flimsy apparatus. Petrus pointed to the bulky marble-and-mahogany hall tree. We shoved it in front of the door. Then we dashed to the back of the apartment to make our own exit. I grabbed my train case, and Petrus gave me a hand navigating the tight window.

"They've shot the bolts," he grunted, passing the suitcase to me, then he followed it out.

The Ivanovs were two flights down the fire escape— Oleg in front with Yelena in back, and Katya in between.

The adults each carried a suitcase and Oleg had a leather satchel slung across his body. The little girl was doing her best, but her short legs simply couldn't move as fast as an adult's legs, and she stepped with such deliberation, I believed she feared the height. One could see to the ground through the metal slats of the fire escape. Petrus and I caught up with them on the third flight.

"We must move faster," I urged Yelena.

Oleg halted our progress, dropped the suitcase, and picked up his daughter. She wrapped her legs around his waist and buried her head in his shoulder. Yelena went to pick up the suitcase, but Oleg barked at her to leave it. Petrus grabbed it as he passed by.

The lot behind the apartment complex had been cleared and was being readied for another concrete structure. Petrus and his long legs surpassed the rest of us, and he led us around the newly laid foundation, through a park, and down an alley road. We came out onto the side street a few meters from his parked car.

We jammed a suitcase and the rucksack into the boot. What didn't fit, we piled onto our laps. The Ivanovs crammed into the back seat with one of the suitcases and the leather satchel. I sat in front with a suitcase wedged between my sweating legs and the train case in my lap. The scene reminded me of a tiny car full of clowns that I'd once seen at the circus. Our situation would have been laughable — if it hadn't been so dire. Petrus started the vehicle, and we motored away in the opposite direction from the front of the building where the KGB sedan was parked.

The car was silent except for our labored breathing and Katya's muffled sobs. I turned to find her head buried in Yelena's bosom. The mother stared blindly out the window as she gently stroked her daughter's hair.

"It's okay, Katya. We've gotten away. The bad men can't find you now," I cooed at her in Russian.

Katya mumbled incoherently.

"She's lost her dolly," Yelena murmured. "That is why she cries."

Oh, dear. I rolled my lips inward and faced forward, because there was nothing I could do to help the child.

A few kilometers away, Petrus spotted a phone booth and pulled over.

"What's he doing?" Yelena asked her husband.

"Reporting a break-in," I answered.

Moments later, Petrus returned, and we were off. "I'm taking you back to the boathouse until I can figure out what to do with you."

I didn't deign to tell him that it wasn't his place to figure out what to do with us.

It was mine.

And I'd already begun running options through my head. Normally, protocol would have had me contacting an emergency number that would connect me to the local directorate, and I would be given directions for getting the Ivanovs out. However, I'd just discovered two Russian agents in our midst, both of them assigned by the Berlin station chief. I didn't know how high the corruption went, and getting the Ivanovs onto American soil would be the safest course of action. The question being—how was I going to obtain new identities for my packages and get us on a flight home?

Whom could I trust?

Jacob's fate also weighed heavily on my conscience. Although I'd gotten a full night's sleep prior to the mission, the thick pressure of fatigue set in. I closed my eyes and attempted to quiet my mind for the drive back to Petrus's place. It wasn't easy with Katya's crying and the turmoil of an operation gone wrong.

Chapter Eleven
A New Plan

Petrus's snug boathouse became even smaller with the four of us and our luggage.

"It's only temporary," I explained to everyone and silently prayed I spoke the truth.

The craft bobbed gently on its moorings, its ropes squeaking against the pilings as we entered. After stacking the luggage in a corner, Petrus poured drinks. Oleg and Yelena gladly took the schnapps Petrus offered, and I found a Fanta in the miniscule refrigerator for Katya. The offer of a sweet, new drink finally halted her tears. I declined the schnapps. Instead, I poured a lukewarm cup of leftover coffee and retreated to the bathroom to change out of my schoolmarm outfit and into a shirtwaist dress with green skirt and striped, orange top. A pair of slingback kitten heels completed my new ensemble. I took an aspirin and spent time covering the ever-darkening bruises with the proper makeup.

When I returned to the living room, Katya was at the kitchen table coloring the newspaper comics with red and black markers, and Petrus was regaling Yelena and Oleg with one of his farfetched, but likely true, war stories.

"I'm going to pick up supplies," I announced in German. "I'll return in an hour. Petrus, walk me out."

Petrus excused himself and escorted me onto the path that took us to the carpark.

"First, I can't thank you enough." I placed my palms together as if in prayer. "I wish I could say, 'I'll take it from here,' but I've determined I still need your help."

"*Ja*, of course. What is your plan?"

"I have contacts back in the States whom I know I can trust. I'm sure there are agency people here in Germany that aren't being paid by the Soviets, but I don't know who they are. I'm not willing to risk the Ivanovs or my own neck. We don't have a Berlin Embassy, and my former contacts at the Mission have moved on. Ideally, I would like to get the family out within the next forty-eight hours. The longer they remain, the harder it'll be to get them out."

"They can defect to West Germany," Petrus suggested. "I can drive them over now."

I chewed my bottom lip in thought. Indeed, I *could* turn the Ivanovs over to the West Germans. I could also imagine the hell I'd pay for doing so. It had been made abundantly clear how valuable the Oleg was to the American intelligence community. The failure of the operation would be placed at my feet, and mine alone.

My attention went back to my "friend." Petrus was no dummy, and I suddenly wondered if he had realized exactly who I'd brought to his boathouse. Any Western intelligence agency would love to get a crack at Oleg Ivanov. What were Petrus's intentions?

"If I allowed you to do that, I would wave goodbye to my career."

Petrus nodded with understanding and placed a

hand above his brow to block the sun. "What can I do to help?"

The thing about being a spy, sometimes you had to go with your instincts and put your trust in someone. Right now, I needed to trust Petrus. "First, keep an eye on the Ivanovs. I worry that Oleg or Yelena will panic and try to go their own way. Second, I need new passports for the Ivanovs. German ones for Oleg and Katya. Also, a French one. Male, age mid-thirties. Can you do that?"

Petrus stroked the scruff at his jaw. "I can get the books and travel papers, but the visa stamps are going to be a problem."

"I've got it taken care of," I said dismissively.

"What about the photos?"

"I have a camera we can use. First, I need to get some new clothes for Katya and change her hair. Is there someplace you can have the film developed quickly?"

"*Ja*, but it will cost many Deutsche Marks," he said, rubbing his thumb and forefinger together.

I didn't blink. "How much?"

His features pulled down, and he frowned in thought. "Fifty each for the passports."

The price seemed a little steep, and I suspected Petrus planned to take a hefty cut. Considering what he'd already done for me, I didn't mind. "An extra fifty is in it for your contact if he can get them to us in the next twenty-four hours."

His brows rose and he rubbed his chin. "I'll let him know."

I checked the pendant watch on my lapel—an item I'd swiped from Eva's belongings to replace my own ruined timepiece. "I need to get going to make purchases before the shops close."

Petrus handed me the keys to his car. He gave me directions to a pharmacy, where I could purchase hair dye, and a store that carried children's clothing.

"Are you sure it's safe for you to be going out?" He scratched his head, and a tuft of hair stood on end.

"I'm going off the assumption that KGB operatives will be searching the train and bus stations, and the airport. I'm also assuming Bernard or Eva gave them the false names the Ivanovs would be traveling under. That's why the new passports are imperative."

"What about you?" He frowned with concern and his chin jutted forward as he asked, "Do they know your name?"

"I've got that covered." I unlocked the car door. "I'll pick up dinner while I'm out and start arranging the airline tickets."

"Are you sure flights are the best way to get them out? What about the train?"

Climbing into the Volkswagen, I replied, "It will be best. I dare not take the duty train." Trains left West Berlin and traveled through East Germany into West Germany. They were only allowed to travel at night, and papers had to be in order when passing out of the East. Military folks called it the duty train. Civilians often referred to it as the freedom train. It wasn't stopped except at the border. "If it's stopped and their papers don't pass muster"—I made an exploding sound—"World War Three."

Petrus must have agreed with my point, for he turned

and lumbered back toward the boathouse without asking more questions.

I rolled down the window and called out, "Petrus, I have one more favor to ask."

He paused.

"Do you still have contacts in the East? Your SPD friends?" The Social Democratic Party of Germany had been around since before the war. Its strongest proponent and anti-Nazi, Curt Schumacher, had died earlier in the year. Though East Germany was a one-party system, the SPD was allowed to exist on the fringes. West German intelligence utilized East German SPD members as sources. Petrus worked with one of them during our Bulgarian Embassy op.

Petrus came back to the car and leaned down, placing his forearms on the window frame. "*Ja*. Of course."

"My leader of this mission is somewhere in East Berlin. Can you see if you can find out what happened to him? I need to know if he's been captured." I swallowed. "Or at the morgue, riddled with bullet holes. Can you do that for me?"

Slowly his head bobbed. "*Ja*, I can do that. It might take time."

"Just . . . find out what you can. I'll be back in an hour."

"What if you are not?"

The question wasn't off base. "I will phone if I'm going to be late."

This seemed to satisfy Petrus, and he stepped back, waving me on my way.

A few blocks from the canal, I located a small, family-owned inn and restaurant called *Gasthaus Bach*. It was decorated in the traditional Bavarian style — cream walls with wood trim accents, flower boxes in the window, and a red awning out front. I talked the bartender into preparing a takeaway order of a family platter of Spaetzle with kielbasa and caramelized onions, two bottles of wine, and a bottle of *limonade*. He told me I could pick it up in an hour.

The little *Gasthaus* was so inviting, and I desperately wanted to move the Ivanovs out of Petrus's tiny boathouse. However, even though the inn was a modest facility, there was still a dangerous possibility KGB would locate them. No. Petrus's boathouse was the safest option for the time being.

I located the clothing store Petrus recommended. It was a specialty boutique, and I paid rather dearly for two dresses, a nightgown, and underthings for Katya. It was nearly closing time, and the squat salesclerk was very attentive, twittering about me with various offerings in an effort to move me along so she could get home to her *abendessen*.

Once my purchases were twined in brown paper, she kindly directed me to the pharmacy two blocks away, which, she assured, would still be open for another hour. I dumped the packages in the back of the car and walked to the pharmacy, where I purchased the popular Poly Color hair dye by Schwartzkopf, various cosmetics, scissors, a few other odds and ends, and a handful of payphone tokens.

Outside the pharmacy stood a glass-and-metal enclosed phonebooth with the word FERNSPRECHER emblazoned across the top. The sun waned, and the streets began to darken into the gloom of evening. The phone booth had recently been painted white with horizontal black mullions across the glass, and a light came on when I closed the door. First, I phoned Petrus to assure him that I was hale and hearty but still had a few more errands to complete and would get back to the boathouse in thirty to forty minutes. He intimated that he had news to be discussed. I promised I would hurry and hung up.

Staring at the black payphone, I debated my options. Berlin didn't house an official American Embassy. Our presence existed under the US Mission Berlin, or USBER, in the upscale neighborhood of Zehlendorf. It was also run, not by the State Department, but by the US General in West Berlin. It did not operate under the authority of the US Embassy in Bonn, but rather under the authority of NATO. Had I known whom I could trust at the Mission, I would have used the government's ability to make a transatlantic voice radio call. On the other hand, if I knew whom I could trust, the entire reason for me to make the call would be moot. Realizing a phone call was out, I knew I'd have to follow an avenue that would both take longer and be more dangerous. I sighed and exited the booth.

The drugstore offered telegram services. As I strode down the aisle toward the telegram kiosk, the cuckoo clock bird popped out of its miniature Swiss chalet, announcing the bottom of the hour—half past six. Closing time. I begged the elderly proprietor for five minutes to complete the telegram. He picked up his pipe and a packet of tobacco and, with a gallant little bow, told me to take my time. While he busied himself with the pipe, I chewed the end of the pencil, contemplating my message.

Knowing I had to pay per word and that the message might be seen by others, it took at least ten minutes to formulate something appropriately vague, but still displaying a sense of urgency to Lily, as the message worked its way to her.

> **TO: LILY MCNAIR, STATE DEPARMENT, WASHINGTON, D.C.**
> **THE FLOWERS IN BERLIN BLOOMING. NEED A FRIEND. NOT A COMPANY MAN. REPLY SOONEST. BUTTERCUP.**

First, blooming flowers had been used many times as a call for help or sign of emergency during our OSS days. Lily, Jane, and I used it on occasion as a codeword at social events when we needed help extricating ourselves from a particularly boorish gentleman. It also provided Lily my current location so she would know where I needed a contact. The most important words, which I prayed Lily would understand—not a company man. I *did not* want her to use her contacts within the agency, of which she still had plenty. Finally, I used my codename that harkened back as far as our OSS days, another sign to Lily that I needed this to be kept confidential.

I'd considered contacting Jane, who was still working at the Pentagon, and if Lily didn't come through, I would go to her. However, I had a feeling Lily's contacts would be better equipped to obtain the flight reservations and visas that I needed to get the Ivanovs out of Berlin.

I handed the form and a pile of D-marks to the kindly gentleman. "Request replies to be sent here. I'll return tomorrow evening to see if there is a response."

His watery gaze peered at me, and he said with solemnity, "I will send it out tonight."

I thanked him and returned to the *Gasthaus* to pick up a delicious-smelling dinner packed in a covered brown casserole dish, which I promised to return the following day.

Chapter Twelve
Cover Identities

Petrus gave his room and big bed to the Ivanovs. I slept on the lumpy sofa, and he took the floor in the main living area. Eventually, the thoughts going round in my head spun themselves out. The slight creaking and rocking from the houseboat lulled me to sleep.

We both awoke before sunrise, sore and bleary eyed. Petrus got the percolator going, and we discussed our schedules for the day over our first cup of coffee. While I'd been out, he'd made a phone call and arranged to meet with his contact during *mittagessen*. My plan was to get our guests ready for their trip out of Germany and visit the pharmacy to see if Lily had returned my message.

The Ivanovs rolled out of bed after Petrus left for work. I refilled the percolator, and we ate leftover kielbasa with boiled eggs around the small dining table.

After we finished, I gave Katya a new windup car that I'd purchased during yesterday's outing. It was a model of a two-seater sports car with a key to wind the spring. She clapped with glee when I wound it up and let it zip down the narrow hallway. While Katya was occupied with her toy, I sat down with her parents to talk about the day's agenda. Considering I needed both of them to understand what was happening, we spoke quietly in Russian.

"I'm sure you've realized, since yesterday did not go as planned, there are new risks getting you out of Germany. Petrus and I are working to get fresh paperwork, visas, and plane tickets. However, along with that paperwork, I'm going to need to disguise the three of you. We'll be making some changes today so I can take photographs for the new passports."

"Even Katya?" Yelena asked.

Both her husband and I nodded. We heard a squeal of glee from the hall as the little car buzzed along, banging into the wall.

"Especially Katya," he whispered, covering her hand with his. "What did you have in mind?"

"Petrus is obtaining German passports for you and Katya. Yelena will be flying out on a French passport. Do you speak any French?" I asked.

"*Oui, un peu,*" she replied.

I let out the tiniest sigh of relief. I'd still have to work with her, but if she had some idea of the language, it would help.

"But Katya speaks no German," she said in a worried tone.

"I speak German." The little girl's head appeared over her father's shoulder. "*Wo ist die Toilette?*" she said with perfect pronunciation, then reverted back to her native tongue. "Papa taught me."

"Yes, my sweet kitten, and you speak it well." He pinched her cheek.

A dimple peeped out as she smiled at her father's compliment.

It was nice to see her smile. After the waterworks

ceased, she'd barely said two words since our precipitous exit from the apartment yesterday. Though she was young, clearly, she knew what danger was and when to stay quiet.

"Katya, do you wish to learn more German?" I asked.

"After I finish playing with my car." She disappeared, and a moment later we heard the buzzing coming from the hall.

"We will make some physical changes, as well."

"What kind of changes?" Yelena asked with trepidation.

"As much as we can. Starting with hair color. I've purchased a dye for Katya," I explained.

Yelena allowed a stricken look to cross her features.

"It is only temporary, my dear." Oleg gripped his wife's hand. After we cleared away the dishes, Oleg sat down with Katya and explained, "Today, we are going to play dress-up and take pictures. How do you like that?"

She jumped with excitement. "Oh, yes, Papa! I want to play Anastasia, the Romanov Princess."

"Well . . ." Oleg faltered.

I crouched down to her level. "Katya, remember you're not in the Soviet Union anymore. We're going to pretend to be German storybook characters."

Her eyes widened and she shook her head. "Is there a German princess?"

"A little girl named . . . uh . . . Heidi," I said, grasping at the first fairytale name that came to me. "We are going to turn your hair to the color of wheat and put on one of your pretty new dresses."

While Katya sat to have her hair colored and cut, Oleg

worked on teaching her more German words and phrases. It became a game.

Katya pointed at Petrus's armchair.

"*Der Sessel*," Oleg said.

"*Der Sessel*," the little girl pronounced and pointed at the couch. On it went—*das Sofa, das Handtuch, die Stuhl, die Puppe.*

When it was all finished, she had dark golden hair with a freshly cut fringe of bangs. I braided and pinned the rest of her hair around the backside of her head. Katya hopped off the chair, spun in her new navy-blue sailor dress, and chirped excitedly, listing off items around the room. She loved the new hairstyle, and with her blue eyes, she couldn't have looked more German. While I enjoyed her lighthearted chatter, I made a mental note to pull Oleg aside and let him know that she'd have to tamp it down the day we left for the airport.

A troubled look crossed Yelena's features as she watched her daughter. It may have been the first time she realized her daughter would change as she assimilated to the new life upon which they were embarking. If she didn't like what we'd done to Katya, she definitely wasn't going to like what I had planned for her.

Oleg was next. Under normal circumstances, one of our CIA officers skilled in disguises would have used Hollywood-quality products to change Oleg's appearance. I had to work with what I could find at the local pharmacy. I enhanced the bits of grey with white shoe polish throughout his hair, especially at the temples, and perched a pair of half-moon reading glasses upon his nose. I'd pilfered them from the woman running the dress boutique when she wasn't looking. Jake's clothing fit Oleg the best. He put on a pair of Jake's pleated brown slacks, a yellow tie, white dress shirt, and a blue button-up V-neck sweater. Bernard's olive Tyrolean-style hat finished the ensemble. I put more gray in Oleg's eyebrows and added Bernard's false mustache.

"Who is Papa pretending to be?" Katya inquired, pointing to the mustache.

Oleg wiggled the new facial hair.

"The Frog Prince," I said, putting the last touches on her father's brows.

Katya's face scrunched up. "He's not a frog."

"Tonight, at bedtime, I will tell you the story of the witch who put a curse on a handsome prince, turning him into a frog." I tapped her button nose, and she scampered off to play with her car again.

Oleg and Yelena tacked a white sheet against the wall for pictures. I stared down at the camera, marveling over the fact that it'd been a full week since I'd sat in the warm Argentinian sun. The photos I'd taken of Helmut were still in the camera.

"Something wrong?" Oleg inquired.

"*Nein. Sehr gut,*" I replied, shaking off the memory.

I photographed Oleg and Katya separately for their new identifications. There were only half a dozen photos left on the film cartridge, and I took two pictures each.

"I want a photo with new Papa!" the little girl cried over and over.

"Katya!" Yelena snapped, pressing a hand to her temple. "Not now!"

Oleg, who'd been doing his best to help amuse Katya

over the past few hours, looked at his wife in surprise. "Yelena?"

Katya clamped her mouth shut and tears brimmed on her lashes.

Yelena's nerves were frayed, and I tried to smooth over the awkward moment. "Yes, my pet. Soon we will take more pictures of you and Papa. But first, I must work on your mama."

Katya nodded solemnly. "What shall Mama be? A Princess? Or a Tzarina?"

"It's a secret surprise. Why don't you take the new coloring book and crayons outside with your papa? I'll call when your mama is done."

"An excellent idea." Oleg took the little girl's hand and led her out to the side deck.

Once they were gone, I turned to Yelena, who still had a hand pressed to the side of her face. "Would you like an aspirin?"

"I'm sorry for losing my temper—" she whispered raggedly.

"Not at all. I know *I* didn't get much sleep. Did you?"

"Bits and pieces."

"I understand this is difficult for you, Yelena. I'm doing everything in my power to get you to America the safest way I can. You just need to bear it a little longer." After she swallowed the aspirin powder with a glass of water, I broke the news. "Yelena, your disguise will be as a man."

She didn't show any surprise; instead, she sighed with resignation. "I thought as much. What do you have planned?"

Because her hair was so short, it was easy to slick it back off her face using pomade. I combed shoe polish into the pomade to give her a salt-and-pepper look. Using cosmetics and shadowing techniques, I thickened her brows, giving them a hooded aspect, enhanced her crow's feet, added a mole to her jawline, and elongated her nose.

With bandages from the pharmacy, we strapped down Yelena's already small breasts. From the rucksack, I pulled out some of Bernard's clothes—a pair of black slacks and a gray tweed sport coat—and a black turtleneck of Eva's. The turtleneck was a little baggy, which worked to our advantage, hiding Yelena's bandages. The pants fit her perfectly in length, but the waist was a few inches large. None of the belts that had been packed would work. Then I remembered an old Fred Astaire movie where he wore a tie as a belt. I found a dark tie from Petrus's closet and added it to the growing pile of favors that I owed him.

I finished Yelena's transformation with men's tortoiseshell sunglasses that I'd purchased and a small black fedora—a donation from Jake's coffers. All the men's shoes were much too large, so I gave Yelena the brown brogues from Petrus's neighbor. Yelena made a rather handsome, if effeminate, French gentleman. I worked with her to elongate her stride and affect a bit of a slouch when she walked. Finally, I invited Katya and her father inside and watched the pair of them clap with delight at Yelena's transformation.

"Is Mama a frog prince, too?" Katya asked.

"No, dear, she is the Changeling. Another story I shall

tell you at bedtime," I said. "Now, I must go out and find—"

"But what about you?" Katya interrupted. "What kind of storybook character will you become?"

"I shall become Brigitte. But, before I transform, I must go to the market—" The shrill ring of the telephone interrupted me.

It was Petrus calling. "The passports will be ready in two days' time."

"No earlier?" I tried to keep the concern out of my voice.

"*Nein.* And the French passport will cost an extra twenty."

I let out a whistle between my teeth but agreed to the upcharge—what choice did I have? "Is it possible to have the girl's passport carry the first name of Heidi?"

"I'll see what I can do," Petrus replied.

I hung up to find all the Ivanovs' gazes riveted on me. "Good news," I chirped, "the papers will be here in a few days." Yelena's face fell, but I continued before she could speak, "I'm headed to the market to pick up dinner. Oleg, why don't you take Katya to the park nearby for some fresh air?" I wanted both of them to get used to being in public in their disguises. It would also allow Yelena some quiet time to rest.

"It's important to speak only German while you are being Heidi," I said in a serious tone to Katya.

She nodded solemnly and replied, "*Guten tag! Ja!*"

We parted at the end of the carpark, and I walked the dozen blocks to the pharmacy.

The same elderly gent stood behind the counter. As

soon as he saw me, he waved me back to the telegram kiosk. "I have your reply." He handed me the envelope.

Thanking him, I tucked the thin envelope into my handbag. His face fell, obviously expecting me to open it and read it in front of him. An action I was unwilling to do, no matter how helpful he'd been. Two blocks away, I sat on a park bench and tore open the telegram.

GOOD TO HEAR FROM YOU. FRANK SAYS HELLO. I UNDERSTAND THE VICTORY COLUMN IS LOVELY THIS TIME OF YEAR. ESPECIALLY IN THE AFTERNOON AT 4. BRING HOME A COPY OF BUDDENBROOKS BY THOMAS MANN. LILY.

The code was straight forward. I checked the pendant watch. It read 3:15 p.m. I had forty-five minutes to locate a bookstore, purchase a copy of Thomas Mann's *Buddenbrooks*, and get myself to the Victory Column to meet with my contact, Frank. It didn't give me much time. If I could find a cab . . .

Glancing up and down the street, I noticed a man on the opposite side, dressed in a shabby suit and trilby hat. The left side of his face revealed a thick scar, puckered and red, that ran from his jaw, down his neck, disappearing beneath his shirt collar. His attention was riveted upon me. A shiver ran down my spine. It may have only been simple male admiration, however, I couldn't take the chance.

I pulled up my coat collar, keeping him in my sight as I pretended to window shop. He remained across the street but kept pace with me. I should have put on a disguise before going out. But then I wouldn't have been able to get the telegram from the pharmacy. Petrus's neighborhood was in such an out of the way place, I'd taken a chance. Since nothing happened when I went out yesterday ... I'd gotten complacent and assumed it would be the same for today.

Damnation! Poor tradecraft! I chastised myself.

Coming upon a shoe store, I went inside. The tinkling bell announced my entrance, and the scent of fresh leather engulfed me. A middle-aged clerk knelt in front of a matronly Frau sliding a pair of low-heeled Oxfords onto her thick foot.

He glanced over his shoulder *"Guten Tag, Frau.* You may look around. I will be with you directly."

A young mother and her daughter were studying the children's shoe section. The girl reminded me of Katya. I moved to the rear of the store and pretended to study a navy peep-toe pump. The clerk rose and headed into the back storeroom to find a larger size for his customer.

Through the display window, I saw the scarred man stroll past the shop and take up residence against a lamppost. He casually lit a cigarette.

"That comes in red, too," the clerk said.

I jerked. "Pardon?"

"That peep-toe." He pointed to the shoe in my hand. "It also comes in red and black."

I thanked him, and as soon as he returned his attention to the Frau, I disappeared behind the curtain from whence he had just come. Rows of shoes were stacked above my head and ran four or five meters in length to the rear of the building. I quickly traversed the center row. At the end, on my left, I found what I was looking for—an exit. I pulled the bolt and was out in a flash. To the left was the main street and my tail. On my right ran a shadowed alley littered with cans and the rank smell of discarded trash. I chose the garbage route, picking my way along the cluttered cobblestones. Eventually, I found myself on the far side of the block. A black taxi cruised up the street, and I flagged it down.

"*Die Buchhandlung,*" I directed, checking out the back window.

"Which one?"

I blurted out the first bookstore that came to mind. "*Literaturhaus. Fasanenstrasse 23.*" I hadn't been in years and prayed the shop was still there.

The cab motored away from the curb. As it turned the corner, a figure stumbled out of the alleyway—body erect, alert, gaze sweeping the area. The leather creaked as I slouched down in the seat. I had a little over half an hour to make it to my meeting.

It took fifteen minutes to get to the bookstore. The driver pulled up in front of the white brick building.

"Wait here. I have another stop to make," I said, climbing out of the car.

A helpful shop assistant located a copy of the book and rang it up for me. Back in the cab, I now had under ten minutes to make it to Victory Column. I knew we wouldn't make it on time. I could only hope my contact would linger.

At ten after four, I stepped out of the cab and dashed into one of the four neo-classical temples that marked the tunnel entrance. Stepping quickly, I passed other tourists in the passageway that crossed beneath the four lanes of the busy *Großer Stern* roundabout. The tunnel brought me up onto the stone tile platform of the Victory Column. The column had been built in 1864 to commemorate the Prussian victory in the Second Schleswig War. A golden statue of Victoria, the Roman goddess of Victory, stood proudly atop four blocks of sandstone decorated by cannon barrels, all of which were anchored by a base of red granite columns.

Its location in the center of a traffic circle intersected by five major streets was not its original location. The Nazis moved it from the Königsplatz in 1939. Lucky for the Germans. If it had remained at its original location across from the Reichstag, Allied bombs would have decimated it. The monument was a popular location for tourists, and even this late in the day, about two dozen people wandered around the site taking photos and admiring the architecture. Visitors could reach the observation deck directly below the statue by climbing 270 steps of a mind-spinning spiral staircase.

Since the telegram was rather slim on details, giving me no way to identify my contact, I ambled slowly around the base of the monument with my book clutched in my hand, its title on clear display for anyone to see. All the while keeping a sharp eye on the traffic circle to make sure there weren't any cars driven by the scarred man. Surveying the shimmering monument, I prayed my contact didn't expect to meet on the observation deck.

On my second trip around the base, a silver-haired man in a red sweater, black slacks, and brown overcoat approached. "Interesting book," he muttered in English.

"Have you read it?" I responded, shading my eyes

from the dipping sun as I looked him up and down.

"Are you Buttercup?"

"Frank?"

"Frank Mueller." He held out his hand. "Edward said you needed help and told me to give you anything you asked for."

So, Lily had gone to her father. Edward held a fairly powerful position in the State Department and had forty years' worth of connections.

"You work with Edward?"

Frank shook his head. "Not since the war."

"I don't understand. What is your job here in Berlin?"

"My family owns a timber company in Bavaria. I live in Berlin, where I conduct business for the company." His explanation was delivered naturally, and I could detect no deception.

"I see. Why do you wish to help me?"

He smiled. "Let us say, I owe Edward a favor, and his telegram was fairly adamant that it was time to pay up, so to speak." While his English was excellent and his accent faint, there was a definitive German flare to it; he pronounced the *W* in Edward's name as a *V*.

Lily had certainly gone out of her way to find a non-company man. Frank wasn't even a man working for the German government. Perhaps it would be for the best.

While we spoke, I continued to search the area for any sign of the scarred man or a person taking an unnatural interest in our conversation. "I need four plane tickets. From Berlin to London. London to New York."

"When do you need to leave?"

"Soon." I kept my comments short and to the point.

"Can you make it happen?"

"Of course," he said in an offhand way, as if it were nothing to purchase expensive plane tickets for four strangers.

"How can I contact you with the details?"

Frank pulled a wallet from his back pocket and removed a business card. "I have my car parked nearby. Can I give you a lift?"

I slid the card into my purse. "No, thank you. I must be getting along. I'll be in touch."

I retreated down a different tunnel than the one I'd originally taken and made my way through the *Großer Tiergarten* to the S-Bahn station. So focused on my destination, I barely noticed the colorful orange and yellow leaves clinging to the trees and crunching beneath my feet, as I walked through the redeveloped parkland. At the station, I ducked into a phone booth and asked the operator to put me through to the *Kriminalpolizei* Kreuzberg district. I released a sigh of relief when, a few connections later, Petrus answered the phone.

"Petrus, can you please look into a man named Frank Mueller?" I checked the white business card. "Of Mueller Timber Holdings."

"I've heard of Mueller Timber. What do you need to know?"

"Just get me what you can about Frank. I need to know if he's got any Russian or CIA connections."

"I'll see what I can find." Petrus rang off.

I took the S-Bahn back to the canal area. On my way back to the houseboat, I passed a market and picked up apples, milk, bread and cheese, and other foodstuffs to last us another day or two.

Chapter Thirteen
Preparation

Petrus arrived home well past dinner time. Katya had already been put to bed and the three of us were huddled around the dining table, discussing the next steps. It became clear the strain of waiting was getting to them. Yelena had taken a short nap while everyone was out, but she was clearly still on edge. She jumped, letting out a small squeal when Petrus let himself into the house. They greeted his return as though he were a conquering hero, scurrying toward him as he stepped over the threshold.

"Did you get the travel papers?" Oleg asked in German. "The passports?"

"Want dinner?" Yelena gripped his sleeve. "I make stroganoff." She'd gladly accepted my groceries when I arrived home and busied herself making a savory beef stroganoff for us. It was delicious, and the scents of the meat and flavored spices still hung in the air.

I remained seated at the table, watching with amusement. A house full of people for a confirmed bachelor must have been disconcerting. He was lucky Katya had been put to bed. When Petrus gave me a wide-eyed look, I simply asked, "How was your day?"

"*Ja, ja*, all is well. Everything is going according to plan. Dinner is good." He spoke the last to Yelena.

Yelena had left a plate warming in the oven for Petrus. I set a place for him at the dining table while she got his meal ready, and he fished a beer out of the refrigerator. I suggested we allow Petrus to eat in peace and talk further over coffee. This led to the three of us silently staring at him like a zoo animal.

He put his fork down rather forcefully. "The passports will be here tomorrow."

Laughing good-naturedly, I said, "Let's allow Petrus to finish his dinner. How about some music?"

The Ivanovs joined me in the living area, and I turned on the radio. I tuned into a classical music station and the melody of a Bach concerto filled the tiny room. Yelena and Oleg sat next to each other on sofa, holding hands. First Yelena's, then Oleg's, eyes drifted shut.

After Petrus finished eating, he put his dish in the sink and stepped out the back door. A jerk of his head indicated I should join him.

"What about the tickets?" he asked in hushed tones.

"The tickets will be available soon. What did you find out about Mueller?" I shivered and rubbed my arms.

"Not much." He patted his pockets, searching for a pack of cigarettes as he spoke. "The business is legitimate, and they've been raking in the money ever since the Brits and Americans joined sectors and the results of the Marshall Plan created a favorable economic environment for German businesses to flourish."

"What did he do during the war?"

He put a cigarette in his mouth and held the pack toward me. "From what I can tell, the Nazi party took over their timber business. The family moved to their villa in Switzerland and spent the remainder of the war in Geneva."

"Frank said he worked with Edward during the war. Any idea in what capacity that would've been?" I took a cigarette and cupped my hands around the lighter Petrus held out for me.

"Nothing concrete." He blew a puff of smoke into the air, which immediately dissipated, snatched by the brisk northeastern breeze. "After the war, it was revealed their villa was filled with refugees—Jews, professors, a priest."

So, Frank's family helped people escape Nazi persecution. That was enough for me. "Do you have the false names for the passports? I need to contact Mueller so he can purchase the tickets."

Petrus stuck the cigarette between his lips, dug out a piece of paper from his shirt pocket, and handed it to me. I held it up to the light coming through the window. Petrus's handwriting was atrocious, and it took me a moment to identify the names through his chicken scratch: *Johann Schmidt, Heidi Schmidt, Gaston Lavigne.*

"What about you?" he asked.

"I have a dark wig and a French passport identifying me as Brigitte Moreau. I'll be traveling as Yelena's companion. I need the film developed for the passports. Can you get that done?" I asked.

He nodded. "I have a friend in the department who is a crime scene photographer. He can develop them."

"Thanks." I tapped ashes into the water and studied my friend. "Why did you bring me outside? What don't you want the Ivanovs to hear?"

Petrus took his time answering. He stared onto the water, watching the gentle waves lap against the lip of the dock. He puffed on his cigarette and, finally, said with gravity, "There has not been any news of your friend."

"Yet."

His gaze turned to me. "Pardon?"

"Yet. You said there hasn't been any news of my friend . . . you mean, yet. Surely, your contacts can't be everywhere at once. Maybe they simply haven't come upon his whereabouts. Perhaps he's crossed back into friendly territory."

Petrus grimaced.

"What? You're not telling me something."

"The brown Skoda you described was located by the East German police. There was blood in it."

I relaxed and waved my hand. "Yes, I know. He'd been struck by a rock during our escape. It caused a scratch above his temple. Some of it must have bled onto—"

"There was a lot of blood. Not from a scratch. There were bullet holes through the passenger windows."

My breath caught. I twisted away from Petrus's pity. Now it was my turn to watch the dark canal, searching it for answers it could never give. "Do you think they've got him?" I asked in monotone.

Petrus sighed. "I could not say. My contacts are looking into it."

I shivered, whether from the breeze or the news, I didn't know. "Anything else?"

The tip of his cigarette glowed red. "Today, an American woman filed a complaint at the train station. She'd been accosted by a pair of men who tried to drag her into their car."

"I'm sorry to hear that. What does it have to do with our situation?"

He tossed the butt into the canal. "She was a blonde, like you, and they called her Claudia Fischer."

I thought about the scarred man following me and sucked in a deep breath of cold air. Clearly the wolves were on the hunt.

Before I could answer, a shadow dropped between us, and Oleg opened the door.

"Is everything alright?" he asked, using his German.

"Everything is fine, my good man," Petrus assured him, clapping him on the shoulder.

I flicked the cigarette into the canal and drew up my features before turning to speak to Oleg. "We didn't want to wake you. However, it is time we talked about the next steps."

♠♠♠♠

After the Ivanovs went to bed, Petrus headed off to take a bath. And I used the phone to contact Frank Mueller.

"*Ja, Mueller.*"

"*Herr Mueller, hier ist . . . Buttercup,*" I said.

"Good evening, Buttercup," Mueller responded, switching to English. "What can I do for you?"

"First, I apologize for the lateness of the hour." Petrus's clock above the radio read ten past eleven. "Second, I have the names for the flights. What did you find out?"

"I can get you on a flight out of Berlin to London as early as tomorrow. Two airlines make daily trips. As for the trans-Atlantic flight, there is a Pan Am Stratoliner that leaves on Saturday, Tuesday, and Thursday." He paused. "I am assuming you would like to fly your guests out of Berlin as soon as possible."

"Yes, that would be best. Put us on a flight the day after tomorrow, Sunday." I'd have to find a hotel to stay in for two nights. Once I arrived in London, I knew there were people I could contact.

"That will leave you with a layover. I can make hotel arrangements for you in London," Mueller offered.

Surprised by his kind offer, I didn't immediately answer. "I—I . . . would greatly appreciate that. Preferably a smaller hotel."

"No problem. What are the names for the airline tickets?"

I rattled them off from Petrus's list. "They need to be purchased in pairs. Johann and Heidi separate from Brigitte and Gaston. Do not get seats close to each other." I figured it would be less likely Katya would make a mistake if her mother, dressed as a man, was *not* nearby.

"British European Airways has a morning flight and KLM an afternoon flight."

I chewed my lip, trying to decide between the British carrier or the Dutch. I'd prefer to get out first thing in the morning, however, the enemy might expect us to take a British airline. Shaking my head, I realized my own ridiculousness. The enemy would be watching every flight, it didn't matter if it was morning or midnight. "Book the first one out."

"Consider it done. Do you want them available to pick up at the ticket counter?"

"Yes. Phone me tomorrow to confirm." I gave Mueller Petrus's phone number and said goodbye.

Chapter Fourteen
Photos and Passports

Petrus left early the following morning before daybreak. Taking the film with him, he promised to return home at *mittag* with the passports.

Oleg came out of the bedroom not long after Petrus left. Rubbing the sleep from his eyes, he nodded and headed toward the percolator.

"How did you sleep?" I asked in German.

He shrugged. "Fine. Yelena . . . not so good."

I sighed. "Let her sleep. I've arranged for flights. We'll be leaving tomorrow morning."

His hand paused, holding the coffee pot above the mug. "We're leaving? Tomorrow?"

"If all goes according to plan, we will be flying into London, and soon you will be on American soil."

He whispered something I didn't understand, but I was fairly certain it was a prayer.

♠♠♠♠

At lunchtime, Petrus arrived home with the passports and the developed film. I heard him arrive and met him on the pathway to the houseboat. He handed me an envelope with the photos, but when I went to take them out of his hand, he didn't release them.

I tilted my head questioningly.

"You have some interesting pictures in here. Where were they taken?" he intoned innocently.

My brows rose in surprise, but then I remembered the photos of Helmut von Schweiger on the roll. "Anyone you know in them?" I matched his innocence.

"Perhaps." He finally released the envelope and repeated his initial question. "Where were they taken?"

I paused before responding, "South America."

His gaze narrowed, and he kept his left hand in his pocket. "Your government's handiwork?"

"Not that I know of."

He paused a moment to consider his next question. "Will you be delivering the photos, along with the Ivanovs, to your superiors?"

My lips flattened. "It wasn't my plan. I took them while on vacation." His face showed surprise at my response. "Is there someone you know who would be interested in them?"

He hesitated, and I could tell Petrus wasn't quite sure how to answer. Finally, he said, "Indeed, I do." Running a hand through his thinning hair, Petrus continued to scrutinize me.

I spun the envelope around with my fingers and tried to determine my next move. I couldn't decide the exact reason Petrus wanted the photos. He used former Nazi contacts for intelligence. Helmut was a former Nazi, and while I'd just entrusted three defecting Russians into Petrus's care, I wasn't sure where his loyalties would lie when it came to another German—especially one as controversial as von Schweiger.

While the rest of NATO saw a man like von

Schweiger as a Nazi war criminal who should stand trial for crimes, there were plenty who worked in the intelligence community that would use anyone they could to gather information. Moreover, I still didn't know if my own country was responsible for putting Helmut in Argentina. During the collapse of the Reich, Allen Dulles and his people made all sorts of deals with fleeing Nazis. Like it or not, they became valuable assets to the CIA.

"Are you familiar with his background?"

"I am," Petrus replied with gravity.

"Who would you give it to? German intelligence?"

Very slowly his head twisted back and forth. "A Frenchman."

My eyes narrowed as realization dawned. *Yes, I bet French intelligence would be very interested in knowing where Helmut von Schweiger currently resides.* I opened the envelope and allowed the photos to slide out of the pocket. The ones I'd taken of the Ivanovs were on top. "The negatives?"

He didn't move for a few moments. Finally, with a deep sigh, he pulled them out of his pocket. I stuck them in the envelope and pulled out three photos. They were of Helmut behind the bar, the front of the restaurant with its name, and of the corner street sign. I passed Petrus the photos. Any intelligence agency worth their salt would be able to find his location with those.

"Give them to your French contact. Keep my name out of it. Understand?"

Petrus slipped them into his pocket. "*Danke.* My friend will be . . . delighted to receive them."

I turned to find all three Ivanovs staring at us from

the front window. Apparently, they'd witnessed my hushed discussion with Petrus.

"Problems?" Oleg asked anxiously as we entered.

"*Nein. Alles ist gut,*" Petrus responded, clapping him on the shoulder.

I spent the next hour doctoring the passports with appropriate stamps and aging them with backdated visas, thanks to Bernard's stamp collection. I'd been trained in document falsification during the war, when a piece of paper might be all that stood between you and a concentration camp. The photos had to be attached with precision, using tweezers and glue.

At two thirty, Mueller called to inform me that the tickets had been purchased and would be available at the airline counter. "The flight leaves at 9:45. I've arranged rooms for you at the Byron, a small hotel near Hyde Park." Mueller rattled off the address, which I wrote down on a slip of paper. "The Pan Am flight to New York leaves at 9:05 on Tuesday."

"Thank you, Herr Mueller. I will make sure you are reimbursed for the expenses."

He made a scoffing noise. "Forget it. Anything for a friend of Edward's. I owe him much more than can be repaid. *Viel Glück.*"

"*Danke, danke.*"

The next few hours were spent preparing the Ivanovs. We worked on German signs and phrases. I also trained them on gait, speech, and gestures, such as counting with your fingers—Germans start with a fist, open with a thumb for number one. Russians generally started with an open palm and folded fingers in while counting. One could either start with a pinky or thumb. The hardest part to teach—behaving with an air of confidence that came naturally to Westerners, but which was incredibly abnormal to those from Communist states.

I'd spent six months interviewing refugees escaping the yolk of East German Communism. I could spot an Eastern Bloc native from sixty paces. They walked, talked, and even ate with a furtiveness when out in public. They checked their surroundings surreptitiously before speaking. They tended to speak in low tones, worried who might overhear, because even the most innocent comment could be misconstrued by government agents who littered the public arena. While Oleg walked and talked with far less restraint, Yelena did not. I noticed she tended to hunch her shoulders in a defensive manner when Katya made loud noises or the phone rang.

Katya had a natural childlike exuberance around her parents, and even around me. However, I'd noticed whenever Petrus was around, she watched him warily and tended to keep her mouth shut. Occasionally, she'd whisper something to one parent or another when she had questions. Clearly, she was already learning to watch what she said around strangers. I felt she'd shown me her other side due to the time we'd spent making her into her Heidi persona and the folktales I'd told her. Even though she was young, she seemed to grasp the notion that, in order to get to America, a place her parents had raved about, she had to "become" Heidi. She walked around all morning, quietly repeating German phrases her father taught her.

However, both parents had warned her to remain quiet at the airport. I had a feeling if she had questions, she would naturally revert to her whispering ways, which would be for the best. Adults would likely shrug it off as simply a child's natural shyness. Oleg and his daughter's cover story was simple—a grandfather taking his only granddaughter on an exciting trip to New York City to see the sights.

Yelena spent the day pitching her voice to a lower octave when she spoke. Her French was mediocre, at best. A native French speaker would know immediately, however, a non-speaker might or might not. I suggested she allow me to do the talking, especially while we were in Germany. Once we made it to London, my fears would dissipate. Yelena's—or I should say—Gaston's and Brigitte's cover story was purely business. Gaston was a history professor at the University of Paris conducting research for a book on World War I. Brigitte would be both a secretary and translator for Gaston.

Because I had to work their cover identities on the fly, the Ivanovs didn't have a litter like I did for Brigitte. There was no paperwork to fill out their wallets— driver's license or state ID, credit card, library card, etc. Leaving from West Berlin, I didn't expect the airlines to need more than our passports, and I prayed they didn't ask for anything else.

That evening, I spent time preparing to become Brigitte. With a pair of manicure scissors, I carefully cut the right side of the lining of my train case. The tiny stitches fell away to reveal Brigitte Moreau's passport, license, and various papers. I retrieved them, along with a small stack of French Francs, then took the time to baste the lining back in place with a travel sewing kit that I always carried with me. My D-marks were dwindling, and I'd need to exchange both the Francs and Marks into British Pounds once we arrived in London in order to feed everyone and take care of any incidentals.

I also discovered the forgotten switchblade that I'd found among Roy's things. During a rare moment alone with Oleg, I slipped him the knife.

Initially, he protested, "*Nein*, you take it. Or Yelena. You both might need it."

"I have my own, hidden here." I tapped my thigh.

"*Ja*, I will take it. Thank you." He slipped it into a pocket.

"I don't expect you to need it, but—"

"I understand. In case . . ."

We decided to cut into the lining on the sleeve of his overcoat and sew a little pocket for the knife so it would be hidden but accessible. A rudimentary fix that did the job.

Our flight left at 9:45 a.m. We needed to arrive in plenty of time to pick up the tickets. However, I didn't want to arrive too early. Sitting around the airport would be both risky and nerve-wracking, knowing agents would be in the area, trying to locate the three defectors.

If they were identified by Russian agents, one of three scenarios could happen. First, they could simply eliminate Oleg—a poison dart to the neck, a dagger slice to the lungs, anything that would quickly and quietly take him out of commission. The enemy wouldn't even need to retrieve Yelena and Katya at that point. After all, it was Oleg who held the vital information. A different scenario had the KGB identifying any one of the defectors and creating a hullabaloo that would have us all dragged away to a security room. All the major players would get involved—Soviet, American, and German alike. It would cause an international incident, and not knowing if there were disloyal players on the American side, the Ivanovs could be taken back to their home country, where Oleg would undoubtedly be tortured and thrown in the Gulag, while his family, if not imprisoned, would wither away their days in squalor. Or the Germans would be able to claim the Ivanovs, and a dirty agent might take care of them later. Either way, tensions between East and West would elevate, and the Ivanovs would be in danger.

These scenarios and plenty more spun through my head as I tossed and turned on the uncomfortable couch for the last night in Petrus's houseboat. Around four in the morning, I gave up. Wrapping myself in a blanket, I snuck out to the deck to smoke a cigarette. The temperature had dropped, and the breeze off the cold water sent goosebumps up my arms. I curled up on the deck chair, tucking my bare feet beneath the blanket. The waterfront was quiet. Three houseboats down, a forgotten exterior light burned low, the only illumination among the handful of homes other than the red glow of my cigarette. A nearby fishing boat rubbed against the dock, its ropes squeaking with the ebb and flow of the autumn breeze.

Twenty minutes later, Oleg joined me.

"Smoke?" he asked, making a smoking motion with two fingers near his lips.

I pulled the pack from beneath the blanket and held it out. "Couldn't sleep?" We spoke in German.

He shook his head. The match flared brightly, showing a quick glimpse of his drawn features before he extinguished it.

"Oleg, you must know, even though we are not in East Berlin, tomorrow . . . it is still—"

"Dangerous. Yes. I know."

Of course, he knew. His dreams were probably far worse than mine. After all, I'd never actually seen the inside of a Soviet gulag. I wasn't sure Oleg had either, however, Communist Party members were told, in no uncertain terms, exactly what happened to captured defectors. He may have even witnessed the execution of a failed defector or spy.

A smoke cloud gathered above his head for a moment before the breeze took it away. "I want you to promise me something," he whispered urgently.

"If I can."

"Should something happen to me—" He paused to take a drag. "—Yelena and Katya must get out." Smoke slithered from his nose and mouth. "Do not allow Yelena to come back for me. Their lives would be hell in the Soviet Union after this."

"I will do whatever I can. What if the roles are reversed? What if Yelena is caught?"

He stared past me as if in another world. Only the glow of our cigarettes lit our little porch. "We have spoken of it. Katya must get to out. It does not matter which of us takes her," he said with finality.

I didn't bother to ask what the plan was should an

agent grab Katya. The child would be the weak link between the parents' pact. The Soviets would know it too. It's why I'd warned Katya to always remain at her father's side and not use the bathrooms at the Tempelhof Airport. Bathrooms could be dangerous places. Any of them could easily be attacked or abducted by KGB in the public restrooms. We'd drink little in the morning and relieve ourselves prior to leaving for the airport.

I stubbed out the cigarette. "We are *all* getting out today. The American military has a motto—never leave a man behind."

Oleg stared at me, and Jake's face came to mind. I cringed and glanced away from his scrutiny. "It is a great motto," he mused. "Perhaps easier to adhere to on the battlefield than it is in covert affairs." The man knew and saw far too much.

"Once you are safe, I will return to find him," I muttered.

He tossed the cigarette into the canal. The end made a quick sizzle before turning black. "I wish you every success. I owe that man my life."

The high-pitched trill of the telephone startled both of us. Oleg jumped up, but I placed a calming hand on his arm. "It's probably Petrus's office. He can be called on at all hours to investigate a case."

Petrus had turned on the lamp by the phone. He stood in a pair of red, long underwear and an undershirt. His expression was hard as he nodded. "*Ja . . . ja . . . jetzt? Ja.*" He hung up and turned to the two of us.

"New case?" I asked.

"*Nein.* KGB knows you two swam through the Spree.

They've traced you as far as the dock where you stole the boat."

Damn! "Where is the dinghy now?"

"I drove it to the opposite end of the canal and tied it to a public dock," Petrus replied.

"Do they know if we've left Germany yet?"

"They aren't sure. They're still searching every vehicle and train making its way west through East Germany."

"Even the freedom trains?" I asked.

He shrugged. "One has been halted inside the East German border. I don't know if it's been boarded. They are searching all boats and ships heading north toward the Baltic Sea."

"And the airport?"

Petrus nodded. "They'll have agents at the airport."

"Yes, but it will be more difficult for them to make a move at the airport," I countered.

"More difficult, but not impossible," Oleg said. "In either case—"

"In either case, we can't stay here any longer." I finished his sentence. "It is too dangerous for Petrus."

Petrus scratched his head and sighed. "KGB is no longer keeping Oleg's defection out of the press. He's been declared a dangerous war criminal who escaped prison. It's not just the KGB and Stasi looking for him."

I turned to Oleg. "Get everyone up and dressed. We're leaving. *Now.*"

"Where will you go?" Petrus asked. "It's not yet five o'clock. The airport doesn't open until eight."

He was correct. My mind raced. Lack of sleep and

stress had me questioning every move I'd made up until now.

"Breathe," Petrus whispered. "I'll think of something. Go get dressed."

I closed my eyes and drew in a deep lungful of air, in and out, five times. Then it came to me. My eyes popped open. "Mueller."

Petrus looked skeptical, but I remembered Mueller's words about how much he owed Edward. I didn't like doing it, but I was going to play on his friend's debt one more time.

The call went through, and after a dozen rings, a gravelly male voice answered. *"Ja?"*

"Herr Mueller, ist Buttercup."

Suddenly alert, he answered clearly, "What is wrong?"

"I need a place to stay until we can go to the airport. My current location is no longer safe." I twisted the phone cord between my fingers.

He rattled off his address. "I can send a car."

"Nein. We will come to you." I rang off.

"I'll take you," Petrus said, pulling on his pants.

"Thank you, my friend."

Thirty minutes later, I climbed into Petrus's car with a dapper Frenchman, a German grandfather, his granddaughter, and a pile of luggage. There was nothing funny about our situation, but I had to bite my lip to keep a giggle from escaping as we once again crammed ourselves into Petrus's tiny Volkswagen.

Petrus looked us all over one more time, and the car puttered to life. "The disguises are good," he murmured.

Chapter Fifteen
Waiting

Mueller's apartment was in the Charlottenburg district in a wealthy part of town. The building must have dated to the eighteen hundreds and had survived the war undamaged. We slipped quietly into the stone-paved courtyard; I knocked softly on door number 102. Behind the window curtains, the lights burned bright, and Mueller quickly answered my summons.

He squinted at me. "Buttercup?"

"Yes, it's me," I whispered in English. "Call me Brigitte."

Mueller pushed the door wide, allowing us to enter.

"Das ist Johann, Heidi, und Gaston." I introduced our entourage as they entered the marble foyer.

"Guten Morgen," Mueller greeted, and shook each person's hand, saving Katya for last. *"Wilkommen."*

"Danke schön," Katya said with a serious expression.

I remained amazed at how well she'd taken the early wake-up call. I knew the lack of sleep would eventually wear her down. Hopefully, she'd be able to make it on the plane, where she could get some rest on the way to London.

"Would you care for breakfast? I have pastries, meats, and coffee in the kitchen," Mueller suggested.

Katya's eyes rounded at the word *Frühstück*, a word she'd already memorized, and gave an enthusiastic nod.

The Ivanovs graciously thanked Petrus and allowed Mueller to usher them upstairs to the kitchen.

"I'll be up in a moment," I said to their retreating backs. Sandwiching one of Petrus's hands between my own, I spoke from my heart, "My dear friend, I cannot thank you enough for the help you have rendered me." He blushed and tried to pull away, but I held tight. "One day, I will repay you."

He shook his head.

"This is for you." From my handbag, I removed the Cuban cigar that I'd pilfered from Bernard and placed it in his hand.

His eyes lit up. "*Ja, ja.* Very nice."

I'd already asked so much of poor Petrus, but unfortunately, I hadn't finished imposing upon his kindness. "As soon as I am able, I want to return to help my friend. If you could remain in touch with your contacts . . ." I trailed off.

His face creased with understanding. "Send me your direction when you can."

I rose to my tiptoes and gave Petrus a kiss on each of his sagging cheeks. "*Danke, mein Freund.*"

He shuffled out the door. Moments later, I heard the *whistle-whuffle* of the car as it drove up the street.

Following the scent of coffee, I located the kitchen. The cabinetry was made of dark oak, the floor was terracotta tile, and a fire burned merrily in the brick hearth, making the kitchen feel warm and cozy.

The Ivanovs sat around the scarred wooden table in the center of the room, happily enjoying Berliner Krapfen, known in America as jelly donuts. Katya licked a glob of red jelly from her finger and gave me a sugary smile. I didn't know if Mueller had the donuts on hand or specifically fetched them following my phone call. I gratefully accepted a lemon curd-filled confection but declined the espresso, though I desperately could have used the energizing brew. Neither of the Ivanovs had any sort of drink at their place. Katya, I noticed, had a miniature glass of milk at her elbow. It was barely past five, and we still had a few hours to wait before leaving for the airport. I would make sure Katya visited the toilets before we left.

Waiting was the worst part. Katya didn't seem to be affected by the general apprehension, but I could see the strain in the vein beating at Yelena's temple, which she would press her fingers against from time to time; in the tautness around Oleg's eyes and by the tensity of his shoulders. My own nerves were tight as a bowstring. It felt as though we'd been waiting for weeks to get out of Berlin, instead of the few short days it'd actually been.

After Katya finished her jelly donut, Mueller brought out a basket of German dolls dressed in traditional dirndls and lederhosen. "These were my daughter's dolls. Would you like to play with them?" he asked the little girl.

Oleg translated, and his daughter reverently accepted the basket. Her mouth O'd in awe of the beautiful porcelain faces. She took the carrier and sat on the rug in front of the fireplace. Speaking to the dolls in her native tongue, Katya gave each one a name and gently fingered the clothing—fixing a cuff, buttoning an undone button, tying a shoe.

The adults made conversation in fits and starts. Yelena said very little, spending most of her time watching Katya. Desperation, love, and unguarded fear played across her features.

The sun rose; light filtered through the sheer curtains, brightening the room. Katya sat in the center of a shaft that lit her newly golden hair like an angel's halo. I sent up a silent prayer for her safety. While the parents were adults who knew exactly the dangerous tightrope we treaded, little Katya was an innocent child, and I would hate to see any harm come to her.

Finally, the appointed hour arrived. We gathered our cases and prepared for departure. This time when Mueller offered his car, I took him up on it.

"Please drive Johann and Heidi. Gaston and I will take a taxi. Leave ten minutes after we depart," I directed.

Yelena wasn't happy with the plan. "*Nyet.*" She shook her head. But Oleg, realizing the wisdom in appearing at the airport in separate vehicles, agreed to my suggestion. Oleg took Yelena out of the room to convince her of the necessity of the plan and to have a last private moment with her.

Meanwhile, Mueller called for a taxi to pick up Yelena and me at the street corner. Then he did an incredible kindness. Crouching to speak with Katya, who was tenderly placing each doll in the basket, he told her she could pick one doll to take with her to her new home. Katya hesitated, unsure if she'd understood, and I translated Mueller's offer into Russian. Her eyes lit up and she took a moment to examine each doll in turn, settling on a blonde doll wearing a pink apron and a green velvet dress with rose flowers embroidered on it. She thanked her benefactor profusely in both German and Russian.

I said my goodbyes and stood on tiptoe to give Mueller a kiss on each cheek.

He blushed and patted my shoulder. Clearing his throat, he said, "Tell Edward he still owes me a chess rematch."

I promised to pass along the message. Yelena hugged Katya tightly and told her to be a good girl for her father. Katya realized we would not be together until we reached England, and the excitement fell from her face. Her lip quivered and her eyes glistened with unshed tears. The new prize hung limp at her side. Yelena whispered something into her daughter's ear. Katya pulled in her lip and mustered up a courageous smile while her mother wiped away the tears. She hugged the new doll tight to her chest. Yelena and I gathered our luggage and left to meet the cab.

Chapter Sixteen
Tempelhof Airport

The airport bustled with activity. Perfumed women and harried men hustled through the entrance, dressed in their Sunday best. Every time a door opened to the tarmac; the scent of jet fuel wafted through the terminal. Tempelhof was considered the third-busiest airport in Europe and had been a lifeline during the Soviet blockade from 1948 to 1949. Operation Vittles, aka the Berlin Airlift, brought in 4500 tons of food, fuel, and other essential supplies to the population of West Berlin on a daily basis. In order to accommodate the air traffic, the US military laid two new runways, demolished the original terminal, and built a newer, larger one to create space for unloading more planes.

My heels clacked against the hard tile floors, blending with dozens of other footsteps. Yelena and I approached the British European Airways, or BEA, desk and took our place behind an English RAF officer and his family. While we waited, I scanned the area. The loudspeaker announced a boarding flight. A porter, wheeling a large steamer trunk, headed down the hall toward the gates, followed by a nattily dressed bald man and middle-aged woman with a mink tippet and matching hat. Other porters shuttled luggage thither and yon while passengers strolled and trotted their way through the terminal.

Even though the American and British military had turned the airport over to the government of West Berlin last year and resumed a full slate of daily commercial airflights, their presence was still apparent. Tempelhof was the main airport for UK and US military personnel and their families to fly in and out of. In addition to those traveling, military guards stood at intervals around the airport with weapons slung over their shoulders. Three American Hiller-Raven helicopters sat on the tarmac on alert status at all times. Additional military planes were housed in surrounding hangars, ready to leave at a moment's notice should the Communists make a move against the West. In truth, Berlin was a pressure cooker of politics and intrigue. If anything were to engage the US and USSR into a new war, it would likely happen on Berlin's soil.

The British family moved on; Yelena and I stepped forward. Setting the suitcase at my feet, I spoke in German, with a French accent. "There should be tickets on hold for us. The 9:45 to London. Brigitte Moreau and Gaston Lavigne."

"Passports, please," said the blonde representative. She wore the BEA's uniform—a gray skirt suit with nipped waistline and distinctive golden lapel pin with a crown and single wing.

I handed her our fake identification, and Yelena stiffened at my side. The representative pulled open a drawer and flipped through a file folder. I coughed and jostled Yelena's shoulder. She exhaled the breath she'd been holding and relaxed her stance, dropping to the slouch we'd rehearsed that I'd assured her was very

French.

"Yes, I have them." The blonde pulled out two thin, rectangular pieces of paper. She glanced languidly at our passports and stamped the tickets. "The flight leaves from gate two. It will begin boarding in about twenty minutes, at nine fifteen. You may wait in the BEA guest lounge until it is called." She indicated a glass-enclosed seating area with the British airline's distinctive red logo emblazoned on the wall next to it. She passed the documents across the desk. "Shall I call a porter for your luggage?"

"We'll take it to the gate," I replied. Should anything go wrong and we needed to make a hasty exit, I wanted to be sure we had our bags.

"Is there anything else I can help you with?" It didn't surprise me the woman addressed the "man" on my left as she spoke.

Yelena simply nodded and grunted a throaty, *"Oui."*

The woman waited with expectation.

I interjected before Yelena could make a mistake, "Apologies, he doesn't speak German, only French. Thank you for your help." I picked up the tickets and passports.

Clearly bored with our transaction, the airline worker looked past the pair of us at the businessman next in line. Behind him stood Oleg with a tentative Katya tucked at his side, hiding slightly behind his overcoat. My glance caught his; neither of us revealed any sort of recognition. Yelena started to turn, but I hooked my arm through hers. I didn't want her to catch Oleg's or, worse, Katya's eye. Guiding her toward the lounge, I stated in French,

"We can wait in here."

Nodding, she seemed to comprehend the French, or at least did a good job faking it.

The seating area was filled with a variety of bright-colored, blocky chairs that were becoming fashionable. They were grouped in twos, threes, and fours, along with small tables and standing ashtrays around the room. Yelena and I chose a pair of sapphire-blue chairs at the far end of the lounge. The businessman in line behind us joined the growing crowd, and a few minutes later Oleg and Katya entered, taking seats near the door.

She gently sat her doll in the chair next to her, and the ever-present crayons and coloring book came out. While Katya remained quiet, her attention darted around the crowd. The little girl's eyes rested longer on her mother than any other waiting passenger. When her gaze shifted to me, my lips flattened, and with the barest of movements, my head shifted back and forth. Katya's face reddened and she returned her attention to the crayons. Oleg had gotten ahold of a German newspaper and perused it.

I'd placed Yelena with her back to the doorway so I could sit with my back to the wall and watch the crowd. The poor dear had taken to chain smoking to calm her nerves. She was like a duck on the water—tranquil on the outside, while her insides paddled madly. Her stubby fingers barely shook as she tapped the ashes onto the glass tray.

From my own observations, nobody seemed to be paying special attention to Oleg and Katya, nor Yelena and me. While Yelena was strung up with anxiety, the busy airport full of passengers calmed me. I was confident in our disguises, and I knew it was easier to hide amidst large groups. Especially a large crowd of international travelers that exhibited a variety of clothing styles, languages, and body types.

At nine fifteen, a loudspeaker announced our boarding call. Many of the passengers in the lounge were waiting for the same flight. They rose ponderously and began filing out the door toward gate two. Yelena and I gathered our belongings. She carried her suitcase in one hand and hat in the other. I hitched my handbag onto my shoulder, carried the suitcase in one hand and the train case in the other, and we followed the throng out the door.

Had Yelena not bent to pick up the hat she dropped, I would not have turned to witness the dull black Gaz Pobeda come to a halt in front of the terminal. From my vantage point, I could see the Soviet license plate. A man leapt from the passenger side and briskly entered the building. An olive-drab Jeep pulled in behind the Pobeda. I'd been expecting an attack to come through covert means. It never occurred to me the Soviets would use a more direct approach via one of their "flag tours." Even though the Soviet would have no authority, he could cause problems that would spell disaster for the Ivanovs and me. Traveling under assumed names and false papers, unsanctioned by either the West German or the American governments, put us in a precarious position.

Yelena's breath caught. I took the hat from her hand, placed it on her head, and giving her my train case, urgently whispered in French, "Get to the plane. Do not wait for me. Do not look back."

Wide eyed, she scurried to follow the dwindling crowd. I fiddled with my suitcase for a moment, opening one of the two locks, and slowly began making my way toward the gate.

The arrival of the Soviet vehicle had put the military guards inside the terminal on alert. Weapons came off shoulders, and a pair of privates left their posts to follow the new arrival. The representative—possibly a KGB agent—bypassed the airline desks and, walking at a fast clip, strode toward the gates. I paced my steps at a diagonal path that would intercept him. Counting silently backwards from ten, I crossed directly in front of the Soviet. He tried to dodge around me. I shifted the suitcase, which knocked his leg, and at the same time, I flicked the second lock. The lid flew open, and my clothes tumbled onto the floor as the man stumbled over the mess.

"*Imbécile!*" I cried out the insult.

The Soviet mumbled an apology in Russian, his gaze searching the crowds ahead, and tried to move past me. However, I stepped in front of him, and my voice lashed out. The French language reminded me of an uppity Siamese cat—all sleek lines and elegance. German, on the other hand, is a wonderfully guttural language. Perfect for scolding someone. My throaty tones rained down upon him, and the infantrymen were at my side in an instant.

"*Was ist los?*" the shorter of the two asked.

"This mannerless lout knocked the suitcase out of my

hand, trod on my blouse—"I indicated the littered floor"—and tried to walk away without so much as an apology." At that point, I sniffed and sank to my knees to begin gathering my clothes.

One of the privates—his nametag read Swindon— crouched to help me, while the other interrogated the Soviet, asking him all sorts of questions—starting with a request to see his identification and his purpose for being at the airport. Another guard, a sergeant, joined the fray. Other passengers going to their gates gave us a wide berth.

The Soviet removed his identification from an interior pocket and held it out.

The sergeant's eyes were slits as he snatched it from the Soviet's hand and passed it to his subordinate. Then, in a friendly tone, he asked down to me, "Frau, are you okay?"

I jammed the last bit back into the suitcase, snapped it closed, and thanked Private Swindon, who helped me to my feet. Demurely, I looked up at the sergeant beneath my lashes and answered in German, "*Ja,* thank you for your help. My flight is boarding, I must hurry."

The sergeant looked me up and down. "I need to see your passport, please."

My ticket was tucked into the passport, and I handed both to him. He glanced at the papers. The two privates flanked the Soviet, who, by now, was red as a bowl of cherries, angry, and growling that it was all a misunderstanding. He insisted he was there on official business to locate a war criminal who had escaped from East Berlin.

The sergeant returned my travel papers and said, "Private Swindon, escort Frau Moreau to gate two."

Giving a serene smile, I thanked him.

He turned to the Soviet. "Comrade Semenov, follow me. My lieutenant will want to hear more about this dangerous war criminal you are searching for."

Semenov sputtered an objection and insulted the sergeant in Russian as he was led away. Returning my attention to my new friend, I witnessed a man with a scar enter the terminal—the same man who followed me into the shoe store. His gaze, like many in the airport, focused on Semenov and his military escort.

I turned my back to him and, with a bright smile, said, "Shall we?"

Private Swindon picked up my suitcase and ushered me to the gate. The last call for boarding rang out over the intercom. Swindon pushed open the glass door. A painted yellow pathway of arrows stretched out in front of us, like the yellow brick road in *The Wizard of Oz*, directing passengers to the tarmac where a Vickers Viking plane awaited, prepped and ready for its trip out of Berlin. The BEA plane would travel through a narrow, twenty-mile flight zone over East Germany, stopping in Amsterdam to refuel before ending up at Croydon Airport in London.

The last travelers climbed the stairs, and Swindon hailed the luggage handler who rolled a wagonful of bags out to the waiting plane. "Hold up! One last passenger."

The handler jogged over to us, and Swindon passed him my suitcase.

I thanked the private for his help, kissing him on each cheek in French fashion, before mincing toward the plane.

He blushed and called out, "My pleasure, ma'am."

One of the nice things about the Tempelhof Airport was the large apron-like overhang that allowed passengers to board and deplane without having to walk in the elements. I appreciated the architect's forethought as the pewter rain clouds that had gathered in the past hour opened and droplets spattered against the concrete. The stewardess awaited me at the bottom of the stairs, welcoming me aboard.

Nine rows of seats with two on the left and a single on the right flanked the aisle. Twenty-one of the twenty-seven seats on the Viking were filled. I counted working my way to my own seat. Oleg watched me with a frown darkening his features. Katya stared out the window, her hand gripped tight around the German doll Mueller gifted her. Three-quarters of the way to the back, I slipped in next to an anxious Yelena, who held a lowball glass of clear liquid in a death grip.

"*Bonjour, Gaston.*" I smiled at her.

Yelena stared at me, her mouth agape.

I patted her forearm. "*C'est bien.*"

She slugged back the rest of her drink in one gulp. Before she could speak, a dark-haired stewardess with bright red lipstick took the hat from my lap—"Let me help you with that."—and helpfully put it in the open rack above our seats. "May I take your coat? Get you something to drink? Would you like another vodka martini, sir?" she asked in German.

Yelena shook her head and handed over the empty glass.

"I'll have a mimosa, once we're in the air," I replied, giving her my coat.

Ten minutes later, the propellers charged to life, their spinning blades creating a steady hum and vibration throughout the cabin. The plane jerked and slowly crawled backward. I shut my eyes and blew out a deep breath between my lips.

Yelena tucked her cold hand into mine and gave it a squeeze. "*Spasibo,*" she whispered.

When learning the language, English speakers will be told that *spasibo* means *thank you,* but it is derived from old Russian, directly translated, meaning, *God save you.* I returned the squeeze and watched the rivulets of rain snake across the window as the plane gathered speed and lifted off the ground.

Chapter Seventeen
London

I fell asleep soon after finishing the mimosa, missed breakfast, and didn't wake until we landed in Amsterdam to refuel. Five passengers exited the flight and three got on. The second leg of the flight was an hour longer than the first, and we were fed a lunch of bratwurst, salami, bread, salad, and beer. After lunch Yelena took a nap.

On approach to our London destination, I debated my options. Contact London station immediately, or take the Ivanovs to the embassy first? I needed to notify someone of the breach and begin an investigation into the Berlin office. Either State or CIA needed to be notified that the Ivanovs were out of Germany and had reached England safely. They needed new identities and secure flights to the US. I was sure our government was raring to have a go at Ivanov and his intelligence. I continued to debate my options as the plane descended through a bright, cloudless sky.

The final decision was taken out of my hands. Yelena and I exited customs, where Katya and Oleg waited for us. Smiles wreathed their faces. Yelena too worked her way through customs relaxed and happy—although that might have been due to the two vodka shots she'd imbibed during the second leg of the flight. As we joined the pair, a gentleman with red-blond hair, a spate of freckles, wearing a tailored dark blue suit and striped tie tapped me on the shoulder.

"Brigitte Moreau?" he asked in a nasal Midwest accent, pronouncing my name as bridge-it mow-row.

My gaze narrowed. *"Oui, Monsieur?* How may I help you?" I babbled at him in French.

"Carl Sullivan, Consular Attaché, from the American Embassy." He removed his hat and held out his hand, which was also covered in freckles. Hesitantly, I shook it. "And you must be our friends from the East. We've been looking forward to your arrival." He winked at Oleg.

The Ivanovs' faces perked up as soon as they heard the words "American Embassy." They shook hands, and Carl, clearly a master at the art of charm, bent to shake Katya's hand. "Hello, little lady." He grinned at her.

"Guten Tag," she dimpled and greeted him.

I couldn't have been prouder of the little girl for keeping her German cover. On the other hand, my own instincts made me wary of our new friend Carl. "I am afraid you mistake—" I spoke in English with a strong French accent.

Carl straightened and his hazel gaze met mine. "Your passport was flagged at Tempelhof Airport. Word got back to us, and we've been awaiting your arrival," he said cheerfully.

My hackles went up. The US Embassy wouldn't have known Brigitte Moreau. It was a non-official cover that only a handful of agency members would have been privy to. Carl either worked for the agency, or he worked for someone else more sinister. I decided to let things play out. I wasn't about to make a scene in the middle of the airport. At least, not yet.

"You must have had quite a time of it, but you can rest easy now, you're safe. I have a car to take you to the embassy." He replaced his hat and picked up my suitcase.

"A car, wonderful, *merci.*" I forced a smile, turned to the Ivanovs, and spoke in German, "Come, we have an escort to the American Embassy."

Oleg, perhaps perceiving my reservations, allowed his gaze to dart between Carl and me. I didn't want to discomfit him or Yelena. I waved them forward, forcing confidence that I didn't feel. "Come. Let us not dally."

Even though we were out of Berlin, I felt exposed standing around. We were beginning to attract attention from fellow travelers. Carl led the way. The building reminded me more of a town hall than an airport with its neoclassical architecture. It was built of white stone block and had weathered hardwood floors, double courtyards, and a domed skylight, all of which flooded the terminal with fresh, natural light. Its whitewashed walls were yellow by the afternoon sunlight. At the front entrance, the doors opened, silhouetting two figures—a man and a woman. They stepped into the light, and recognition flared in my chest.

I blew out a relieved breath. Waving a greeting, I darted past Carl. "Edward! Lily!"

Edward's face revealed confusion with a deep pair of columns between his eyes; Lily's was guarded.

"Come, say you have not forgotten me . . . it is Brigitte. Brigitte Moreau." I gave the pair one of my genuine smiles.

Lily's face lit up with recognition. "It is *so* good to see you." She whispered in her stepfather's ear, and Edward smiled.

"*Oui*. And I am happy to see you as well." Our greetings brought the entourage to a halt.

Edward gave me a fatherly hug. "I'm glad you made it," he murmured in my ear. "We left the day after your telegram arrived."

Carl cleared his throat. "Excuse me, but—"

"Edward Jolivet, Deputy Undersecretary of Public Affairs," Edward said to Carl in a steely tone. "Secretary Acheson sent me to escort our 'guests' home." Edward turned to the Ivanovs, who hovered nearby in a confused fashion.

Carl's jovial assurance faltered. "But . . . I've been given a directive to take these folks—"

"Unless your directive came down from the president, I'm fairly certain my orders outrank yours, son." Edward clapped Carl on the shoulder, and the younger man knew he'd been beat. "Now, if you'd like to follow us to Grosvenor Square in your vehicle, feel free. It's where you were headed anyway, isn't it?"

"Of course," Carl said, heartily replacing his ingratiating smile. "I can put the luggage in my car."

"No need. We've plenty of space in our boot." Edward opened the exit door to reveal a black-and-gray Daimler limousine idling in the front loop.

Carl swallowed.

The driver, wearing a black chauffeur's uniform—including the spiffy hat, got out of the driver's seat and trotted around to open the door for us. Edward directed him to put the luggage in the trunk, while Lily ushered the Ivanovs into the Daimler. The three climbed onto the gray, velvet-covered rear seat of the luxurious vehicle. Lily followed, flipping down one of the two jump seats.

Edward turned to me and said, "We've only one space left in the rear. Would you like to ride in the back with our guests or up front with the driver?"

I gently closed the suicide door and switched to English. "I think I'll go with Carl," I spoke quietly, eyeing the Jaguar Mark VII that had just pulled up with Carl behind the wheel.

Edward glanced at the black vehicle. "Are you sure?"

I realized he wasn't simply asking my preference. "You don't know Carl?"

Edward shook his head. "It's been a long time since I've been to London. I don't know all the embassy personnel."

"Yes. I'm sure. I need to do some intelligence gathering, and I think Carl may have the answers. Or at least have access to obtaining those answers. I'm assuming the packages are safe with you."

"Indeed. Getting Ivanov was quite a coup on your part. However, as you've learned, it's clear he's made enemies with his defection. The Soviets would rather see him dead than in our hands."

"Is he safe in London?" I asked.

"As safe as he can be. That's three-quarter-inch thick bulletproof glass." My brows rose. Edward grinned. "Borrowed from one of the lower royals."

"How are you getting them to the US?"

"Aboard a military transport. It may not be as

comfortable as the Pan Am flight you were supposed to be on, but it's safe. Our friends will remain at the embassy until we fly out tomorrow morning," Edward assured me.

"Then I will leave them in your capable hands for now. Please see the plane tickets are refunded to Mueller. If I don't see you before you go, thank you for all your help." I held out my hand. "I couldn't have done it without you."

He gripped it with both of his hands. "My pleasure."

"Your friend Mueller says you owe him a chess rematch."

The trunk closed, and the driver came around to us. He noticed I still held my train case in hand. "Have you any other luggage, miss? Would you like to put your carrying case in the trunk?"

I realized Carl had helpfully taken my suitcase and must have loaded it into his car. I switched on my French accent. "Thank you, no. I will keep it with me. I join ze gentleman in the vehicle behind yours."

We all glanced at Carl, whose face was pinched and fingers wrapped tight around the steering wheel. I gave a little wave. Carl's face relaxed into a tight-lipped smile that resembled a grimace. The driver tipped his hat to Edward and went around the Daimler to slip into the driver's side.

I opened the rear door to find Lily chatting with Oleg in German. Yelena clasped her hat in her lap while Katya knelt on the back seat between her parents, staring out the window at the plane ascending overhead, the doll gripped tightly in her hand.

"I will take the second vehicle with Carl. See you at the embassy," I said.

Yelena and Oleg exchanged a look.

"You are in good hands. I promise. Lily and I are old friends, and our Secretary of State has sent Edward to escort you home," I assured them.

Edward climbed in back with Lily. "Good luck," he said. The Daimler's heavy door closed with a soft *whump*.

I tossed my train case, coat, and other paraphernalia onto the back seat of the Jaguar and climbed in after it. The car smelled of leather and cigarette smoke. The Mark VII was certainly a spacious, comfortable vehicle. Not as luxurious as the Daimler . . . still, beggars couldn't be choosers. Carl lifted his sunglasses and scrutinized me.

"Are we going to ze embassy?" I asked cheekily.

He shifted into gear and motored away from the curb. The Jaguar followed the Daimler onto the main road leading away from the airport. Carl seemed comfortable driving on the opposite side of the road and the right side of the car, shifting with his left hand as the car accelerated into traffic.

"How long have you been working at ze American Embassy?" I inquired.

"About a month." He slowed and maneuvered around a bicyclist.

"But you have been in England longer. *Non*?" I commented.

"How do you figure?"

"You drive so easily on ze left side—you have been here longer. *Oui*?"

There was a pause. "You're very observant, aren't

you, Miriam Becker?"

And the gloves were off. He didn't even use one of my aliases. I dropped my faux French accent and asked flatly, "Who do you work for?"

"Same as you."

"Were you sent to take the Ivanovs to the embassy?"

He watched me from the rearview mirror. "I was."

"But by whom?"

He didn't respond.

"That *is* the question, isn't it?"

When he still didn't respond, I dug into my purse to find my lipstick and compact. I was applying a coat of Elizabeth Arden's Victory Red when he replied, "The Ivanovs were to be dropped at the embassy. *You,* on the other hand, had an appointment with the station chief."

I lowered the compact and our eyes met in the mirror. "And now?"

"Now, I'm taking you to Grosvenor Square, because I am certain if I do not, the Secretary of State will send out a search party," he muttered.

Directly ahead, the Daimler came to a stop at a light, and we rolled to a halt behind it. I did my best to keep from grinning. "Yes, it is nice to have friends in high places. Once I am assured my packages are safely stowed at the embassy, you may take me to the office."

Carl's brows rose.

"I have important information." I stuffed the cosmetics back in my purse and murmured, "And I don't have a lot of time to waste."

Chapter Eighteen
The Brass Compass

It took an hour to get the Ivanovs comfortably settled in an apartment at the American Embassy at 1 Grosvenor Square, in the elegant Mayfair neighborhood. The embassy—a well-designed, sprawling building of redbrick and granite with eight ionic columns lining the front—occupied the entire west side of Grosvenor Square.

During the war, Eisenhower was headquartered on the opposite side of the square, Naval command and other military installations lined the edges of the square. Brits referred to the zone as Little America. The gardens in the courtyard had been stripped of their blossoms, and huts were built to house additional military personnel and to cultivate victory gardens. Today, the temporary housing was gone, replaced with flowers and greenery. In the center, a statue of Franklin Delano Roosevelt had been erected—funded and built by the people of London in 1948, during a time when they could ill afford it.

The Ivanovs were settled into a two-bedroom apartment on the top floor overlooking the square. I said my goodbyes Katya, who thanked me for her beautiful blonde hair.

I crouched to her level and told her, "Be a good girl and do your best to learn English." She'd picked up German so easily, I had no doubts English would come just as quickly for her. I only hoped the language would develop for Yelena as well.

Still dressed as Gaston, my travel mate gripped my hands tightly, and thanked me profusely. "You have saved our lives," she whispered with tears rolling down her face.

I handed her my handkerchief. "All in a day's work." I smiled shakily at her, willing my emotions in check. After all, I was a professional and could not allow for any sort of blubbering goodbyes. My part in Operation Blackbird was mercifully complete. Now I could pass the trio over and return my attentions to the man we'd left behind.

Oleg clasped my hand and, pumping it heartily, said, "You have the heart of a lion. I shall never forget you."

"And I, you."

Edward wished me safe travels, but it was Lily who joined me in the lift down to the first floor, where Carl waited.

After the doors closed, she turned, pulling something out of her pocket. "Miriam, I want you to take this."

I held out my palm, and she placed a necklace in it. I turned over the pendant to find a miniature brass compass. It was tarnished, with a noticeable dent on one side. I frowned in confusion at the strange gift.

"It brought me luck and helped me find safety during . . . troubled times."

I realized she was speaking of her time during the war.

She stared at the little compass and whispered, "Charlie gave it to me."

Shaking my head, I held the necklace toward her. "Oh, I don't think . . ."

She curled my fingers around the compass. "Take it. You are planning on returning to Berlin to find Jake." It wasn't a question but a statement.

"Lily, I don't—how did you—"

"Oleg. The description he gave me of the man who helped him escape East Berlin left no doubt who it was," she explained.

A lump of guilt formed in my throat, and I mashed my lips together. Charlie and Jake were in the same airborne company during the war, which made them lifelong friends. It was funny how Jake was both a tie to my childhood friends and those I made as an adult. He was a connecting link of my past, present, and . . . future?

"This compass is . . . good luck. It will help you find your way and bring you home. It always did so for me," she whispered urgently.

Clearly the compass held a great deal of significance to her. Whether or not it was lucky, I couldn't deny that a compass might come in handy. Nodding, I hung the trinket around my neck. "Then I shall consider it a loan and return it to you when I get home."

Chapter Nineteen
Old Mentor

Carl drove us to Belgrave Street in the Pimlico neighborhood—not far from Westminster, where Parliament was located, along with a number for foreign embassies. He parked in front of a six-level, white stucco and stone, eighteenth century rowhouse with a covered front entry. The modest brass plaque on the door read Vandermeer and Associates Imports, Inc. A nice, generic-sounding company for the CIA to function under.

An unpretentious receptionist went with the generic sign and was the only person in the shallow entryway. The woman was somewhere between forty and sixty. She wore a blue suit, no makeup, and a pair of reading glasses, which sat atop her fuzzy, gray-brown hair. Her hand disappeared beneath the heavy, dark desk the moment we entered.

"How may I help you?" the woman greeted us.

"The nightingale sings at dawn," Carl said, digging into his pocket.

"The mockingbird sings at dusk," she replied.

"Good afternoon, Margaret." Carl presented an identification card.

I knew Margaret was the first line of defense, and a weapon was pointed at me from beneath her desk. Besides Margaret, there wasn't much else in the room. An aged, red-and-blue oriental carpet covered the scuffed hardwood floor. A pair of maroon leather wingback chairs sat in the front window, and the only thing on the walls was a hunting party painting. To the right was a set of open French doors that led to a small room with a conference table that sat six. Margaret's desk held a typewriter, a neat stack of papers atop a desk blotter, and a black telephone. Behind Margaret was a heavy wooden door, which she guarded like a dragon at the gate.

"Carl," she said through a pinched mouth. "Who is your friend?"

"Brigitte Moreau," I answered.

"The chief should be expecting us," Carl replied, tucking his ID into his pocket.

Margaret jerked her head. "He's in his office."

There was a buzzing noise, and I followed Carl through the four-inch-thick door behind the dragon. On one side was a narrow hallway, dotted with closed doors, and on the other, a steep staircase. Behind one of the doors, I could hear the steady clicking of a typewriter. I followed Carl up the staircase to a wide hallway. He led me past an empty desk with a phone, typewriter, files, and papers piled in a corner box, to an unmarked door.

Carl knocked.

"Come!" a muffled male voice called.

The station chief's office was large, spanning the front of the building, with two floor-to-ceiling windows. My worries receded as I laid eyes on the man behind the desk.

He must have been about fifty now. White sprinkled through his dark hair and across his brow, which only enhanced his aquamarine blue eyes. They were now lined with wrinkles. He'd gained weight since the war, and a small potbelly strained against the lower buttons of his shirt. A suit jacket hung on the back of his desk chair, his tie was askew, and he'd rolled up his shirtsleeves. A cigarette burned in the ashtray at his elbow. He rose at our entry, greeting us with a tobacco-yellowed grin, and came around the desk.

Carl started, "Sir—"

The station chief cut him off. "My dear, it's been a while."

"Hello, Greg." I let out a low whistle between my teeth, glancing around the well-appointed office, which included a seating area with loveseat, pair of club chairs, and coffee table; a round table that sat four; luxurious new blue carpet; and a wall of bookcases filled with leatherbound books. "You've come up in the world. London Station Chief, I had no idea."

Whereas the downstairs entry had been stark and minimalist, Greg's office was personalized with *objet d'art* and little knick-knacks. I picked up a family photo of Greg with his wife and dark-haired daughter of about twelve.

"Nice. I never thought of you as a family man." I smirked.

"Thank you, Carl, I'll take it from here," Greg said in a dismissive tone.

Carl took his ejection with aplomb. "Yes, sir." He closed the door with a snap on his way out.

"How is Gisele these days?" I asked.

"She retired and married her French diplomat. They are living in a villa on Lake Geneva," he said without emotion.

"Why do you keep the photograph?"

Greg took the photo out of my hand and replaced it on the little side table from whence I'd retrieved it. "Sentimental reasons."

I allowed the breath of a laugh to escape. The woman in the photo was no more his wife than the girl was his child. Gisele had been an excellent agent, infiltrating the Vichy French Embassy in Washington, D.C., by becoming the mistress of a French diplomat. She flipped the diplomat, and he provided intelligence to us throughout the rest of the war.

Greg had been a mentor to me during my training and eventually my handler. He had a rugged sexiness about him and was known to be quite the playboy. However, on a harrowing ride in the trunk of a car together, he'd told me he wasn't the marrying type. While other women hadn't, I'd taken him at his word. The photo had been crafted half a dozen years ago when he'd been on assignment with Gisele.

"How sweet." I meandered around the room, picking up and putting down little bits of bric-a-brac—a nineteenth Century porcelain figurine, a small brass Buddha, a souvenir ashtray with the young Queen's face on it. "I should have realized it was you. After all, you're the one who created Brigitte Moreau."

Greg eyed me as I casually moved around the chamber. "I thought that cover identity had been retired."

"I kept her around for emergencies." I replaced the ashtray and moved to the bookcase. *So many places to hide a listening device.* I drummed my fingers before randomly pulling a book from the shelf.

Greg didn't move or discourage my nosiness. "Rather dangerous, no?"

I closed the book with a snap and pulled out another. "Only in Yugoslavia."

"Still..." He waited for me to give further explanation. When I didn't, he shrugged and indicated the sofa. "Have a seat."

It wasn't an invitation. It was a command. The book went back in its place, and I sank down onto the plush cushions.

"Would you like a drink?" he asked. Opposite the bookcase, a silver tray with three decanters, a half dozen cut crystal lowball glasses, and a small ice bucket rested on a cherry credenza with brass knobs and walnut inlay.

A drink sounded heavenly. "I'll take a brandy if you've got it."

Ice plinked into the glasses and liquid splashed. Greg handed me the golden topaz liquor and kept a glass with clear liquid for himself.

"Gin?"

"Vodka." He clinked my glass and took a sip before settling in one of the club chairs. Pulling a pack of Lucky Strikes from his front shirt pocket, he offered one to me.

I declined with a head shake. The ubiquitous Lucky Strikes were not a brand I cared for.

Even though a cigarette still burned at his desk, Greg took a fresh one from the pack. Lighting it, he spoke around the fag, allowing it to bounce between his lips. "Tell me what happened."

"What do you know?" I sipped the fruity, sweet whiskey. Its warmth hit my stomach and spread from there, slowly seeping into my bones.

Shaking out the match, he sat back and crossed his legs. "I know three operatives are dead and Greyhound is missing," he said, referring to Jake by his codename. "As were you and the Ivanovs, until this morning, when Brigitte Moreau popped up on my radar."

"What does the Berlin Station Chief have to say about all of it?"

"Not very much. I imagine because he's trying to clean up the mess and explain to Washington how he lost an entire team, along with one of the most valuable Soviet defectors we've seen since Igor Gouzenko."

I waved away a cloud of smoke. "What are you orders regarding me?"

"I'm to bring you in, of course. They expect a full debrief until the higher-ups are satisfied. So, what is the story, Little Girl?"

The hint of a smile crossed my features. I was young when Greg and I began working together, barely twenty. He called me "Little Girl" in the early days. I supposed, even when I was fifty, Greg would continue to call me by the moniker.

I leaned against the sofa and dove into the disaster that was Operation Blackbird, while Greg chain-smoked and occasionally asked questions. "And you don't know where Greyhound is?"

"No." I jumped up and paced away from the seating area. "Do you?" When Greg didn't immediately answer, I spun around to find him contemplating me. "Well, do you?" I snapped.

He took a long drag and blew the smoke out before answering, "*I* do not."

"Do you know if he's still alive?"

"We believe so."

An uncontrolled gasp of excitement escaped me. "How? Why?"

"Because our Soviet counterparts are still searching for him," Greg replied in measured tones.

That *was* good news. "I wish to return to Berlin and help with the search," I blurted.

"Miriam . . ." He stubbed out the cigarette. "You seem to be unaware of the fact that you're in a tricky situation. Your entire team is either dead or missing. You are the only one left, and you are asking us to trust you at your word."

"I also safely retrieved and delivered the packages, and I'm sure when you depose our Soviet comrades, they will tell you a similar story." I tried to make the statement firmly and not to sound as defensive as I felt.

"Which I would have been happy to do"—Greg rose ponderously—"had you not turned them over to your friends at the embassy. Refill?"

I suddenly realized the precarious position I'd put myself in. The narrative sounded farfetched, even to my own ears. Without the Ivanovs to give credence to the story, I was asking for a lot of trust from an organization that spent their days performing duties precisely because they didn't trust anyone.

While Greg refilled his own glass, I noticed the phone sitting on his desk. "The Soviets won't be leaving until tomorrow. Make a phone call."

Greg swished his fresh drink and studied me. "How would I know it is them?"

My brows V'd. "How many Soviets are staying at the American Embassy?"

He didn't seem moved by my argument.

"Come now, Greg." I sighed and crossed my legs. "Edward Jolivet can supply appropriate validation. Moreover, I know for a fact, there are secure communication lines at the embassy."

He resumed his seat and lit another cigarette. "I don't speak Russian."

"Is that all? Ivanov speaks excellent German." Greg opened his mouth, but I continued before he had a chance say anything, "Don't tell me you've forgotten your German. It was far better than mine. Really, Greg, I think you're being overly dramatic. *I* am the one who has been betrayed while my neck was on the line. Two"—I held up two fingers—"operatives were turncoats and more than ready to put a bullet through my head or slit my throat. If it weren't for me, America wouldn't have its shiny new Soviet defector, whom, I might add, is *more* than willing to provide valuable intelligence. I am the patriot. You *know* me. We worked together during the war. Why do you doubt me, Greg? *Why?*" My speech, which started calmly enough, became more impassioned as I went, and I was practically shouting by the end.

That was a mistake. My only excuse—it had been a long couple of days.

Smoke curled above Greg's head, he sipped his drink, tapped ashes in the tray, and shifted in the chair. "Are you finished?"

I bit my tongue, holding back a childish eyeroll, and indicated with a flick of my wrist that he should continue.

"As I was about to say, you make a valid point. I'll make the phone call."

"Thank you." I slugged back the rest of the brandy.

"In the meantime, Carl will take you to a hotel where you can freshen up and get some rest. We will arrange a room for you at the Savoy."

"I've a reservation, at the Byron." I waited to see if he would insist on the Savoy. If he did, I would go on the assumption that the agency had planted bugs in my room.

"Suit yourself." He rose from the chair, and I followed his lead. "I'll pick you up at seven. We'll have dinner."

"I'd like that."

He opened the door for me. "Carl?"

Carl popped his head out of an open door. "Yes, boss?"

"Please take Brigitte to the Byron Hotel and see that she gets settled." Greg turned to me and held out his hand. "It's been a pleasure."

Chapter Twenty
The Byron Hotel

Carl drove me to the Byron, a quaint little hotel in the Bayswater area of London. He found street parking a few doors down. I tried to put him off, but ignoring my refusals of help, he carried my suitcase to the registration desk. I assured him I could take it from here and waited until he exited before giving the white-haired gentleman the name for my reservation.

I was given a room with twin beds, an Art Deco armoire, and matching dressing table with a needlepoint bench seat. The attached bath had a lovely clawfoot tub, which I put to immediate use. I washed my hair and face, removing all traces of Brigitte Moreau. To my surprise, I fell asleep. When I awoke, the water had gone cold, and my fingers and toes had turned to prunes.

Chilled from the frigid bath, I dressed in my underthings and wrapped myself in a blanket from the bed, while I put on fresh makeup. Fifteen minutes later, I realized my mind was a million miles away. My cheeks had overly bright slashes of red, and I'd been too heavy-handed with the eyeliner and shadow, making me look ready for a vaudeville stage. I wiped it off and started over, focusing on the task at hand instead of worrying. I chose to wear a black tea-length dress with white piping, nipped waist, and flared skirt, with a pair of red pumps. My hair was again tucked beneath Brigitte's wig. Her passport remained in my handbag. Since Greg continued to refer to me as Brigitte in front of Carl, I needed to continue to assume her identity while in London.

At half past six, I trotted downstairs to visit the front desk. The septuagenarian at check-in had been replaced with an orange-haired teen with spots on his face. I gave him a bright smile. "Good evening. I need to send a telegram."

He bobbed his head and replied, "Yes, ma'am. If you will please fill out the form." Reaching beneath the desk, he pulled out a Western Union form.

I addressed it to Petrus's home and hoped he would get it by tonight.

AM IN LONDON. HOPING TO RETURN SOON. ANY NEWS?

"Please have responses directed to the hotel," I said, passing over the payment for the telegram and adding a generous tip.

The boy's face lit up. "Yes, ma'am. I'll see it gets sent immediately."

"Is there a public room where I could await my dinner date?"

He directed me to a library down the hall. The darkened room was empty. A fire crackled in the hearth, giving off an amber glow that created unearthly shadows. I flipped on a lamp. The ghostly forms vanished, and I found myself in a cozy, rectangular room. Two of the four walls were laden with overflowing bookcases. The other wall had a tall, narrow window with heavy brocade curtains, and masculine, dark leather wingback chairs were scattered about.

A glance into a hanging mirror made me realize I'd forgotten to put on fresh lipstick. Rifling through my purse, I came across Lily's brass compass. Drawing the pendant out, my thumb swiped across the crystal. The tiny arrow bobbed and settled in place.

A forgotten childhood memory popped into mind.

♠♠♠♠

I must have been seven or eight, the sun was high, and the summer heat beat down on the concrete sidewalk. Fred, Hugh, and Jake had earned money painting a neighbor's fence and they were headed to the Five & Dime to buy candy. I'd saved five cents from my allowance and begged to go with them. Gra-mere wouldn't let me go alone because it meant crossing a set of railroad tracks and a busy road. It was a time in my life when Fred considered me nothing more than a pesky little sister and my very existence seemed to irritate him.

He refused my pleas as I chased after them. The concrete sidewalks were broken and heaved from a bad winter. I tripped and fell, scraping up my hands and a knee and ripping my baby-blue cotton dress. Sobbing, I called out my brother's name for help. However, it wasn't Fred who returned to pick me up and dust me off.

Jake's prepubescent, narrow face, untidy dark hair, and crooked front tooth came into view. "Don't cry, Miriam," he said, wiping dirt off the back of my dress. "Give me your nickel. I'll buy you a candy bar."

I sniffed. "A Ch-charleston Ch-chew s-strawberry?"

The other two boys, having made it to the next block, had turned and were yelling at Jake to hurry up.

"Leave her be. She's a pest!" Fred shouted.

Jake ignored them and replied, "If that's what you want."

Nodding, I wiped my eyes with a corner of my dress. "C-can I c-come with you?"

His lips turned down. "You're bleeding. Go home. Your granny will clean you up. I'll bring the candy bar later."

I surrendered my nickel and watched Jake run to catch up with his jeering buddies. I continued to stand on the sidewalk, blood running down my leg into my white, frilled sock, until the trio turned the corner out of sight.

Of course, I tattled on Fred, and he got in trouble when he returned home hours later, which only sought to make our relationship more combative. Gra-mere restricted Fred from playing with his friends for the rest of the week. I thought I'd never see my nickel or the Charleston Chew. However, true to his word, the following day, Jake spied me playing with my dolls in the backyard. He climbed the fence to give me the coveted candy bar.

I wrapped my skinny arms him and cried, "I love you, Jake! I wish *you* were *my* brother."

Embarrassed, and probably afraid Fred would see him, he shrugged me off and retreated back over the fence.

♠♠♠♠

So caught up in the memory, I didn't heard Greg enter

the room until he cleared his throat. "Brigitte?"

The pendant dropped back into my purse. "Just freshening up my lipstick. Have a seat."

Greg removed his black wool overcoat and sat in one of the wingback chairs in front of the fireplace. "What were you daydreaming about?"

"Nothing of importance," I said dismissively. Taking the other seat, I crossed my legs and waited for him to begin the conversation. When he didn't, I finally said, "Well?"

Greg merely raised his brows questioningly as he dug out the Lucky Strikes from his suit pocket. He was baiting me.

I should have waited, but I was out of patience with this nonsense. It felt as though I'd spent an entire afternoon wasting time, when I could have been returning to Berlin to find out what Petrus had discovered. "How was your phone conversation?" I enunciated each word with slow precision.

"It would seem—" He stuck a cigarette in his mouth and lit it before proceeding. "That you are quite the hero. At least, in the eyes of Oleg Ivanov."

"Pish." I flapped a hand at him. "Stop it. You know what I mean, Greg. Am I cleared? Are the powers-that-be happy with the story? Or are you still looking at me with cockeyed mistrust?"

He puffed out three smoke rings in a row and grinned. "Well, I, for one, completely believe in you."

"But . . ."

"Come now, Little Girl, you didn't think they'd send you straight back to Berlin without a debrief? They may not send you back at all."

"Damn," I hissed, popping up from the chair. I strode across the room only to stride right back. "We're wasting time. Can't you see that? If Greyhound isn't dead yet, he will be once the Commies find him. He needs our help. *My* help."

"Sit down, Miriam," he said in a calm but steely voice. I sat.

"While I can appreciate your concern, it is not your responsibility to rescue him. Greyhound is an agent, a very skilled one, and he knows the dangers."

My mouth dropped. "Your plan is to let him rot?"

"You know, as well as I, there are pathways for him to communicate. We are waiting until he can make contact, and then we will determine the best course of action."

"Who is *we*? The Berlin station chief who put the assassination team together?" I replied with asperity.

Greg licked his lips. "On my recommendation, the station chief has been removed, pending an investigation."

That was good news, but . . . "Who else in the Berlin office may have been a part of it?"

"The Bonn station chief reports tomorrow and will take over. He's bringing along some of his own men. Trust me, the situation is being handled. Samuels will get to the bottom of it."

"That's wonderful news. However," I drawled, "I would think by now, Greyhound has his own concerns regarding the trustworthiness of Berlin's station chief and may not reach out through traditional channels." I allowed Greg to stew on that for a few moments before continuing, "I, on the other hand, have already begun to make inquiries through my own contacts, and might be able to make a connection that could lead us to him."

Greg finished his cigarette and tossed the butt into the fire. "It is not my call, Little Girl," he said softly.

Ducking my head in defeat, I sighed, "It was worth a try." I rose. "We'll be late for our reservation."

Greg would've been a fool if he thought I would leave it alone, and Greg was no fool. But I realized we'd reached an impasse. I would simply have to bide my time and hope Petrus came through with information, which I could use to argue my way back to Berlin.

He placed a hand on my arm. "I was able to arrange for you to be debriefed here in London, instead of back in Washington."

Well, that is something.

Greg returned me to the hotel at the solemn hour of nine thirty and declined an after-dinner drink, claiming an early morning meeting. More than likely, he had a woman waiting for him. Frankly, I didn't mind. After spending the past few nights on a lumpy couch, I looked forward to a comfortable bed and a night of unbroken sleep.

Chapter Twenty-One
In the Hot Seat

The following day felt like being put through a washing mangle. I reported to the Belgrave Street house, where Margaret left me cooling my heels in the front room for thirty minutes. Luckily, I'd retrieved a copy of *Pride and Prejudice* from the hotel library and completed the first two chapters while waiting for my escort.

After getting me past the dragon, Carl ushered me to a tiny room on the fourth floor. "You can type your report in here."

I surmised the room had been a linen closet in a former lifetime. Musty shelves filled with file boxes lined one side, a mop, bucket, and pair of broken ratan carpet beaters rested in the far corner, and a bare bulb hung from the ceiling. There was a dusty wooden chair and square table shoehorned into the room. I surmised, they'd been found in the attic and brought down ten minutes ago. A hulking behemoth Underwood typewriter, circa 1925, sat in the center of the table with a pile of snow-white paper next to it.

"I see you brought out the best for me, eh?"

"Nice, isn't it?" He smirked.

"Whose idea was the broom closet? Greg's? Yours?" It wasn't as though Carl and I had gotten off on the right foot.

The smirk turned into a grin. "Margaret."

I gave him an incredulous stare. I barely knew Margaret and couldn't figure a reason why she'd taken a dislike to me.

Carl gleefully filled me in. "She doesn't like your familiarity with the chief and means to—how did she say it . . ." He looked down his nose at me. "Oh, right, 'put you in your place.'"

"I'll tell you; I once shared the trunk of a car with Greg for many hours. We couldn't be any more familiar with each other." Enlightenment dawned in Carl's eyes, but I crushed it immediately with my next sentence. "Except in the biblical sense, of course."

"Never?" Carl asked cheekily.

"*Never,*" I replied, decisively shutting down his unholy curiosity.

"This afternoon you'll meet with Howard."

"Howard?"

"He'll review your report."

Ah, the interrogator. The person who would go over my report frontwards, backwards, and sideways, trying to poke holes in it or catch me in a lie.

The smirk returned. "I assume you know how to type."

Of course. I took typing class in high school. All the girls did, but I wasn't quite ready to be cooped up alone in this dreary room. It may have also been that I enjoyed poking at Carl, too.

"Why do you assume I type?" I fluttered my lashes at him.

"Because all the girls do," he blustered.

"Women, *Carl.*" While I didn't mind when Greg

called me "Little Girl"—because I knew he meant it as a term of endearment, a remembrance of a time when the world was going to hell and we were working together to save it—when Carl called me a girl, it sounded demeaning.

He blinked. "I'm sorry."

"We are women, *not* girls. Girls gad about in pinafores and pigtails, not high heels and suits, and they most definitely *do not* engage in espionage," I snapped, catching sight of Margaret at the top of the stairs.

Wonderful. I'm sure she heard my little lecture to her favorite agent. She pivoted and retreated down the steps.

Redness bloomed across Carl's cheeks, and he rubbed the back of his neck. "You're saying you need a typist?" he asked, dodging the "girl" reference.

I decided to let it drop and entered the room. "No. I'll take care of it."

Carl shrugged in confusion. "Door open or closed?"

"Closed. I wouldn't want the clacking from the antique on the desk to disturb any of my other colleagues," I said drily.

Carl paused, mid-close. "Is there anything you want? Tea? Coffee?" Perhaps he felt bad for his earlier jibes.

"Tea would be lovely. Also, where can I find the water closet . . . for future reference?"

"Go past the stairs to the end of the hall. Tea and coffee are on the first floor. Back of the building, you'll find the kitchen."

I sighed and nodded. Of course, he wasn't actually *offering* to get me a cup of coffee.

"I'll be leaving for the embassy in an hour. If you need

something, Jim Jones is in the office to your right. He should be arriving any minute and can answer your questions."

The heavy wooden door closed with a clunk. I was alone with my thoughts and a rusty, old typewriter for company. I found a dry rag in the bucket, dusted off the chair and table, placed my handbag on a shelf, and situated myself behind the Underwood. This was the part of the job I despised. Running around, pretending to be someone else, the fear that flooded my system during an operation giving me a sense of heightened emotion—that I fed off of. If only these damned reports weren't necessary, it would be the perfect job. Sighing, I wound a piece of paper around the platen and typed the date.

Hours later, a knock drew me away from the Bennet household and the rolling hills of Longbourn, England. My watch read just past noon. I quickly closed the book and shoved it onto the shelf between two boxes. "Come."

When Greg opened the door, I was removing the final page of my report. He stopped short.

"What on earth..." His gaze darted around the meager room, taking in the mop, bucket, and rickety old typewriter.

"Are you here for my report? I've just finished." I gathered the papers, tapping them on the table to straighten them into a neat pile.

"I'm here to take you to lunch. Why the devil did Carl put you in a bloody broom closet?"

"You've been in London too long. You're picking up the vernacular. And I believe it was Margaret's idea," I said, squeezing past the table.

He frowned in confusion.

"The broom closet. And you are not to say a word." I shook a finger at him. "Margaret's already taken a dislike to me. I don't need you lecturing her and making it worse."

"Why do you care what Margaret thinks?"

"Because I have a feeling, while you men storm about making decisions and believing *you* run this place, it is actually Margaret who does so. I'd rather earn her respect to win her over. Besides, she already believes that I'm too friendly with you."

"Bloody hell," he muttered.

"Where are we going for lunch?" I grabbed my coat and handbag off the shelf.

"The Red Fox. It's a pub a few blocks away."

"Can we walk?"

"If you like." He motioned for me to precede him down the stairs.

Stepping out of the building, I felt like a bear emerging from hibernation. The air was crisp, but the sun shone bright, and I slid on a pair of sunglasses. Rolling my shoulders released the stiffness of typing a ten-page report.

Lunch was the highlight of my day. Greg had nothing new to provide, and since I'd not heard back from Petrus, I had nothing to tell him. We reminisced about old times, speculated about Queen Elizabeth's coronation, and spoke of the atomic bomb the UK detonated last week.

Upon our return, Margaret greeted Greg with munificence befitting a king, or at least a prince, and handed him a stack of correspondence. She then turned to me and announced in a flat, uninviting tone, "Howard is looking for you."

"Very well," I replied demurely. At the top of the stairs, I asked Greg, "Where is Howard's office?"

"Third floor, first door past the stag," Greg replied absently, sorting through the mail.

My brows furrowed. He looked up to find my confusion.

"You'll see." The phone in his office rang. "I need to take that."

"Thanks for lunch!" I hollered as Greg stepped into his office.

The third-floor stag was a six-point buck's head mounted on the wall. I knocked on the door next to it.

"Come in!" said a sharp voice.

"Howard?" The office was of average size, but Howard sat behind a rather imposing desk that seemed to take up most of the room. He was a tall, lanky, balding man in his late fifties.

"Moreau, it's about time! Sit down! No smoking!" He pointed to a hard, wooden, straight-back chair.

The report review, aka the interrogation, went as I'd expected. For the first hour, Howard hooked me up to a lie detector machine, and asked yes and no questions. Polygraphs had become standard operating procedure for the CIA, and I was used to the methodical questions. Besides, I had nothing to hide. After establishing a baseline, Howard asked pointed questions about the operation and my loyalty to the United States government.

Once he finished with the polygraph, we headed into

a more detailed discussion about the operation parameters, my report, and subsequent operational failures. Howard alternately mumbled and barked questions at me. It was an interesting tactic. He'd start off murmuring in gravelly tones, forcing me to lean forward to catch what he was saying, then he'd raise his voice so much, I'd jerk back in my chair. In either case, the questions were conveyed in such a manner to put my back up and rattle me in turn. I did my level best to answer coolly and maintain my composure. The only time I lost my tranquility was when Howard muttered a question about the knife Eva used.

"What? Speak up, Howard. What's your question?" I snapped.

"What kind of knife did Eva use?" he barked.

"How the hell should I know? It was a kitchen knife of sorts. I didn't get the manufacturer details after she slit her femoral artery and bled all over it! Call the Berlin police if you must know." We'd been at it for hours. My back was stiff, my derriere numb, and I desperately needed a cigarette. I started to rise.

"Where do you think you're going?"

I straightened to my full height and looked down my nose at him. "To the loo." My lips puckered saucily around the *O*s, and my hips swayed arrogantly as I strode out.

On the way back to Howard's office, I stopped short, noticing a comfortable-looking cushioned armchair outside of the office door, opposite the stag. Howard must have stepped away while I'd had a quick smoke, and I dragged the heavy wooden beast into the hall.

When he came back to his office, Howard found me sitting in the new, comfortable chair. The rest of the afternoon went about as well as the first part, except for the fact that I was no longer uncomfortable—a point which seemed to irritate Howard but made me relish our sparring match even more.

He finally called it quits at five thirty.

Back at the Byron, I found the pimpled youth manning the front desk. "Room 216. Have I any messages?"

He shook his head and solemnly handed over my key. "I made sure the telegraph office sent your telegram. Nothing yet."

Chapter Twenty-Two
The Polish Diplomat

Day two started off slightly better than day one. I brought Margaret a pecan muffin from a bakery near my hotel. Placing it on her desk, I delivered the code phrase, "The nightingale sings at midnight."

Margaret stared at the little paper bag as if is held a snake. "*What* is that?"

"A pecan muffin from the bakery. I had one this morning with my coffee. It is delicious. The nightingale sings at midnight."

"The mockingbird sings at dusk." Tentatively she opened the bag and looked inside, then up at me.

I waited. *Will she accept the gift, throw it in the trash, or try to hand it back to me?*

"That is very . . . kind. Unnecessary, but kind of you," she said gruffly.

"I thought you might enjoy it." I shrugged and took a seat in one of the wing chairs to await my escort.

"You were right, you know."

"Right about what?" My head tilted.

"We are *not* girls." She adjusted herself and sat up taller. "We are *women*."

So, she *had* heard, and agreed with the set down I'd given Carl. I couldn't help the grin that broke across my face. I held up *Pride and Prejudice* to hide it.

"You may go in," Margaret said with gravity, as if

bestowing an honor upon me.

The door buzzed.

"Lovely. Do you know if Howard has arrived?"

She shook her head. "Not yet. He usually arrives at nine on the dot."

My watch read quarter 'til. "Thank you," I said and trotted up to the third floor. Howard's door was closed and locked, so I patted the stag's head and took a seat in the uncomfortable wooden chair that I'd hauled out of his office the day before.

At five after nine Howard rounded the staircase, and I rose to greet him.

"Good morning, Miss Moreau. What can I do for you?" he asked in a genial voice.

Shocked by his about-face attitude from the previous day, it took me a moment to gather my thoughts and respond. By the time I did, Howard had unlocked his door and entered his office.

I followed him inside. "I, uh, assumed you had more questions for me. Shall I come back after you've had a chance to get settled?"

"No need." He hung his coat and hat on a hook behind his desk. "I believe we covered everything yesterday."

I frowned in confusion. "You mean we're . . . finished?"

"Correct. Unless there is something else you wish to add, I'll be submitting my own report along with yours by the end of today." He sat behind his desk and began sorting through a pile of correspondence.

That's it? "Then, I'll . . . return to my office?"

"That will be fine," he replied absently.

At the staircase, I stepped aside to allow a pudgy woman in a flowered dress to chug past me, while I debated going up—to the lackluster broom closet—or down to Greg's office to see if there was something he needed from me. I decided on the latter.

"Come!"

Greg, still in his overcoat, stood at his desk, with the phone to his ear. He waved me into the room and pointed at the sofa, while continuing his phone conversation. "I understand, but I don't care! Find him, *now!* That's an order!" He slammed the handset down and turned to me, his face still mottled red with anger.

Meanwhile, I folded myself onto the loveseat. "Anything I can do to help?"

Greg studied me for a moment, and his color returned to normal. I could almost see the cogs rolling in his mind, but eventually he shook his head. "I wish I *could* place you into this operation."

"It would seem Howard has finished with me, which puts me at a loose end." I left the comment hanging.

Greg removed his overcoat and tossed it at the coatrack. Surprisingly, it found its mark and stayed hooked. He picked up a sheaf of messages on his desk and began sorting through the pile, tossing them either into the metal wastebasket or back onto the desk. "You'll be happy to hear the Ivanovs landed safely at Naval Air Station Anacostia."

"Good. I hope his intelligence is lucrative and the operation was worth it." Greg merely grunted, and I continued, "I came to ask if you've heard anything new from Berlin."

He paused at the final message, rereading the sharp script before tossing it in the trash, all of which would be incinerated. "As a matter of fact, I received an interesting call this morning that was put directly through to my flat. A gentleman came to the Berlin Mission asking to speak to Claudia Fischer."

I perked up, leaning forward. "That *is* interesting. What did the gentleman want?"

"To speak to you, apparently. When no one knew who Claudia Fischer was, the gentleman left."

"Did they get his name? A description? Anything?"

Greg sat behind his desk, and the chair gave a punctuated squeak. "About five feet ten, brown hair. He wore a black suit and scuffed shoes."

"Describes a number of men. Anything else?"

"He also had a scar that ran across his jaw." Greg patted his pockets in search of a pack of cigarettes.

I sucked in a breath and jumped to my feet. "A scar, you say? On the left side? Did it run down into his collar line?"

His hands froze mid-search. "On the left side, yes. You know this man?"

I paced in front of Greg's desk. "He followed me on the streets in Berlin." I pivoted and tapped a finger on my chin. "And he was at the airport . . ."

"Tempelhof Airport?" The search resumed as Greg opened and closed desk drawers.

"Mmm . . ." My mind's eye reanalyzed the two times I'd seen the scarred man. "I'd assumed he was KGB or Stasi and was afraid that he'd got on to me. I ditched him the first time, and I don't believe he saw me the second, or if he did, I was undercover as Brigitte, and it's unlikely he'd have recognized me," I mumbled, walking over to the wall of books to stare sightlessly at them.

Was he an East German or could he be someone else?

"Little Girl," Greg said in a singsong voice.

I turned, blinking away my musings.

A match flared. Greg had located a pack of Lucky Strikes. "Want to let me in on your brainstorm?"

"It's nothing—or, I don't know, maybe it is something." I tossed up my arms. "Clearly, the scarred man wants to speak to me. Could it be KGB wanting to let us know they've captured Greyhound?"

"Why be surreptitious about it? If they captured an American spy, they'd be crowing about it from the rooftops."

"What if they're hoping to trade him for Ivanov? If they can get Ivanov back before his defection to the West becomes public knowledge?"

"Possibly." The end of the cigarette glowed red while Greg pondered my suggestion. "There are better avenues than sending this scarred man to speak to you. Besides, the politburo knows Ivanov and the family are gone by now. Moreover, there are other back-channel options, should the Soviets wish to make a trade. Especially in Berlin. They don't need to go through you." Smoke poured from his nose as he spoke.

"What if . . ." I watched Greg tap his ash into the morning's clean tray. It would be filled with a pile of cigarette butts by the end of the day.

"Spit it out."

Our gazes met. "What if I was mistaken? What if his intentions were something different? What if Greyhound sent him with a message?"

He put the cigarette down.

I placed my palms on the edge of his desk and leaned forward with arms stiff. "Am I being ridiculous?"

"No. It's not out of the realm of possibility."

My arms relaxed, and I took a step back from vulturing over Greg. "What am I to do? How can we find this man?"

"*I* am going to call the Berlin office and see if we can get an ID on this character."

"If he's KGB? Stasi?"

The cigarette was back between his lips, and he spoke out of the side of his mouth. "Let's find out who he is. Then we can discuss a plan."

"What should I do in the meantime?"

"Sit tight." Ash dropped onto the desk blotter, and he wiped it to the floor. "There is a high possibility you'll be called upon to give a further account of the Blackbird Operation."

"In Berlin or Washington?" I crossed my arms and set my mouth.

"Washington," he murmured.

My eyes turned to slits.

"Now, don't look at me like that. An investigation will take time. Eventually you *will* be called back to Foggy Bottom." Greg referred to the location of CIA headquarters. "I can keep you here for only so long before I either need to put you on temporary assignment or send you back to D.C."

"Great!" I threw my hands up. "Put me on assignment . . . in Berlin. Call your new station chief pal from Bonn. I'm sure he can find a use for me."

Greg delivered an arch look to my suggestion, and I knew we were talking in circles. I decided it was time to retreat and hope information came through via Petrus. Greg's phone rang.

"That's my cue." I waved and exited the office, closing the door behind me.

My next stop was the kitchen, at the rear of the first floor, to make myself a cup of tea before braving the broom closet. The whistle of a teakettle guided my footsteps. A short, balding man in a tweed coat, whom I had yet to meet, was dunking a teabag in a dainty, flowered teacup.

"Hello. Is there any hot water left?" I asked.

"Enough for another. Cups are in that cabinet." He pointed to his left.

"What kind of tea is there?" I picked through a basket of bags.

"Only plain black tea and Earl Grey, I'm afraid." He placed the kettle back on the warm stove. "There's milk in the icebox, sugar on the counter. I'm Jim Jones, by the way." He nodded at me. "We didn't meet yesterday. I believe our offices are next to each other."

"Brigitte Moreau," I replied, removing a chintz-patterned Royal Doulton mug from the cabinet.

"Welcome to the London office," he said on his way out of the kitchen.

Immediately, I decided I liked Jim Jones. Beside Greg, Jim's was the friendliest introduction I'd gotten since arriving. I estimated the London office housed about twenty to twenty-five people. I'd passed a few of them on the stairs or in the hallways. Most either ignored me or gave me a simple nod before moving along. Jim was the first to introduce himself.

This behavior didn't surprise me. Doors tended to remain shut. Secrets were locked away in desks and file cabinets. Somewhere in this building was a room filled with coding machines and teletypes spitting out information. Offices were swept regularly for listening devices. Intelligence work tended to be compartmentalized. Each analyst or small group was a part of the larger puzzle. People who'd worked in a normal office environment might find it strange and, at times, a lonely place to operate. It was one of the reasons I enjoyed my time in the field.

The liquid turned dark, and I removed the Earl Grey bag. I added a touch of sugar, then trudged up the four flights to my broom closet. Jim's door was closed, and I could hear the murmur of conversation coming from it.

Someone had visited my office since yesterday. A brown cushion had been left on the wooden chair, the shelves were dusted, and the mop, bucket, and rug beaters were gone. A desk lamp sat on the table, its cord snaking along the wall, beneath the door, and into a hallway plug. Two pencils, a pen, and pair of scissors sat in a blue ceramic mug next to a glass ashtray. With a click of the switch, a soft glow emitted from the lamp, and the room didn't seem quite so stark and uninviting as it did yesterday.

I wondered who gave my office the improvements. I

hadn't seen Carl since yesterday, and I simply couldn't imagine him doing such a thing. Margaret? No. I shook away the thought. Definitely *not* Howard. Perhaps Greg had said something to the cleaning crew, or a kind soul simply took pity on me. Jim Jones? It didn't matter. Instinct told me I wasn't long for the London office. If I couldn't convince Greg to ship me back to Berlin, I'd be returning to Washington within days.

Ingrained habit had me closing the door and searching for bugs. Yes, if the powers that be were still uncertain about me, they would not hesitate to place a listening device in my office. Although, considering I had no phone, I'm not sure what they would have discovered. Perhaps they thought the same thing. I didn't find a bug.

I laid my coat and handbag on a shelf and settled myself at the desk. Pushing the antique behemoth aside, I placed a piece of white paper in the center and, with the two pencils, began sketching the scarred man from memory. I'd always had a natural talent for art and took classes during high school. If I'd spent more time practicing or taken some college-level courses, my skills would've been much better. I couldn't quite get the shadowing correct, and wore one eraser down to the nub, but after an hour and a half, I felt as though I'd rendered a fairly good resemblance of the man.

The desk outside Greg's office was no longer empty. A young brunette wearing a brown-and-black plaid dress and bright pink lipstick typed rapidly, her gaze fixed on a pad with shorthand writing on it. I envied the quiet clicking her new Royal machine made, as opposed to the teeth-rattling clacking of the Underwood in my broom closet.

"Hello." I interrupted her concentration.

The clicking paused. She looked me up and down, and her pink lips split into a friendly smile. "May I help you?" she chirped with an Irish lilt.

"Yes, I am Brigitte Moreau. I do not believe we have met."

"Petunia Fernsby." The name suited her.

"I was wondering if Greg was available. I have something to show him."

She glanced at the black phone at her desk. One of the keys at the bottom blinked on and off. "I'm afraid Mr. Dunbar is on a call. Have you an appointment?"

"No." I shook my head.

"I can have him ring you when he gets a moment. What is your extension?"

"I don't, uh, have one."

"Everyone has one," she said matter-of-factly. "What floor do you work on?"

"The fourth, but I don't have a phone in my office."

"New, eh?" She nodded sympathetically. "It can take a bit to get a telephone in your office."

"Right." I doubted the broom closet would be wired for a phone. I was lucky to have a desk lamp.

"Would you like to make an appointment?" She opened a large, black scheduling book.

"It isn't necessary. Can you please give this to him?" I held out the sketch. "Tell him, it's the man with the scar, whom I saw in Berlin."

She eyed the sketch. "My goodness, a rather forbidding-looking fellow, isn't he?"

"Fernsby!" Greg's voice bellowed through the door.

Petunia jumped up, grabbing her notepad and a pencil. "He's in a touchy mood today." She made a face. "I'll pass it along."

"Do not let him bully you." I gave her a wave and retreated back to my closet.

Once I got there, I realized I had nothing to do but pace my miniscule office. The report and debrief materials were being sent along the chain of command. Greg would decide what to do with the sketch, perhaps send it off to the Berlin Mission or to the new station chief. Perhaps he'd file it in the trash. I hadn't been given a new assignment. The reality of the situation was, I wanted to be reassigned back to Berlin. However, I feared if I started making waves, I'd be shipped home to D.C.

Sighing, I retrieved *Pride and Prejudice* from my handbag, lit a cigarette, and hunkered down with Jane and Elizabeth Bennet on a visit to Netherfield. All my worrying was for naught, for within ten minutes there was a knock on my door.

Jim Jones stood on the other side with a stack of file folders in his hands. "You're fluent in French?"

"Oui."

"The chief told me you've got Top Secret clearance, and I could use your help. These communiques are from French Intelligence. They've been decoded and need to be translated." He passed the folders over to me. "You have a typewriter?"

"Such as it is." I pushed the door wide and pointed at the monster.

Jim's lips turned down and he tilted his head. "Is

there something wrong with it?"

"I think it's a prototype, built at the turn of the century," I drawled.

Understanding crossed his features, and, grinning, he rolled back on his heels. "I'll see what I can do to help you find something built within the decade."

"I appreciate that, Mr. Jones—"

"Call me Jim," he corrected.

"Jim." I dropped the pile onto the desk. "Shall I return the completed translations to you?"

"That will be fine. I'll have more for you following lunch."

At noon, upon a recommendation from Margaret, I walked to a nearby café for lunch, then took the tube over to Westminster. The sun shone bright and there was a crisp breeze upon the air that played with my faux locks as I strolled. I always enjoyed seeing Big Ben and the surrounding Parliament buildings up close.

The exterior of the medieval complex hadn't made it through the war unscathed, and reconstruction was completed only the year before. The clocktower took a hit from an incendiary bomb, and the new, clean, sandy limestone starkly contrasted with the older, coal-darkened stone, making it look like a patchwork quilt. It didn't matter—the structure was magnificent, the fact that it was still standing a testament to the British fortitude displayed throughout the war.

I didn't go inside and regretted leaving my camera at the hotel, though I had plenty of photographs of the building from previous visits. The roadways were busy. Red, hulking double-decker buses dwarfed normal-sized cars, and Londoners walked across the neighboring Westminster Bridge at a fast clip, hunched against the breeze off the cold water.

To the west, I followed the pathway to the famous Westminster Abbey, with thoughts of taking a stroll inside the ancient church. I'd not been inside of it since the war. My watch read quarter 'til one. I should probably head back to the office, but I didn't relish the thought of returning to the linen closet and a fresh pile of translation work.

Putting a hand above my brow to block the bright sun, I caught sight of a freckled figure. "Carl?"

He spun around. "Brigitte?"

He'd been speaking with another man, the embodiment of the cliché "tall, dark, and handsome." They both wore hats and unbuttoned coats over their business suits.

I dragged my gaze away from the Humphrey Bogart doppelgänger back to Carl. "Good afternoon."

"What are you doing here?" he asked.

"I thought I might visit the Abbey. It's been years since I've been inside." I glanced significantly at the gentleman to his left, and Carl remembered his manners.

"Brigitte Moreau, meet Radoslaw Lewandowski. He works for the Government of the Republic of Poland in exile," Carl said, referring to the expelled government which formed in 1939 after the invasion of Germany and the Soviet Union.

Though the exiled government was no longer in control of the Polish Embassy in London and only recognized by a few entities, including Vatican City, they continued meeting at the Polish president's private residence in London. Their mission had become a symbolic resistance against the Soviet occupation of Poland. The Republic was anti-Communist, and although NATO did not officially recognize the exiled government, their members were still connected to the underground movement against Communism inside of Poland.

"Nice to meet you." I held out my hand. Instead of shaking it, Radoslaw bent in an old-fashioned gesture to kiss it, keeping eye contact with me while doing so. His cologne smelled outdoorsy, like cedarwood, and I'll admit the action produced a tingle of goosebumps up my arm.

"The pleasure is mine," he said with a mild Polish accent and a wolfish smile. Without releasing my hand, he looked to Carl. "How do you know this lovely creature?"

"We're, er—" Carl's face went blank.

I gently slid my hand from his grasp. "Friends. I am visiting from . . . Paris."

"How long are you in town?" Radoslaw asked.

"Oh, a few more days," I replied offhandedly. "What do you do, Mr. Lewandowski?"

"Call me Rado, all my friends do. I provide consular liaison services for the president," he said with pride.

This completely generic title could mean many things. Radoslaw could truly be a diplomat making efforts to reestablish his president's government, or he could be a spy. Most likely he was both.

"How long have you been in London?" I asked.

"Since the war. It has become my second home." He made an expansive gesture.

It was a silly question, but I had to ask, "Do you miss Poland?"

"Of course, but there is a vibrant Polish community here, and we keep each other company."

"Mm-hm," I murmured.

"As a matter of fact, there is a concert tonight. Do you enjoy Polish folk music?" Radoslaw asked, his gaze brimming with excitement.

"I—I do not know if I have heard any," I replied guiltily, fearful my ignorance would let him down. Ridiculous, I know. How many people outside of Poland listened to Polish folk music?

"There is a concert tonight at Wigmore Hall. If you haven't other plans, allow me to take you." He delivered a winsome smile, then, remembering our third party, he turned. "Carl has refused my invitation."

"As I mentioned earlier, I already have plans," Carl declined again.

The melting gaze returned to me. "What about you, Miss Moreau? Please, say you haven't other plans."

The fellow is a persuasive rogue, I'll give him that. Carl, standing slightly behind Radoslaw, delivered a fierce frown with the slightest shake of his head. I pretended not to notice. "*Oui*, I would be honored to attend."

Radoslaw put both hands on his heart and went into an ecstatic Polish monologue, none of which I understood. However, I believed the gist to be—he was in raptures over my acceptance of his invitation to the concert and his life was now complete. Finally, he paused the foreign oration and returned to English. "I shall pick you up at seven thirty. What is your direction?"

I couldn't help the grin and the flushing warmth that spread across my cheeks at his flattery. "I am staying at the Byron Hotel."

"Perfect. Unfortunately, I have a late meeting, so we haven't time for dinner beforehand, but I assure you, the concert will be magnificent. I shall take you for drinks at the Savoy afterward." He kissed his fingers in the manner of an Italian gourmet complimenting the chef on the penne a la carbonara.

"Sorry to interrupt." Carl didn't look in the least sorry. "However, I must be getting back to the office. Can I give you a lift somewhere, *Brigitte*?"

Clearly Carl wanted to have a little tête-à-tête, and I almost said no, just to tweak at him. On the other hand, a car ride back to the office would be quicker and easier than the tube, and Jim's translations awaited me. "I would appreciate that."

"What about your visit to the Abbey?" Radoslaw inconveniently remembered my initial plan.

"*Non*, I haven't time." I fluttered my lashes at him. "I must return to the hotel to prepare and have them press my dress for the evening."

Carl made a gurgling noise in the back of his throat, but Radoslaw's face brightened, and he gave an elegant little bow. "Until tonight."

"Tonight," I murmured.

Carl offered me his arm. We walked in silence, a block and a half to the car. Once inside, Carl didn't start the engine. Instead, he turned to me, putting his arm across the back of the seat. "Why did you accept Radoslaw's invitation?"

I shrugged with innocence and dropped my French accent. "Why not? I haven't anything better to do tonight, and I enjoy music as much as the next person."

A *V* formed between Carl's brows. "You should watch out for Rado. He's a known womanizer."

"Oh, I have no doubt of that." I smirked in both knowledge of Radoslaw's character and surprise that Carl felt he had to warn me. "He's quite the charmer. And handsome too."

The *V* deepened and was accompanied by a severe scowl.

"Of which, I'm certain, he is fully aware. He utilizes it to get his way, you know. Not just with women," I added.

Carl merely grunted in agreement.

"Is there another reason you didn't want me to attend tonight?" I searched for a pack of cigarettes in my handbag. "Do you believe Rado is dangerous?"

"It's just . . ." He shook his head at my silent offer of a cigarette. "You're aware of NATO's stance regarding the Polish Government in exile."

"I am aware the Allies were highly annoyed that the exiled government wouldn't accept the newly proposed Polish border with the Soviet Union. They were over a barrel. In the end, Stalin took what he wanted and installed a Communist-dominated government." I shuffled objects in my purse in search of a lighter. "Personally, I can't blame them for continuing the farce in hopes that one day the situation will change. I am also aware that covertly we have supported their anti-

Communist actions."

Carl nodded, producing a silver Lumet pocket lighter for me.

"Is he a person I shouldn't be fraternizing with?" I inhaled, allowing the tobacco to flow deep into my lungs.

"Just don't . . . shag him, as the Brits would say," Carl said baldly.

I coughed and gagged, and the smoke burst inelegantly out my nose and mouth. Carl's face reddened as deeply as a rooster's comb.

Recovering, I sputtered, "Not that it's any of your business, but it wasn't in my plan to do so."

"Good." He turned the car over and drove in agitated silence back to the office.

I cracked the window and smoked with a nonchalance I didn't feel. I was both irritated at Carl's forwardness and flattered by his dreadful attempts to protect me from a known womanizer. Clearly, the thought of using me in the field had not occurred to Carl, so I put it in his head. "Since I *am* going with him to the concert, what should I watch for?"

He drummed his fingers on the wheel before replying in a serious, but much friendlier, tone, "Pay attention to the people he speaks with and take note if he spends time alone with anyone in particular." He maneuvered the car into a tight parallel parking spot with an ease of skill. "Report back to me tomorrow."

"Very well." I stubbed the cigarette into the ashtray.

My afternoon bore an alarming resemblance to the morning—a fresh cup of tea, a cigarette, and a slowly dwindling heap of files kept me company. Determined to finish the stack, my fingers pounded savagely against the stiff keys, and the forgotten cigarette burned down to the filter. I don't know how long the knocking had gone on for, when I finally paused my attack on the typewriter. Whipping open the door, I found Petunia wringing her hands.

"Hi," she squeaked, stepping back. "Mr. Dunbar would like to see you now." She glanced past me. Taking in my squalid office, her face turned down. "Oh, dear. It might take longer to get that telephone."

I couldn't help the snicker that escaped at her understatement. "I think you might be right."

"He said you may go in directly," she whispered. Returning to her seat, she began typing at top speed.

The door was cracked, and pushing it fully open, I found Greg on the phone again. This time the cord stretched across his desk and behind his chair, as he stared out the front window. "*Damnit!* What do you *mean* you can't find him! I don't care what it takes! *Find him!*" He spun around. *Wham!* The phone slammed into the cradle. "*Fernsby!*" he hollered.

Petunia gave a little jump. I waved her back into her seat. His infuriated gaze landed on me.

I thrust my shoulders back and said serenely, "Miss Fernsby stepped away from her desk."

Petunia's eyes rounded big as teacups, and she put a hand to her mouth.

"I understand you wanted to see me." I strolled into the room, pulling the door closed behind me. "I seem to be repeating myself, but is there something I can do to help?"

"No," he snapped, hunting for a cigarette.

"There's one burning in the ashtray." I pointed.

He snatched it up. "Well, Picasso, I understand you drew this," he said, holding my sketch by the corner with two fingers.

"Picasso was an abstract artist. I think Degas or Vermeer might be more appropriate." Neither one was appropriate. I was the merest dab compared to those masters, but I was trying to leaven Greg's mood.

He got the joke and snorted. "Okay, I get you. I'm to assume this is the scarred man?"

"It is." I wandered over to Greg's bar and poured myself a finger of brandy. "Scotch or vodka?"

"Vodka," he harrumphed.

I poured two fingers for Greg. It seemed like he could use it.

"I'll see about getting it into a diplomatic pouch headed to Berlin. *Fernsby!*"

My hand jerked and vodka splashed over the rim of the glass. "Confound it, Greg! Please stop yelling. You are terrorizing that poor girl," I said, shaking liquor off my fingers.

The door opened and Petunia peeked in, her gaze wide. "Yes, Mr. Dunbar?"

"Miss Fernsby," he said, his voice softened noticeably, "see if Carl is still in the building, and if so, send him to my office."

"Right away, sir." Her head disappeared and the door closed with a thump.

"Charming. How long has she been with you?"

"Six months. She's lasted longer than the rest. I don't

understand why it's so difficult to keep a good secretary." Greg scribbled a note and put it, with the sketch, in a manila envelope.

"Perhaps if you stopped shrieking at them, they would be more likely to stay," I suggested.

"I need a girl with a backbone. Someone like you. How about it, Miriam? Are you ready to give up life in the field?" He addressed the outside of the envelope.

"A tempting offer, but I must regretfully decline." I allowed only the tiniest lilt of sarcasm to taint my refusal. "Speaking of returning to the field, if you sent me with the sketch, I could take it to Berlin and make sure it reached the proper people," I suggested, leaning casually against his desk, legs crossed, sipping the brandy. The liquor warmed me to my bones.

Greg didn't deign to answer my volley. A firm knock interrupted my next comment, and he hollered, "Come!"

Carl entered. "You wished to see me, sir?" He nodded an acknowledgement to me. "Brigitte."

"Carl." I held my drink toward him with a brow raised. "Drink?"

"He hasn't time for a drink." Greg held out the envelope. "See this gets coded and into the next diplomatic pouch headed to Berlin."

"I'll make sure it goes out immediately." He took the packet. "Any word on . . ." He let the question dangle.

Greg shook his head. "Not yet."

Carl cleared his throat. "You should know, I ran into Brigitte at lunch."

Greg stared blankly at Carl.

Carl swallowed. "I was with Rado Lewandowski."

Greg's gaze pivoted to me. "So, you met our charming Pole. Did he make love to you on the street? He has a penchant for brunettes . . . and women in general."

"As a matter of fact" —I sipped— "he invited me to a concert tonight."

Greg's stare turned to a glower directed at Carl. Carl blanched.

I almost felt sorry for him.

Almost.

"I saw no reason not to go with him. Shall I put him off?" I asked.

Carl spoke up before Greg could respond. "She offered to gather intelligence." He shrugged. "Who knows? She might hear something useful."

Greg finished his cigarette before responding, "Very well. See to the pouch, please."

Carl swiftly exited with the packet.

The station chief drank deeply, and I perceived the strain the job placed upon him. His eyes were tight, and a world weariness hung heavily across his shoulders. Clearly something was not going as planned, and the failure would be on his head.

"I don't envy your position. Are you *sure* I can't be of some help?"

"If the situation doesn't change soon . . . it may be too late for anyone to help." He sighed, leaning back in his squeaky chair. "Be careful tonight, Little Girl."

"You're the second person to warn me off Radoslaw." I stared down at the topaz liquid.

Greg's brows rose. "Carl?"

"In his own clumsy way." I grinned at the memory of

his beet-red face.

Greg slugged back the rest of the vodka. "He's right. There have been . . . rumors . . ."

Intrigued, I put down the glass. "Rumors? Worse than womanizing?"

"Don't—don't allow Radoslaw to drive you home, at the end of the night. He has difficulty hearing the word *no*. Especially from women," Greg said solemnly. "Take a cab back to your hotel."

The lightbulb of understanding turned on. I read into the words Greg did not speak.

He pulled one of his business cards from a drawer and scribbled on the backside. "This is my home number . . . in case you need it. Call anytime."

Tucking the card away, I finished the brandy and took my leave. "Thank you."

Chapter Twenty-Three
The Concert

The youth with the spots was not in his usual place when I arrived at the hotel that evening. A girl in her early twenties manned the front desk. She handed me my room key and shook her head when I asked if there had been any messages. At seven thirty, wearing the trench coat over my black dress and black elbow-length gloves, I stood out front beneath the portico, waiting for Radoslaw. The weather had turned humid, and leaden clouds hung dense in the heavens, threatening to burst at any moment. Taking Greg's and Carl's warnings to heart, my knife was strapped to my thigh. Its solid weight provided me a sense of security. In addition, I had formulated a surefire plan to put Radoslaw off at the end of the concert. No better way to kill an amorous mood than with a raging case of Delhi Belly. As the first fat drop of rain splatted onto the sidewalk, Radoslaw rolled up in a forest-green two-seater Jaguar.

The concert turned out to be more than just a musical event. The sextet of musicians played from the back of the stage beneath the cupola, while a variety of dances were performed in the forefront by small ensembles of beautifully costumed, lithe young dancers. Folk music styles included the mazurka, krakowiak, and polonaise. Before each piece the band leader would come forward to explain the history and origin of the music to the audience in both Polish and English. Most of the songs had upbeat rhythms with clapping and quick footwork. I enjoyed the performance so much, it surprised me when the houselights came on, indicating we'd reached the intermission.

"Shall we stretch our legs?" Radoslaw asked.

The large foyer was abuzz with chatting audience members. Different languages blended together while tuxedoed waiters roamed the room with trays of champagne.

Constructed at the turn of the century, Wigmore Hall was originally known as Bechstein Hall, after the German piano manufacturer who built it. During World War I, tensions between Britain and Germany forced the piano company to sell the grand building, and it was scooped up by Debenhams for half of what it cost to build. It was also renamed at that point. The hall was known for its black-and-white marble floors and alabaster walls. During the war, free concerts had been held for military members.

The head usher, wearing a maroon-and-gold uniform, mounted the stairs and clapped his hands to gain our attention. When the din of conversation lowered, he announced, "Thanks to donations from the Patronesses of Wigmore Hall, biscuits and mini cakes can be purchased in the anteroom to my right. The proceeds will benefit the Polish Performing Arts Foundation." He left his perch and the noise level resumed its previous level.

Radoslaw caressed my back and leaned close. I could feel his warm breath upon my ear. "Shall we visit the refreshment room?"

Warnings from Carl and Greg rang in my mind, and it took an effort not to cringe at his closeness. A tall, balding man with black-rimmed glasses waved at us, but Radoslaw's attention was too focused upon me to notice.

I cleared my throat and spoke above the chatter, "*Monsieur*, I believe that man is hailing you."

Radoslaw pulled his attention away from my decolletage, and a Polish exclamation escaped his lips as the man approached us.

"Rado, it's good to see you." The two men shook hands.

"This is a surprise," Radoslaw responded. "I expected you to be at—"

"My dear man, be so good as to introduce me to your beautiful companion," the bespectacled fellow interrupted, heartily clapping Radoslaw on the shoulder.

Taken aback by his friend's impoliteness, Radoslaw shifted out of arm's reach. Recovering, with reluctance, he said, "Brigitte, may I introduce Jako Kovac? Jako works for the International Bank for Reconstruction and Development. Jako ,this is Brigitte Moreau, a visitor from Paris."

While Radoslaw made introductions, a woman slid into place next to Jako. She wore an emerald-green cocktail dress, white gloves that had a slash of red lipstick on the forefinger, and a silver fox stole across her shoulders. Her pretty, heart-shaped face was surrounded by a mass of thick black hair. She was perhaps five or six years my junior.

"A pleasure to meet you, Miss Moreau." Jako

beamed, shaking my hand. His English was excellent, and the accent wasn't Polish. I couldn't quite place it. "This is my niece, Sara Kovac."

She nodded at the two of us and muttered a pleasantry.

"How did you meet?" Jako asked, rather brusquely.

"Brigitte is a friend of Carl Sullivan. We met outside Westminster Abbey this afternoon, and I invited her to attend the concert," Radoslaw replied, scrutinizing his friend with confusion.

Sara absentmindedly tapped her foot and allowed her gaze to wander, as if bored by the entire exchange. However, at the mention of Carl Sullivan, she zeroed in on me like a torpedo.

Radoslaw missed Sara's sudden interest and continued, "We were about to purchase refreshments to support the cause." He took my elbow and, clearly, did not invite the Kovacs to join us.

"Sara"—Jako turned to his to his niece—"would you mind taking Miss Moreau to the refreshment room?" He pulled a money clip from his pocket and peeled off a few bills as he spoke. Then he turned to me with an apologetic tone and said, "Pardon me, but there is some business I must discuss with Rado. You understand, Miss Moreau." He tilted his head to the side as if the word "business" explained away his impoliteness. He ended with a condescending, "I wouldn't want to bore you ladies."

Radoslaw sucked in a breath, squeezing my elbow tight, and a thunderous expression crossed his features. His lips pinched. I had a feeling, if I allowed it, the next words out of Radoslaw's mouth would be far more impolite than what his friend had already delivered.

I had no interest in being part of a scene amongst the sea of concert goers. I placed my hand upon Radoslaw's and forced a soothing smile and tone. "But of course, I understand." With a tinkle of laughter, I continued, "You men. Work, work, work. That is all you seem to think about. It is different in France." Rado's hand relaxed, and I pulled my elbow free. "Shall we, Sara?"

"Of course, right this way," she murmured, ducking her head in compliance.

She wove effortlessly through the throng of concert goers, dodging around a rather robust woman in blue velvet, a short man, and a mother and her young son. I kept up for a bit, then lost sight of her when a group of senior citizens walked between us. I realized there was no reason for me to chase after this aloof character.

A waiter came into my orbit, and I plucked a champagne coupe off his tray. Sipping the fizzy drink, I stepped behind a potted plant.

From my vantage point, I observed Radoslaw and Jako by the stairs, deep in discussion. Radoslaw jammed one hand in his pocket, and the other clenched in a fist at his side. He shook his head with an exclamation that carried above the general drone of conversation, and his face turned ruddy with anger. A few people surrounding the pair turned their attention to the contretemps. Jako put a calming hand on Radoslaw's shoulder, and he leaned in, speaking in low tones. I couldn't read lips, and I didn't know what language they spoke, but Jako's body language said it all—"calm down, we are in public." Radoslaw realized he'd drawn unwanted attention and made an effort to relax. Jako released his shoulder and jerked his head toward the left. The pair tucked deeper into the corner of the stairs, out of my line of sight.

Checking my watch, I found I had time before the concert resumed to visit the ladies' room. Sara was still nowhere to be seen. I asked a passing waiter where I could find the toilets. He took my empty glass and directed me downstairs to the lower floor.

Once behind the sturdy stall door, I took a moment to scribble on a receipt I found in my purse—

Jako Kovac, International Bank of R and D
Sara Kovac, niece, knows Carl

While washing my hands, the lights dimmed, indicating intermission would soon be at an end, and I took a moment to put on fresh lipstick. Taking a final swipe along my lower lip, my eyes locked with Sara's in the mirror.

"*Bonjour.*" I recapped the lipstick tube and dropped it in my purse. "I did not know where you went. We lost each other in the crowd."

She stood stiff, two sinks away, and when she didn't answer immediately, I pivoted to face her. Her eyes darted around the room. She chewed her lip. I wondered if her English was subpar, or perhaps she didn't understand my French accent.

"Shall we walk back upstairs together?" I made a walking motion with two fingers and pointed upward.

While I didn't feel threatened by Sara, my instincts told me there was something . . . odd about her manner. A plump woman waddled out the door and we were alone in the bathroom.

"Are you really a friend of Mr. Sullivan?" she asked in stilted English, with an Eastern European accent similar to her uncle's.

"Why, yes, I am. Do you know him?" I pinched my purse closed with a snap.

"He was supposed to be here with Rado. I *must* get a message to him," she whispered urgently.

My brows rose, and for the first time, I noticed the crumpled piece of paper she held tight in her gloved fist. *What is this? Is Carl having a tryst with pretty Sara?* "I can pass a message to him, if you like."

"Tonight, *please*. It must be *tonight*. By tomorrow, it— it will be too late," Sara whispered with anguish in her eyes.

"It will be late by the time we leave the concert. I'm not sure I should wake him. Can it not wait until tomorrow?"

Her gaze silently pleaded with me, and I thought I saw a tear well up.

What theatrics. I sighed with resignation. "Yes, yes, tonight, if you insist."

She furtively slipped me the piece of paper, as if someone might be watching. "Hide this in your purse. Tell him *they* know. He—he will not make it until morning. Car—Mr. Sullivan will understand."

That sounded rather ominous. I dropped my voice and asked, "Sara, is Mr. Sullivan in danger?"

"Sullivan? In danger? No, no. It is . . ." She put a hand to her mouth. "He . . . I—I cannot say. He told me it was imperative to keep it secret . . . but he—he does not realize the danger he faces. Tell Sullivan. He will know what to do. *Please.*"

Like beads on an abacus, things started adding up. Greg's concern all day over a missing officer. At least, I had assumed it was an officer. Perhaps it wasn't an officer at all, but rather an agent—a source in the field. Someone Carl knew. A person who'd gone dark and was in trouble due to information he'd been providing to the American government. "Carl is not in danger, but someone else is?"

Her head quickly bounced up and down.

My gaze narrowed. *"Votre amour?"* She looked confused, and I translated into English. "Someone you love?"

She blushed and ducked her head. Her fingers plucked at the lipstick stain.

I realized it was time to enact my exit strategy. "Sara, I will leave the concert now to go speak to Mr. Sullivan—"

Her hair billowed as she shook her head and cried, "You must not. You *cannot* tell Radoslaw! Nor my uncle! They will know something is wrong."

"Calm yourself. I won't tell them, but I need your help to leave. Do you think you can do that?"

She took a steadying breath. "Tell me what to do."

"Simply affirm the lie I am about to tell Radoslaw. Can you do that? *Oui?*"

"What lie?"

"We haven't time. Do I have your word?"

"Yes." Her head bobbed and she stiffened her spine.

Together we walked up the steps to the main floor. Both Radoslaw and Jako awaited us at the head of the staircase.

"Hurry, ladies, they are closing the doors. The concert is about to recommence." Radoslaw beckoned us forward as his eyes hungrily watched our figures ascend.

I placed one hand on his arm and the other to my stomach. "I am terribly sorry, but I cannot stay for the rest of the concert."

Radoslaw's face registered astonishment. "But, my dear—"

"Tummy trouble," I groaned. "Something I ate."

Radoslaw took in the hand at my stomach, and his lips turned down in disappointment. "You are certain?"

Clearly, my illness didn't work into his evening plans.

"I must say, you do look a tad flushed," Jako commented.

"I believe Miss Moreau would be more comfortable returning to her hotel," Sara urged.

With a resigned sigh, Radoslaw said, "Very well, I shall take you back to the hotel."

"Oh, no," I exclaimed, "I would not dream of ruining your evening. A taxi can take me. You must stay here and finish the concert."

"I could not allow—"

Sara cut off Radoslaw. "Uncle, you and Mr. Lewandowski may finish the concert. I will drive Miss Moreau back to her hotel and return to pick you up at the end of the concert." Sara played the coquette, batting her eyes at Jako, who was not immune to his niece's charms. She leaned toward the two men, held a hand to the side of her mouth, and said sotto voce, "I think Miss Moreau would appreciate the help of another woman, if you know what I mean."

Radoslaw was one of those men who was as charming as they come, but I doubted he had patience for a woman's frailties. He proved my theory when his face perked up at Sara's suggestion.

"You are too kind, Miss Kovak. I would not want to put you out," I replied. Dragging Sara along didn't fit into my plans. "A taxi will do fine."

"It is no trouble. Uncle knows I only came to keep him company. This type of music is . . ." She made a side-to-side flicking motion with her hand.

"Very well. If Miss Moreau is amenable," Jako said, removing a valet ticket from his pocket.

Humbly, I acquiesced. "Thank you. Please, now, return to the concert before you miss any more of the music."

Sara kissed her uncle on the cheek. Radoslaw succinctly bowed over my hand. "Until we meet again." And the two men hurried to the usher standing outside the closed door with a flashlight in his hand.

While Sara went out to the valet stall to have the car brought around, I retrieved my coat from the cloakroom. The rain had come to an end, but dampness remained in the air, and the wet streets shone in the moonlight. The temperature had dropped, and across the road a man strode at a fast pace with his dog. A red-coated valet rolled up in a silver, four-door Vanguard sedan, and we climbed inside.

The tires swished through a puddle as Sara pulled away from the curb. "Shall we go to Mr. Sullivan's home directly?"

"*Non*, unfortunately, I do not know Carl's direction. I

would say the best thing to do is find a telephone box. I shall ring him."

A few blocks from Wigmore Hall, Sara found an open parking space near one of London's iconic red booths. My watch read half past ten—late to be calling, but not obscenely so. I suspected Greg would still be awake. The coins clinked into the slot, and I dialed. Waiting for an answer, I reviewed the paper Sara had given me. There was an address on it, today's date, and a time—11:00 p.m.

"Hello!" a male voice barked.

"Greg? Is that you? It's me."

"Little Girl? What's wrong?" his voice boomed across the line, and I could hear the concern in his tone.

"I'm fine," I assured him. "Listen, I met a woman at the concert who insisted I contact Carl. She gave me an address and a message."

"What's the message?" he asked gruffly.

"'They know. He won't last the night.'"

Greg went quiet. "Who is the girl?"

"Sara Kovac. She's the niece of Jako Kovac. The man works at the International Bank of Recon—"

"Reconstruction and Development," Greg cut me off. "I know who he is. I didn't realize he'd be at the concert tonight."

"He and Radoslaw had an argument." My fingers fidgeted with the cord as I spoke, "They spent the entire intermission holed up in a corner. Sara and I were summarily dismissed to the refreshments table, and I was too far away to hear what they talked about. Whatever their discussion entailed, Rado was *not* pleased with Jako."

"Where are you?"

I glanced up and down the sidewalk to orient myself. A few cars came down the street, but there was hardly any foot traffic. "I'm a block from Portman Square."

"Get to the office, *immediately*."

"I'm with Sara."

"What the devil are you doing with the girl?" he barked.

"She helped me escape the clutches of our friend Radoslaw," I explained.

"Hell and damnation!" Greg swore. "Pump her for information, then ditch the girl and get back to the office."

"I'll be there directly—" The line went dead before I could finish the sentence.

"What did he say?" Sara asked as I slid into the passenger seat.

"Sara, what can you tell me about this address?" I held up the paper. "Is he hiding there? Are they holding him? Carl needs to know."

"It's the Lomond Club. The membership is made up of foreign service diplomats."

My mouth pinched. "Eastern or Western countries?"

"Both."

"Where does your *amour*, your boyfriend, work?"

She stared down at her hands.

"Sara?"

"The Hungarian Embassy." It came out in a whisper, and she didn't bother to deny her relationship status.

My eyes narrowed, and I rubbed my thumb and forefinger together in thought. The puzzle pieces clicked into place. Kovac was a Hungarian surname, which explained Sara's accent. The pair probably met through her uncle and likely socialized in the same circles. They shared a language and home country.

"Is he aware of the situation? Does he know there is trouble?" I prodded.

She continued staring at her hands, which plucked agitatedly at a loose string on her coat. "No. I mean, I—I do not know. He gave me the note yesterday and said Mr. Sullivan would be with Rado, but then I heard Uncle . . . I—I tried calling his office, but . . ."

"Tell me about the Lomond Club. Why is he there and you are not with him?"

Her saddened gaze met mine. "He—he has a fiancée . . . in Hungary. He does not love her, and he is going to break it off . . . but her father is a well-connected party member. It is how he was appointed the embassy position. Our relationship . . . it is not . . ."

"Yes, I understand." I understood it all.

This poor, foolish girl had pinned her hopes on a diplomatic playboy. He'd never break off the engagement to the daughter of a high-powered party member. He'd continue to use her to elevate his professional life and make a little money on the side by feeding intelligence to the West. Undoubtedly, this was the type of man who enjoyed the thrill of taking chances. He and Sara most likely arranged secret trysts around the city or in little hamlets outside of London. He would not take her to a fete with his colleagues. And Sara—she'd simply be one of a score of broken hearts he'd leave behind in his wake as he worked his way up the diplomatic ladder.

"And the Lomond Club?" I probed.

"Tonight, there is a casino party. It is being hosted by the Romanian ambassador and his wife. They are raising money for a charity. All the Eastern Bloc countries will have a representative there, and some of the Western countries, too. The Romanians want to—how do you say . . ." She tilted her head in thought. "Make a good impression, but more than that."

"Show off," I supplied.

Her head bobbed, and she turned her palm upward. "Yes, as you say. Intelligence agents will be there."

"KGB?"

"I do not know. Hungarian secret service, to be sure." Her shoulders crawled up to her ears and her head dropped. "He—he will not leave the party alone."

"How will it happen?" I pushed.

"Too much alcohol? A drugged drink?" She bit her lip. "Because there are Western countries in attendance, they do not want to make scene. They may escort him to their car."

I frowned. Once he got in the car, agents could incapacitate him and take him for questioning to their embassy, or a secret site, or they could put him on a ship, and he'd wake up behind the Iron Curtain.

I squeezed the handle on my purse. "How do you know all of this?"

She turned her head away from me to stare out the side window.

"Sara, please." I placed my hand on hers. "I want to help your lover, but I need to know—"

"I overheard my uncle's telephone conversation. He did not know I was home. I live with him and my grandmother, and my cousins. My aunt and parents died in the war," she explained, her voice petering out at the end.

I bit my lip. Not only a diplomat's toy, but a war orphan to boot. "What does Radoslaw have to do with it?"

She shrugged. "I do not know. I was told Carl would be with Radoslaw tonight. That is why I came with Uncle."

It felt as though I'd gotten all the useful information Sara had to offer, and time was not on our side. Turning to face the windshield, I said, "Take me to Oxford Street."

The car purred to life, and she turned at the next stop sign. "What is on Oxford Street? Does Mr. Sullivan live there?"

"*Non,*" I replied succinctly. "Please, hurry."

Buildings zipped by as Sara drove faster than the speed limit. A parked car door opened and she swerved to miss it, honking at the man who almost stepped out in front of the Vanguard. We cruised through an intersection without stopping. I didn't discourage her speed. It was already a quarter to eleven. Who knew how long the card games would last before the party broke up? For that matter, the man may have already been escorted away. The light turned red, Sara jammed on the brakes, and we came to a screeching halt at the corner of busy Oxford Street.

I opened the door to exit; Sara grabbed my arm. "Where are you going?"

"I am getting a black cab. Go back to the concert. Tell your father and Radoslaw you dropped me at the hotel. Say nothing further." I yanked my arm out of her grasp and slammed the door.

Lying across the seat, she rolled down the window and hollered, "How will I know if he is safe?"

"I will have him contact you." I knew I'd spoken a lie as soon as it came out of my mouth.

If this Hungarian had been feeding intelligence to Americans, he'd continue to be in danger here in London. If he was important enough and willing, he could defect, and we'd send him to the US with a new name and a new life. If he didn't want to cooperate with us, we'd toss him back into the shark pond, and he'd likely end up with a bullet to the head after being tortured until he had nothing left to tell.

Sara would never see him again.

Chapter Twenty-Four
Trust Issues

A burly man with a crooked nose and short, clipped hair sat at Margaret's desk. It looked as though he'd seen his share of fisticuffs—along with the nose, he had a cauliflower ear and scar that split his right eyebrow in half. The sole burning light came from the muted desk lamp, which flung shadows upon the walls and made him look even more fearsome.

His presence jarred me, and I stared at him for a long moment. He didn't move a muscle, and I realized his body was tense as a coiled spring, waiting for me to say something.

I spoke the words in a rush, "Thenightingalesings-atmidnight."

His body relaxed. "The mockingbird sings at dusk." His voice was gravelly, as if he chewed tacks for breakfast. The door buzzed. "They're in the chief's office."

I slipped behind the guard, giving him a wide berth.

Greg's door was open, and topping the stairs, I heard Carl's strident tones. "What on earth does this girl have on you, Chief? What kind of dirt? Because for the life of me I can't understand the leeway you've given her, or why you insist on inserting her into this operation!"

I froze in the hallway with gritted teeth and clenched fists. *I thought we'd moved beyond this.*

Technically, I knew things about Greg that might not get him fired but would probably lose him the station chief job. Nothing to compromise national security, but it had to do with a certain former ambassador's daughter. An ambassador who was now a sitting senator. I'm not even sure Greg realized I knew. However, he likely had his suspicions. I would never hold it over his head or use the information as blackmail. We all had skeletons. Greg had been my mentor during the war, and I respected him too damn much.

"First of all, Sara made contact with Brigitte tonight. Not you. Second of all, that *girl* once kept me from losing my goddamn mind when we were locked in the trunk of a car for over eight hours." Greg's voice continued to rise as he counted off his arguments. "Finally, as I've already explained, Brigitte had nothing to do with the deaths of those two traitorous agents. Moreover, the intelligence we're getting from Oleg Ivanov would have taken us years to gather! She's an excellent officer and a goddamn patriot. I don't want to hear another word about it!" Greg thundered. He must have slammed his hand on a table because I heard the sound of flesh smacking against something hard.

Silence followed. Someone mumbled something, and I decided it was time for my entrance. "Good evening, gentlemen."

Greg, Carl, and Jim Jones stood at the round table in Greg's office. Per usual, Greg's face was mottled with fading anger—an emotion I'd seen on him all day today. Carl too was red-faced, whether from anger or embarrassment, I didn't know. Jim showed neither emotion. As a matter of fact, Jim's face seemed immobilized into a mien of neutrality.

However, Jim was the only one to greet me with any sort of enthusiasm. "Hullo, Brigitte. Nice to see you again."

Carl did not acknowledge my entrance.

Greg grunted, "Took you long enough."

I sashayed to the table and took a seat. "Apologies. I thought you wanted me to pump Sara for information before coming in."

"What did you find out?" He yanked out a chair and sat.

The other two men followed suit, and I gave the crew a rundown of Sara's story, making sure to highlight the fact that there was very little time to make plans if we were to successfully retrieve the source before he disappeared for good.

"Should we wait for him to leave the club to take him?" Carl asked. He must not have been lying to Radoslaw about having other plans tonight—he wore a black double-breasted dinner jacket, stiff, pleated shirt, and bowtie.

On the other hand, Greg was still wearing the same shirt he'd had on earlier in the day, but he had on no tie, nor a coat. The sleeves were rolled to his elbows; the shirt was wrinkled and yellowed at the collar and armpits. He shook his head. "We need to get in there."

"Are any of you members of the Lomond Club?" I asked.

"I am," Carl replied.

"Is this casino night by invitation only?" Jim must

have thrown on whatever was handy. He wore a heavy, wool fisherman's sweater, a pair of brown corduroys, and army-green Wellingtons on his feet.

"No. Any member can attend, but you must bring your wallet. It's five hundred pounds, sterling, to walk through the front door," Carl explained.

Jim let out a whistle.

"Is there a back door? Perhaps a dishwasher willing to look the other way for fifty quid?" I suggested.

Greg shook his head, his hands searching for the elusive cigarette pack. "Forget it. We can't have you getting caught sneaking in. I'll front the money."

I pulled a pack out of my purse and passed it to him.

"Thanks." He tapped the box against his thumbnail. "Carl, you and Brigitte will go in."

Carl crossed his arms. "What about Jones?"

We all turned to Jim. He looked down at his clothes and shrugged apologetically.

Greg's brows rose, and he growled, "Jones will be waiting in the car. He isn't dressed appropriately to go inside, and we haven't time to get him kitted out." He flung the cigarette pack on the table in frustration.

To my surprise, Carl continued to argue. "She doesn't know what László Kiraly looks like."

I must have offended Carl rather badly by accepting Radoslaw's invitation. I pulled a cigarette from the box.

"That's what we have dossiers for. She goes, and that's the end of it," Greg snapped.

The room went silent, the only sound the scratch and flare of the match. All eyes turned to watch me light the ciggy.

I shook out the match and blew smoke at the ceiling. "Well, gentlemen, when do we leave?"

"Jones, get László's dossier for Brigitte. You can read it on the way." Greg's tone had softened, but it was still gruff with irritation.

"Sure, boss." Jim jumped up.

Greg looked me up and down. "Well, Little Girl, are you ready for this?"

"Of course."

Beaten, Carl jammed his hands in his pockets and hunched his shoulders.

Greg pointed at him with his unlit cigarette. "Your mission—find László, retrieve him as quietly as possible, and escort him to the embassy. If you can't get him out, pump him for information with whatever promises you can. Try not to draw attention."

"He's being watched," I reminded my old mentor. "A distraction might be necessary."

It took a moment for that to sink in, before Greg replied, "Very well. Try not to cause an international incident."

I grinned. "I'll do my best."

Carl let out a windy sigh. "Time is ticking. Let's go."

Chapter Twenty-Five
The Lomond Club

The Lomond Club was one of many gentlemen's clubs on St. James Square, an area of London built around 1720 that was once inhabited by the fashionable British *beau monde*. The architecture was predominantly Georgian and Neo-Georgian. Clubs, banks, a few embassies, and other commercial businesses now surrounded the well-manicured garden square.

Women weren't allowed to cross the hallowed threshold of the gentlemen's clubs except for special occasions, Carl informed me on the ride over. "During some of our events, the need for female companionship—"

"You mean something prettier to look at than a bunch of men's ugly mugs?" I sneered, still stinging from the overhead conversation in Greg's office.

"As I was saying," Carl continued drily, "since women aren't normally allowed inside, when they are invited, a female guest's behavior is considered to be a reflection of the member."

"In other words, if I behave badly, it will reflect poorly upon you, and you might get blackballed?" I drawled.

His head bounced up and down. "In a manner of speaking."

I rolled my eyes and my voice oozed with irritation and sarcasm. "Poor Carl. You wouldn't be able to meet at your favorite boys' club."

He made a noise in the back of his throat and spit out, "Why the devil Greg puts up with you is beyond me. What happened in the trunk of that car? Did you—"

"Carl!" Jones exclaimed.

My gaze narrowed to slits, my jaw clenched, and my hand itched to smack those freckles off his face. If looks could kill, Carl would have fallen over dead right then and there. I turned away to stare sightlessly out the window and suggested, "Why don't you ask him?"

Years ago, I'd managed to block those frightening hours from my mind. Greg's reprimand had those memories flooding back like an unwanted tidal wave. I wasn't thrilled with tight spaces, but Greg . . . the poor man had a raging case of claustrophobia ensue. He'd held it together for the first half hour. However, as time ticked by, he became more and more agitated, to the point that he started rocking and making pathetic mewling noises, which I'd feared would turn into terrified screams. By stroking his hair, humming quietly in his ear, and talking nonsense, I kept him from having a mental breakdown and giving away our hiding place as we traveled through Nazi-occupied France.

Neither of us spoke about the incident, and I never put it in a report. It was the type of thing that could have had repercussions for him, including removal from the field, which would've been a mistake. Greg had been a damn fine field agent.

The brilliant flash of a car's headlights lit up the interior. Carl flinched and said in a less vitriolic tone, "I belong to this club for business reasons. Back-channel negotiations and important information is exchanged there. I would go so far as to say it is vital for our national security to keep these types of backdoor communications open."

My eyes dropped to the black-and-white photograph in my lap one more time. The man had dark, slicked hair, a round face with a wide nose, and a walrus-style mustache. The file listed him as thirty-three, five feet nine, one hundred sixty pounds, with blue eyes. Firm in the belief that I could identify László Kiraly from across a room, I closed the dossier. Even though I was still irritated about Carl's nastiness, I could certainly see the value in a club where diplomats could meet, off the books, to try and lessen tensions among Eastern and Western countries. Moreover, we needed to work together tonight, not against each other.

As an olive branch, I asked in nicer tones, "If we need to create a distraction, what is your plan? Obviously, we don't want to have a lover's spat or otherwise embarrass you in front of the other members."

"Gas leak," Jones commented from the back seat. He leaned forward with two small atomizers in his palm. "Each of you carry one. The smell will last for fifteen to twenty minutes, which should be long enough to clear a room and retrieve our man."

I plucked one from his hand and put it in my purse. Keeping his eyes on the road, Carl blindly took the other and tucked it into an inside pocket. We didn't pull up to the front door; instead, he stopped a block away from the club and handed the keys over to Jim. The two of us walked the rest of the way to the Lomond Club.

We needn't have worried about the party breaking up early. A short line of cars waited to drop off patrons beneath the portico. Lights shone brightly in all the windows, and the doorman regularly opened the iron-and-glass doors for incoming partygoers.

The foyer was a grand, sweeping affair with dark wood-paneled walls, red carpeting, and an opulent marble staircase to rival the one at the Butler mansion in *Gone with the Wind.* To the right was a cavernous, two-story stone fireplace tall enough for a person to walk inside. A log the size of Paul Bunyan crackled and hissed within it. Nearby the fireplace, a small crowd gathered around a temporary bar. On our left was the cloak check—to which we did not avail ourselves, figuring our exit might be a hasty one—a desk manned by a bespectacled, white-haired gentleman in a spiffy black uniform, who greeted Carl by name. In exchange for his five hundred pounds, Carl received a roll of green-and-white casino tokens.

Well-dressed patrons of all shapes and sizes roamed through the foyer as they passed in and out of the various rooms. Most of the men were dressed in dinner jackets and the women in cocktail or floor-length gowns. A few diplomats chose to wear the formal dress from their own country. A handsome man with skin the color of walnut wore a particularly colorful golden-and-orange tunic, with a hot-pink sash, and matching turban. His height along with the outfit made him stand out like a peacock among a flock of penguins. A variety of languages buzzed around me—English, German, Polish, Hungarian, Romanian, and Russian were just a few I recognized. Eastern Bloc military uniforms interspersed with the dinner jackets and suits.

We entered the barroom first. It echoed with the binging and bonging of a dozen slot machines that had been set up along the wall opposite the bar. The seats were all occupied and primarily filled with women. The room smelled of ale and hard spirits. It was fairly crowded, and the buzz of conversation was loud over top of the slot machine noise. Moving through the throng was slow going but allowed us to ascertain that László Kiraly was not in this room. A few of Carl's acquaintances hailed him, but he was skilled at avoiding conversations or the need to introduce me.

Next, I found myself in an enviable library. Thick, leather tomes lined three of the walls, while windows lined the fourth. A fire burned in the hearth. A spiral staircase wound its way up to a second-floor gallery, where more bookcases were stuffed to the ceiling. Poker tables had been spread throughout the cigar smoke-clouded room. Compared to the barroom, the library was uncannily quiet as gamblers focused on the cards and their opponents' bets. Only a few wives or girlfriends hung around, watching their loved ones' play, and conversations were muted as if in deference to the purpose of the room itself.

Carl moved us quickly into what I imagined was normally the dining room. However, all the dining tables had been removed and replaced with blackjack tables. A roulette table dominated the center of the room and was surrounded by a crowd two deep. The blackjack tables were also busy with gamblers. It was going to take a bit longer to work our way through this room, and time was not on our side. That is, if we weren't already too late.

I plucked at Carl's sleeve to stop his forward motion. "How many more rooms are there?"

Carl's gaze continued sweeping the room as he spoke. "One more. There is a room with craps and baccarat."

"We can move faster if we split up."

"You take the left; I'll take the right." He handed me half the tokens. "If you find him, start playing at the same table."

First, I visited the blackjack tables. Walking behind the dealers, I could see each player and check them off my list. None matched László's description. The roulette table was more difficult to surveille. A number of men, taller than I, surrounded the outer rim of the crowd. I stood on tiptoe, only obtaining glimpses of the players. Luckily for me, a couple decided to depart, and I slipped into their spot before others could do so.

The roulette wheel spun, and the croupier called out, "Place your bets!"

A man across the table from me was half turned away. He had slick, dark hair and was of the height to be László. He spoke to a petite, apple-cheeked brunette with fake eyelashes.

"Do you need help playing?" A gentleman with a handlebar mustache startled me out of my scrutiny.

"*Pardon?*"

"The table?" He indicated with an elegant hand. "Do you need help placing your bet?" He spoke with a high-brow British accent.

"Oh." I realized being at the front of the table held the

expectation of betting. *"Non, merci. Neuf* is my lucky number." I plopped a chip on the red nine and continued to study the other players at the table.

My possible László bent to whisper in the brunette's ear. Her eyes widened, her face flushed, and she giggled into her hand. He took that hand, kissed it, and began working his way clear of the table, towing the giggling brunette in his wake.

I made a move to follow them when the gentleman next to me sent up a cheer. "You won, my dear! That's a thirty-five to one payout."

The croupier shoved a pile of chips at me. *Damn.* I began gathering them up to leave the table.

"Aren't you going to play again?" the kindly gentleman asked as he helped me stack my winnings.

"Non. I believe in quitting while I am ahead." I was having trouble gathering all the chips in my hands; they kept falling out.

With gravity, he nodded. "A wise move. Here, take my bucket. I don't think I'll be needing it." He dumped half a dozen chips out of a small metal pail, like those I'd seen other gamblers using to hold their chips, and scooped my winnings into it.

"Merci, Monsieur."

Once the bucket was filled, I thanked the kindly gentleman again and tossed the croupier a fifty-pound chip.

By the time I got away from the table, my quarry had exited through the door at the far end of the room. I did my best to elegantly weave my way around the throng to try and catch up, while keeping an eye out for Sullivan.

Bursting from the blackjack room into the foyer, I found the pair had stopped to chat with an elderly couple and breathed a sigh of relief. Sidling over to a high-backed chair near the foyer fireplace, I found a place to surveille Kiraly and his companion.

Carl must have noticed my precipitous exit, for he was at my elbow in moments. Staring at my bucket of winnings, he said, "What the—"

Stepping in front of him, I whispered urgently. "Two o'clock, over my right shoulder."

His gaze transferred to the direction I'd indicated, and he breathed, "Kiraly."

I lightened my features and brushed a piece of lint off Sullivan's lapel. "We need to separate him from the girl."

His eyes narrowed in thought.

A waiter carrying a tray full of champagne passed by, and I reached for a glass. "So serious, *Monsieur*, have a glass," I tittered in an effort to lighten Sullivan's features.

He stopped his intense scrutiny of Kiraly and shifted it to the waiter, who had paused to offer him a glass.

"*Bien, merci.*" I nodded at the waiter, and he continued his rounds. "I'll take care of her. Once she is out of the way . . ."

"I'll arrange to meet Kiraly in the men's room. Underneath the stairs. I expect to be out within five minutes or less. If I can, I'll leave with him."

I nodded in affirmation. "I'll be ready with the gas, in case we need to cover our exit."

"Are you carrying a weapon?" Carl tapped his side, where he carried a gun.

"A knife." I placed a hand to my thigh, where it

rested.

Carl's face turned hard, and he leaned down to whisper in my ear, "Not giving you a pistol was an oversight on my part. I apologize."

"I should have requested one. But don't you think a shot will bring undue attention?"

"I'm hoping I don't have to use it."

I nodded and passed him my bucket. "Take my winnings. Maybe they'll come in handy." I took a sip of my champagne. "Wish me luck."

"Good luck."

The conversation between the two couples seemed to be winding down. The gentlemen shook hands, and I wandered none to steadily toward my prey. The older couple walked away, and Kiraly whispered in the girl's ear. When I was in spitting distance, I pretended to trip. Stumbling into the brunette, I spilled my champagne down her golden taffeta dress.

She gasped, throwing her arms up, and stepped backward, bumping into Kiraly.

"Oh! *Mon dieu, Mademoiselle*! So clumsy of me, *un million de pardon*. My heel, it caught on the rug. Please forgive me for ruining your beautiful frock." I clumsily pawed at her dress, trying to wipe off the alcohol.

"No, no. It is fine," she said in a German accent. Her face bloomed rosily with embarrassment as she pushed away my hands.

"Please, let me take you to the retiring room. I will help you wash it off. I can give you my direction to pay for the cleaning to make it right."

Kiraly opened his mouth to speak when Sullivan

walked across his line of sight. Whatever he'd planned to say caught in his throat.

Our gazes met, and I delivered a hard look.

Kiraly coughed to cover up his hesitation. "She is right, darling. Go fix your dress. I will meet you at the foot of the stairs."

"Very well," she said mulishly and led the way to the ladies' room, on the opposite side of the men's, beneath the stairs.

We stepped aside to allow a woman in a black gown to pass us. There were only three stalls, which were thankfully empty. The brunette went to the sinks, and used one of the hand towels to wipe at the champagne.

"*Non, Mademoiselle,* do not wipe with the water. The cleaners will get it out. It was the only way I could think of to get you away from *him*," I whispered conspiratorially.

She paused her ministrations, and her big, spider-like lashes blinked once. Twice. "I am—I mean . . . I do not understand."

I switched to her native language, making sure to keep my French accent, "Herr Kiraly. I am sorry to be the one to tell you, *Fräulein,* he is engaged to be married."

She swallowed.

"Next month," I added for emphasis. "He did not tell you. Did he?"

Her head rotated back and forth.

"No, he—he takes advantage of lovely young women, such as yourself. I promise you, he will take advantage of you tonight, and then you will never hear from him again. He will marry the Hungarian girl because her father is an important man in the Communist party."

"Bastard." She threw down the hand towel. "I should have realized. You say next month?"

"*Oui.*"

She gathered her purse, mumbling German obscenities beneath her breath. "I suppose I should thank you," she said through a pinched mouth.

I lifted one shoulder. "It is a man's world. Women need to look out for each other. *Non?*"

That thought had not seemed to occur to her. Her lips softened and she muttered, "*Ja. Danke.*" Then she stomped past me, whipping open the bathroom door so hard it slammed against the wall.

I casually leaned against the balustrade at the base of the stairs to wait for Sullivan and Kiraly. One hand was tucked into my handbag, the atomizer at the ready, when I witnessed a man in the Lomond Club uniform check over his shoulder before walking into the men's room. I could hear nothing unusual over the din of general conversation, which bounced off the marble floors and stone fireplace of the foyer, but something of the furtive manner the man displayed, and the tightness of his coat, touched a wary nerve. That instinctual feeling of danger slithered through my stomach, and I left my position.

Bit by bit, I tugged the bathroom door open to reveal turmoil. Time froze and the world stopped churning as my brain assessed the disorder. Kiraly's clouded gaze stared at me as blood pooled from a cut at his throat. One of the heavy wooden stall doors hung drunkenly off its hinges. The Egyptian cotton hand towels were scattered across the counter, and a wet bar of lavender soap sat in the middle of the floor, leaving behind a slippery trail.

Meanwhile, the man in the Lomond uniform held Sullivan in a wicked headlock, choking the life out of him, while my partner struggled ineffectively to extricate himself. He stood well over six feet tall, had at least fifty pounds on Sullivan, and had the coldest blue eyes I'd ever seen. Once the reality of the situation settled in, my heart started pumping faster than a wild cheetah.

I stabbed the man up to the hilt, three times in quick succession. Sliding my knife between his ribs, I made it impossible for him to call out. He released Carl and reached for the injury. Carl stumbled aside, gasping to catch his breath, a hand at his throat. I balanced my weight on the balls of my feet and stood ready should the attacker come at me. He did not. A gurgle wheezed from him, and he slowly collapsed.

Carl righted himself, fumbled for his gun, and aimed at the man's head.

"No! You don't have a suppressor. Too loud," I hissed, pushing the muzzle of the compact .22 away from its target. My gaze darted to the door, fearful we'd be discovered by another enemy agent or random guest.

"We have to finish it," he insisted.

The guard flopped and struggled to get air.

"He *is* finished. I punctured his lungs. He'll suffocate in less than five minutes." I used the tails of my coat to wipe the blood off my knife. Thank heavens, I'd worn all black. It would hide the blood spatters. "Have I got any blood on my face?"

Carl pointed his weapon at the ground. "There's some on your . . . erm . . . chest."

Looking down, I saw pinpricks of red along the line above my breast. "Thanks." I wetted one of the hand towels and used the mirror to remove lingering splatters.

Meanwhile, Carl found a *Closed for Cleaning* placard and hung it on the outside of the door, then he locked it.

"Did I get it all?" I spread my arms wide. Carl assessed me, and I realize a purpled bump bloomed near his left temple. "You're hurt."

Gingerly, Carl touched the injury. "I'll be fine. Check Kiraly's pockets. I'll pat down the gorilla."

I found a postcard of the London Tower Bridge, a house key, Kiraly's wallet, and a roll of breath mints. Carl came up empty; the mercenary was clean. No identification. No keys. Nothing but lint. The goon's blood crept along the white marble floor to intermingle with his victim's.

"Professional hitman or KGB?"

"Who knows?" Carl grunted with disgust. He crawled beneath the counter to retrieve the knife that must have been used to kill Kiraly. Balancing it on his palm, he said, "It's an NR-40."

"Looks like a Soviet Finka to me."

"Same thing." He wrapped a towel around the blade.

Someone tried to open the door, and we froze. Angry voices could be heard through the thick wood, but we couldn't make out what was being said.

"Bloody hell," Carl hissed. Curling his fingers around the weapon's handle, he jammed it into a pocket and reached for his gun.

I laid a restraining hand on his stiff forearm. The voices dispelled, and we breathed a sigh of relief.

"It'll have to be the gas if we want to clear people out and have time to get away before these two are discovered." I waited for Carl to agree. When he didn't answer immediately, I said, "Unless you've got another idea."

"No, it'll be the gas. Ready?"

"When you are."

"You go left, I'll go right."

Within minutes, Carl and I flowed out of the foyer with dozens of other guests, the scent of a gas leak left behind in our wake. Jim, having handily parked nearby, flashed the headlights.

We slid into the back seat, and Jim zoomed away from the curb. "Where is Kiraly? Did you miss him?"

"Kiraly got his throat slit, and we left a KGB agent dead on the bathroom floor." The adrenaline that had poured into my body when I saw the beefy hitman choking Carl now exited my system. My fingers shook so much, I couldn't light the cigarette.

"It may not have been KGB. Soviets supply that weapon to a number of Eastern Bloc countries." Carl leaned forward with a lighter at the ready.

"Thanks," I muttered.

"Got an extra?" he asked.

I passed him the pack and sucked in the tobacco to calm my overcharged nerves. "Did you get anything from Kiraly before . . . well . . ." I made a slicing motion to my neck.

Drawing on his own cigarette, Carl shook his head.

We fell quiet, only the grind of the gears and the hum of the engine could be heard. My heartbeat returned to normal as the smoke filled and exited my lungs.

Finally, I broke the silence. "What are the repercussions going to be on this?"

Carl exhaled a cloud. "I don't know."

The killing had been fast but sloppy, and I couldn't be positive no one had seen me enter the men's room. If one person remembered seeing me go in there . . .

"Chief's going to be angry," Carl commented. "He warned you *not* to create an international incident."

"Oh, stuff it," I mumbled, sinking lower in my seat.

To my surprise, Carl's chuckle turned into full-fledged, gut-busting laughter.

Jim just shook his head. We all realized it was a post-operation reaction.

"Wait." I sat upright. "I did find something on Kiraly. A postcard." I drew the piece of cardstock from my pocketbook. "Have you a light?"

Driving with one hand, Jim leaned over to fish around in the glovebox with the other. He passed the flashlight back to us. Carl flipped it on, and we studied the backside of the postcard. Nothing had been written, not even an address. No words were circled or underlined. However, in the right-hand corner, the Queen of England delivered her Mona Lisa smile on a fresh, carmine-red stamp.

"Did Kiraly have the capability to create a microdot?" I asked, running my thumb over the stamp. I could detect no bumps or ridges, but that didn't mean it wasn't there.

"Yes," Carl replied, switching off the flashlight. "He was reaching for his breast pocket when the agent sliced his throat."

"That's where I found it." I handed the postcard over

to him.

Streetlights alternately brightened and dimmed the car's interior. Carl sat back, smoking, and silently contemplated the photograph on the front.

I'd done my job. It was up to the men to ascertain if there was a microdot beneath the stamp and extract it for evaluation. Exhausted, I asked Jim to drop me at my hotel.

My teenage admirer was behind the front desk, his cheek lying on a math textbook, asleep. A little drool trickled from his mouth. I couldn't bring myself to wake the poor kid, so I went around and plucked my room key from its wooden cubby. No messages awaited inside.

Chapter Twenty-Six
Unexpected Intelligence

Bracken and fallen leaves crunched beneath my bare feet. I bolted through the forest, dodging trees and leaping over underbrush. Mist tugged at the hem of my torn nightgown, and I panted in cold-clouded breaths. My right hand held a bloodied knife, but I must not have completed the job, as I could hear the thrashing sound of pursuit behind me. My left hand hung at my side, heavy and useless.

Jake's voice in the distance called out to me, "Miriam! I need you! Where are you, Miriam?"

Not wanting to give away my position to the pursuers, I didn't respond to Jake's cries, but in my mind, the words *I'm coming, I'm coming* repeated over and over.

Something wrapped around my legs, pulling me downward. As the ground rose to greet me, I shouted. The scream dragged me from the depths of the horrid nightmare. The dream retreated, lumbering from my waking consciousness as slowly as a hippo on the savanna on a hot summer day.

The blankets had fallen to the floor, and the remaining sheets were wrapped around my calves. My left hand, twisted at a painful angle behind my back, had gone numb from lack of blood flow. My other hand was fisted so tightly around the brass compass necklace, which I'd left on the side table before falling into bed, that I could feel the pain of the half-moon indentations left behind by my fingernails. I shook away the pins and needles of my left hand, while unwinding the sheets with my working one. The ashen grey of predawn light hovered outside the window, and I flopped back down on the pillow. The bedside table clock read 5:52. As the pounding in my ears receded, I heard the rumble of a lorry and a lone yap from a small dog break the morning quiet.

My subconscious was about as subtle as a punch to the head.

Jake.

I felt useless translating communiques and swanning around concerts with Radoslaw. My hands had been bloodied in the dream, and I looked down at them. The room was too shadowed to see much, but I'd bathed before bed and had taken pains to clean off all traces of the incident at the Lomond Club. Closing my eyes, I replayed the night, starting at the moment I left the concert with Sara.

The *brr-brr* of the telephone startled me out of my musings. A call at six in the morning was never good.

"Hello?"

"Call from Gregory Dunbar. Hold, please, while I connect you," the Cockney-accented operator stated.

"Hello? Brigitte?" Greg's tired voice came over the lines.

"Yes, I'm here, Greg." I yawned.

"You need to get into the office. There have been developments."

Shooting upright, I flicked on the Tiffany-style lamp and had to blink rapidly as my eyes adjusted to the brightness. I must not have been fully awake, because if my faculties had been fully working, I never would have uttered the following word: "Jake?"

"Just get in here," he growled. "We'll talk more when you arrive."

The line went dead.

Fool! I chastised myself. I never should have said his name over an unsecured phone line. The covers fell away as I rose from the four-poster bed, and I spotted an envelope on the hotel's stationary. It must have been shoved beneath the door. A message was written on the missive in crooked handwriting:

This came last night. – Nigel

I drew in a sharp breath and ripped the envelope. The telegram read:

There is news. Come back to Berlin. Petrus

Pressing it to my breast, I let out a triumphant cry.

Chapter Twenty-Seven
New Assignment

The burly fellow still manned Margaret's desk. After exchanging the code phrase, he jerked his head to the left and said, "In the kitchen."

Drinking coffee, Greg sat at a tiny, square table, which was covered with a stained, yellow cloth. Deep circles hollowed his eyes, and his entire complexion held a slightly gray tinge to it. Carl's bowtie hung undone around his neck, he had removed his jacket, and his shirtsleeves were rolled to his elbows. His face also held the haggard lines of sleeplessness.

"Have you two been at it all night?"

"Yes," Greg replied and took a swig of coffee.

I played with my pearl earring. "Any word on the fallout from the Lomond Club?" All eyes turned to me. "Should I be concerned?"

Greg's head bowed. "Apparently, we weren't as special as we thought. Kiraly has been feeding information to the Brits and the Dutch. Hungarian secret service believe Dutch intelligence was a part of the mess in the bathroom. Because of this, they are following the wrong leads, which affords us some time."

"Coffee?" Carl offered, holding up the percolator.

"Yes, please. Cream and sugar," I replied. "Any good information on the microdot?"

"Dots. Plural. Three, to be exact," Greg answered,

"and yes, the information was valuable."

"So, the mission can be considered a success?" I mouthed the word *thanks* to Carl as he handed me a steaming mug. I welcomed the nutty aroma that filled my senses.

"Let's say, it wasn't a complete disaster." Greg drank the dregs of his coffee.

Carl and I remained silent. Waiting. My gaze darted between the two men. Finally, I asked, "Someone want to tell me what I'm doing here?"

"Sullivan, go home." Greg leaned back, draping his arm over the back of the chair. "Get some rest. I'll phone if I need you."

"You're sure, Chief?"

Greg's head jerked an affirmation.

Carl went to pass me, but instead paused. Our shoulders almost touching, he stared down at his shoe and murmured, "Tonight, you were . . ." He cleared his throat. "I misjudged you."

A weary brow rose. "You wouldn't be the first."

His bloodshot gaze flicked up to mine. "Thank you . . . in the bathroom . . ."

"You're welcome."

He shuffled out.

I slid into the seat across from Greg, cupping my cold fingers around the mug to warm them. "I've had news from my contact in Berlin. He urgently requests that I return."

Greg licked his lips. "It sounds like Greyhound is still alive."

"Send me," I whispered.

Greg studied my features. It wasn't his normal, fierce take-on-the-world expression. His mouth and cheeks drooped in sadness.

I'm surprised the mug didn't crack beneath the pressure; I was gripping it so tight. "Please, Greg."

"Against my better judgement, I got you on a military flight out of Welford."

My spine straightened to attention, and I bit my lip to keep the grin off my face.

"Return to the hotel and pack. A car will pick you up in forty minutes. You have to get to Welford before ten. The new Berlin station chief is Robert Samuels."

"Thank you." I placed a hand on his forearm.

He stared at my hand and replied, "Don't thank me yet. Your source in country better have good information. Otherwise, Samuels will never send you further than the front door."

"My source is connected. I'm sure he's got the goods," I replied with an assuredness that I hoped Petrus could support.

Greg's head bowed, his shoulders sagged forward, and I swore I heard a defeated sigh.

"Is that a sigh of fatigue?"

He raised his head, and his tired gaze stared at me as if he was looking straight into the depths of my soul. "I'm afraid this is the last time I will see you."

"Don't be silly. Maybe I'll seek an assignment in London. Maybe I'll retire from the field and become your secretary." I teased.

He said nothing but continued to regard me, as if memorizing every wrinkle and curve of my face.

I mashed my lips together. "You think if I go in, I'll never come out."

Silence.

"Berlin is a sieve. Once we locate him, it'll be a quick car ride to get him to safety." Quirking a lip, I tried to leaven his mood. "You're overtired. Besides, you'll never get rid of me that easily."

"Little Girl . . ." He couldn't finish the sentence. His head shook, and to my horror, tears glistened in his eyes.

I gripped his arm again. "Greg! Stop it. This is the fatigue talking. You've had a hellish few days. I'll be fine. After you get some rest, you'll feel better."

Pushing his fingers into his sunken eye sockets, he harrumphed and said gruffly, "You're right. You'd best get going. The military flight won't wait for you."

I rose and gave a gentle squeeze to his drooping shoulder. "Thanks, old friend. I owe you."

"Be careful."

Chapter Twenty-Eight
Return to Berlin

"There he is." Franz passed the binoculars to me.

I adjusted the heavy glass magnification, and the scarred man came into focus. He spoke to a hatless fellow in a frayed brown overcoat and scuffed shoes. The men stood in the shadow of a brick wall from a bombed-out building as the sun set behind it. The shabby fellow handed our scarred man a paper bag. Scarred man checked the bag, shook his fist at the shabby gentleman, and started a heated discussion.

"Tell me what I'm looking at," I replied in German.

"Scar face is an East German named Wolfgang Zollner. Officially, he works in his family's clothing shop—a sad little store on the outskirts of East Berlin. Out the back door of the shop, he deals in black market goods from the West. Shoes, clothes, cigarettes, chocolates, candy—you name it, he deals it."

"Who's the guy without a hat?" I adjusted the focus to zoom in on him.

"That's a lowlife named Hans Schweitzer. He provides expired medications to Wolfgang," Franz said.

"Which Wolfgang, in turn, sells out the back door?"

"Correct."

I watched the pair continue their argument. We sat a football field away in a generic black sedan that blended in with the rest of the vehicles parked around us in a warehouse borough of West Berlin.

Greg must have put in a good word for me, because the new station chief had been direct and to the point. Two days ago, Mr. Samuels met with me as soon as I arrived at the nondescript office and told me, in no uncertain terms, "I don't have a lot of resources to put toward this mission, which I believe is folly. That being said, I'm willing to allow you to investigate further. I'm assigning Donald Madden as your handler for—"

"Excuse me," I'd interrupted, "may I ask, did Mr. Madden come with you from Bonn?"

Samuels's shaggy brows turned down, which only sought to enhance the deep creases between his brows, and he said in brusque tone, "While I can appreciate your uneasiness working with people from this office—"

"Considering two of them tried to kill me, you mean?" I'd said with forthrightness.

He'd cleared his throat. "Yes, well, you can rest assured you will be in good hands with Madden. You may assuage your worries; he did come with me from the Bonn office." Samuels paused, waiting for me to comment. I simply made a hand gesture indicating he should continue.

"We have one source who can help you follow up on leads. You will observe and report back to Madden. I'm giving you a few days to obtain information. If we receive confirmation that our man is still alive, then a course of action will be determined."

"Exfiltration?" I'd asked.

"Let's see what you find out first," he'd said. "Messing around in Soviet territory is a delicate affair."

I'd next met with Donald Madden, a rather nondescript gentleman with brown hair and brown eyes. He epitomized the word *average*—not too tall or too short, too thin or too fat. Wearing the right suit, Donald Madden would have blended into the wallpaper.

Since Claudia Fischer had been known to Eva and Bernard, it was determined to be an unsafe cover identification for me to utilize. I spent twenty-four hours learning my new identity—a West Berlin interior house painter. She didn't need a wig; instead, she wore her hair braided, with a kerchief. A pair of brown contacts, thickened eyebrows, heavier crow's feet with glasses, and padding around my middle was enough of a change from Claudia Fischer to Gerda Scholtz. A bandage wrapped tightly around my knee to change my gait rounded out my new persona.

The following day, Madden gave me directions to a furniture store, the name of his source, and a phrase to identify myself. That's how I ended up sitting next to Franz—he worked the loading dock at the store. I'd given him my homely new cover identity of Gerda Scholtz.

"What else do we know about Wolfgang?" I asked Franz.

"He's a good Communist party member." Franz wore corduroys, a heavy black sweater, and a knit cap, which he drew off his head, revealing a mop of receding blond hair, which he pushed back with one hand to keep it from falling across his brow.

I rolled my eyes. "When he's not dealing black market materials out the back door?"

"District Stasi tends to look the other way for

Wolfgang. He provides them a steady stream of Western cigarettes, chocolates, Italian-made leather boots, and ten percent of his take. As long as he stays under the radar of the long arm of the Soviets, the Stasi leave him alone. On occasion they bring him in for 'interrogation' to keep up appearances for their superiors. He feeds them whatever intelligence he can acquire during his visits West."

Wolfgang and Hans seemed to come to an agreement. Hans nodded. Wolfgang handed over an envelope.

"A nice little organized crime syndicate, there. And everything that goes against the Communist indoctrination of selflessness and doing for the collective good of the regime. Does Stasi keep an eye on him when he travels West?"

"They do, but he probably has more leeway than other East Germans. Stasi knows what he's doing. As long as he keeps funneling money and goods . . ." Franz shrugged.

"I get it. They leave him alone." I tilted my neck back against the headrest and held the binoculars out for Franz. "What else do we know about Wolfgang? Can we trust him?"

Franz took the binoculars to watch our targets depart. "We can trust Wolfgang to look out for Wolfgang."

"Should we follow him?"

He pulled the glasses away and glanced at me. His pale blue eyes were surrounded with deep wrinkles that spoke of many hours squinting against the sun. "*Nein.* It's time for him to head back home. There is an S-Bahn station two blocks from here. That's where he's going."

I trusted Franz to know what he was talking about, so

I didn't question him. "Do we think he knows something about Greyhound?"

"It's possible. But working with a man like Wolfgang will come with strings." He placed the binoculars on the dash and unzipped the duffel bag sitting between us. "*Kaffee?*" He pulled out a thermos and untwisted the metal cup.

I nodded. "*Ja, bitte.*"

Franz's thick, calloused fingers passed me the tin mug, and I held it steady as he poured the dark liquid. Its strong, aromatic scent immediately filled the small cab. "Going under the assumption that Wolfgang knows anything of the whereabouts of Greyhound is a risk. The man is an opportunist. We can't discount the possibility that he heard about an American agent in East Germany and is simply using false intelligence to extort money." He drank his coffee directly from the thermos.

I cupped my hands around the metal to warm them and allow the steaming brew to cool. "If we sent someone inside, perhaps he'd finger that person to the Stasi to gain himself more goodwill."

Franz nodded. "I hadn't thought of that, but you're right. Working with Wolfgang is dangerous."

"I'm not sure we can risk making contact." I stared out the windshield in frustration.

Franz, too, stared broodily out the glass. "Problem is, if he *does* know the location of Greyhound . . ."

I shook my head. "I have another source. We'll have to see if it bears fruit."

"When are you meeting?"

"Tonight, at nine." I took a sip of the coffee and used

all my willpower not to gag as the dark sludge went down. There was no sugar or cream in the bitter brew, and it was so strong I could have used a fork to chew it.

"Do you want me to accompany you?"

I cleared my throat. "*Nein*, I trust him."

"If you say so." Franz shrugged. "More *Kaffee*?"

"No, thank you."

♠♠♠♠

Petrus met me in the restaurant of a rundown hotel in the Spandau district. The once white grout between the brown tiles had darkened to black, and the wooden tables were scarred with deep scratches and old water marks. The murals across the walls, representing mountains and Swiss chalets, were flaking and dirtied from years of candle and cigarette smoke.

Petrus half rose to greet me, but I waved him back into his seat and leaned down to kiss his cheek. He looked worn out; his skin seemed to hang off his skull like a basset hound, and his eyes were bloodshot.

A pretty, young waitress, who looked out of place in this dive, arrived as soon as I slid into the booth, and began reeling off the day's specials. Petrus ordered a Dunkel beer, I ordered a Gewürztraminer, and we both ordered the chicken-and-mushroom spaetzle in cream sauce for dinner.

"Rough day?" I asked, pulling a crunchy breadstick from a mug in the center of the table.

He ran a hand down his face and sighed. "Rough couple of days." He answered my question in English. "There has been a rash of break-ins throughout the district. Yesterday it escalated to murder when the owner arrived home in the midst of the burglary. Now that it is no longer theft, the director wants everyone he can get working on apprehending this crew. We are putting in overtime."

"Is that why we are meeting so late in this dodgy restaurant? Were you working in the area?"

"No. They have good beer, and it was far enough away from my home and work to be safe from prying eyes and ears." He glanced around the room. The booths rose high above our heads, and because it was so late, most of the tables in the middle of the room were empty. A handful of guests patronized the bar.

"*Danke*," I said to the waitress as she placed our drinks on the table. Once she left, I asked, "Is that why we are speaking English?"

He leaned forward, and I followed his move. "Stasi has a network here in West Berlin. One cannot be too careful."

"Very true," I murmured.

We both sat back as the waitress arrived with our silverware rolled up in red cloth napkins, and our salads. We made a silent agreement to make small talk until after our meal arrived and the waitress left us alone to eat.

Speaking in German, I told Petrus about the Polish folk concert, and he regaled me with a childhood story about a visit to his aunt's farm that included a pig, a homemade saddle, and a race that ended in a nearby pond. The story had me in stitches. I was still chuckling when the waitress delivered our dinner. We both tucked into the meal, and our discussion turned serious and back to English.

"What have you heard from your friends?" I asked

"It would seem your package remains in the East."

"Alone, or has it been picked up?" I stabbed a mushroom and piece of chicken.

Petrus swallowed a bite before answering, "Alone. It's been narrowed down to a building in the Hellersdorf borough."

"Is this information from your special friends?" The spaetzle was cooked to perfection, and the flavors mixed well with the garlic cream sauce.

"Yes." He popped another bite into his mouth and chewed quickly.

"It is credible?"

Nodding, he cut up a piece of chicken, stabbed a mushroom, then piled spaetzle on the back of his fork with the knife. "As credible as it can be."

"There's been visual confirmation?"

The loaded fork paused midway to his mouth. "The day you left the East. By a veterinarian."

Veterinarian? I allowed Petrus to finish chewing before asking the next question. "Why hasn't the package left?"

"I have been told the goods are damaged."

I drew in a breath. "How bad?"

Petrus's mouth turned down, increasing his hangdog features. "Bad. I do not have specifics."

My stomach muscles clenched with concern, and the half-chewed food went painfully down my throat. I took a gulp of the sweet wine to help it along. "I'm to assume the package will need help getting to the West?"

"Yes."

"Is daytime retrieval an option?" I asked, remaining outwardly calm even though the news, while not unexpected, concerned me greatly.

Petrus's head gave the tiniest shake. "It is not recommended."

"Night, it is." I cleared my throat and took another bite.

Petrus finished his beer and eyed me. He spoke in low tones, "I have a contact in East Berlin to help you locate the package. You will need additional personnel for retrieval."

"Have you time to help?"

Ruefully, he shook his head. "Five months ago, I did a job that put me on the wrong person's radar. My presence would endanger the mission. I cannot work in the East at this time. Do you have someone you can trust?"

That was a letdown. I'd been hoping for Petrus's help in East Berlin. "I believe so," I said, spearing a mushroom cap. "There's been a turnover in staff."

He swallowed his next bite before asking, "What is your company's plan for recovery once the package is located?"

Licking my lips, I turned my attention to my plate. "At this time, no options for recovery have been offered. Resources are limited. With your information . . . I am hoping something can be worked out."

It was quite possible I would be forbidden from helping with exfiltration. The question that lay before me—would I sit back like a good girl and do what I was told? Or would I disobey orders and make myself part of the mission, jeopardizing my career and possibly my life?

He wiped a drip of cream sauce off his chin with his napkin. "I can contact my source tomorrow morning. Give me your direction, and I will phone you."

I told him the name of the *Gasthaus* where the company had placed me. "The telephone is a party line."

After the meal, we went our separate ways—Petrus, back to the houseboat for some much-needed rest, and I returned to the Berlin office to share my intelligence and argue my way into a trip across the border.

Madden begrudgingly allowed it. "Observe and report. I'm sending Franz in with you."

I wasn't sure if Franz was there to help me or keep me on Madden's leash. It didn't matter. I was glad to have him. Franz's job loading furniture at the store kept him strong, and we might need that strength if Jake was injured too badly to walk.

Chapter Twenty-Nine
East Berlin

Franz and I sat abreast in the front bench seat of a blue Volkswagen-T1 panel van, across the street from a brick building pockmarked with bullet holes and shrapnel. The rest of the building had been left intact, and the landlord must have not seen fit to correct the wartime blemishes. Considering the general rundown condition of the entire street, perhaps the landlord simply didn't have the money to make improvements. The building was four stories high, with a faded, blue door for an entry. Communist propaganda posters with Stalin's profile were plastered across the front of the first floor. Windowpanes on every level had been damaged during the war and replaced with wood or heavy cloth, instead of new glass.

"Your man is in there," said our East German driver, a thin fellow with hair the color of maple syrup and a ferret face. He wore a black wool peacoat and olive army pants. The lettering along the side of the van read *Handwerker Dienstleistungen*, along with a phone number. Handyman trappings littered the back of the van— random lengths and sizes of wood piled along the floor, cans of paint, and metal toolboxes.

Petrus had introduced the man as Lars. We came to understand that Lars had family in West Berlin who lived not far from Petrus. To his bad luck, his own home happened to be in East Berlin when the four powers split up the city, and he hadn't bothered to move west. Lars's handyman business sent him all over East Berlin, so he was quite familiar with the streets and always had an ear to the ground. It was his intelligence that had the three of us visiting the dubious neighborhood in the Hellersdorf borough of East Berlin.

"You don't know the apartment number?" Franz responded in German. He was hatless and wore a pair of work pants and boots, and a scruffy navy-blue short coat.

"It's been narrowed down to four apartments," Lars explained. "2D, 3C, 3A, or 4B. Residents in the others have been identified, but those four apartments have been dead ends."

"What do you mean dead ends?" I tucked an errant curl beneath the grey head kerchief I wore.

"No one knows who or where they are. The residents may have been picked up by Stasi and put behind bars, or perhaps they are on vacation. Right now, they are just a name on a mailbox."

Chewing a toothpick, Franz squinted out the window. "Why do you believe our man is in this building?"

"Your agent visited a veterinarian two blocks away. The vet stitched him up. He had glass and shrapnel embedded in his hip and leg and a bullet in his arm, which the vet tried to clear out. While the veterinarian's attention was diverted, your man walked out under his own steam. When the vet realized he'd left, he followed and saw your man enter this building. You must realize, the veterinarian has a family. He did not want to get further involved."

Franz switched the toothpick to the other side of his mouth. "How did you get this information from the vet?"

Lars gave a gallic shrug and said simply, "It is what we do."

I wasn't quite clear what organization Lars was connected to. He may have been a Schumacher agent or had ties to Gehlen Org. Both organizations worked in the East providing intelligence to the West. Kurt Schumacher had been the chair of the Social Democratic Party of Germany and held tight connections to Communist party oppositionists in the East. Gehlen Org was run by a former Nazi who opposed the Communist party and was the eyes and ears for the CIA and MI-6. It was also possible Lars was simply Petrus's source, nothing more, nothing less.

I studied the rundown building. Three of the windows had curtains covering them, and one had a white sheet hanging drunkenly. One of the windows, with a cracked pane, had a green chair in front of it. "Do you have the names of the residents in question?"

Lars pulled a folded paper from an inside coat pocket. "Johann Kowalski, Mika Durchdenwald, Benji Dovcal, and Werner Michaels."

"Do any of those names mean something to you?" Franz asked.

I shook my head. "Can we drive around the building?"

Lars cranked the van to life, and we rolled around the corner. There was additional battle damage along the side of the building. A frilly pink curtain covered a window on the fourth floor, a second-floor window held a dead plant with a red piece of cloth hanging out of it. A third-floor window must have been completely shattered, because the entire window frame was covered in rusted sheet metal that looked like it came from a scrap pile.

A gray-haired woman carrying a bag full of groceries limped down the sidewalk, while across the street a young brunette pushed a black pram with a crooked wheel that squawked repetitively as she walked. The brunette paid no attention to us, but the elderly woman paused to stare at the van as we drove to the end of the building and Lars turned down the alley. Our presence was being noted.

The back of the building revealed a zig-zagging fire escape so rusted that it looked as though it wouldn't hold the weight of a stray cat. A rear door stood open, but we couldn't see inside, for the hallway was black as midnight.

The alleyway ran behind another damaged building before ending at the cross street. We watched a Soviet military truck pass by with a pair of soldiers in the front. The soldier in the passenger seat stared out the window at us, and we all held our breath, not making eye contact as the truck drove by.

Lars had East German identification. Franz and I had paperwork classifying us as West Berliners. It was more difficult and would have taken longer to build an East Berlin cover identity for the two of us. And time was not on our side. As West Berliners we were within our rights to be in East Berlin, however, military soldiers and East

German Volkspolizei, aka VoPo, could stop anyone and request to see their papers. Since the East Germans had built their interior wall and closed the borders into West Germany earlier this year, soldiers and VoPo had increased their harassment toward Westerners. Two West Berliners with an East Berliner made our trio suspect, especially this close to the edge of the Berlin/East German border. Being with Franz and I could lead to hours of interrogation for Lars.

The military truck turned left at the end of the street, and we all breathed a little easier. Lars cruised a four-block radius, passing a tank and another military transport, before returning to the same parking space.

"Any ideas on how to figure out which apartment he's in? Beyond knocking on doors and drawing attention to ourselves?" I asked, slumping back against the seat.

"Further surveillance," Lars responded.

An answer I expected, but not one I wanted to pursue. First, because Madden had put me on a short time frame. Second, my instincts were telling me that Jake's injuries were bad. It'd been over a week. If he'd recovered enough to walk, Jake would have made his way back into West Berlin. The fact that he was still holed up here was a sign that he needed physical help to get out.

An image of Jake hovered in my mind like a Dickens ghost from Christmas past. The last moments I'd seared into my brain of Jake driving us next to the Spree River — the cut on his cheek, the scar beneath his ear, the pin-striped suit, the . . .

And there it was, so clearly in front of my face, I

couldn't believe I'd missed it the first time.

I gasped and shot upright. "I've got it!"

Both men turned to me, and Franz made a shushing sound.

"Lars, may I see the list of names?" I held out my hand.

Ponderously, he pulled the paper from his pocket and passed it over. The names were penned in a column.

Johann Kowalski – 3C

Mika Durchdenwald – 4B

Benji Dovcal – 2D

Werner Michaels – 3A

"He's in apartment 2D," I crowed triumphantly.

"Why 2D?" Franz asked, glancing at the list.

"Benji Dovcal is an anagram of—" I coughed, stopping myself from revealing Jake's real name. "It's an anagram that I recognize. And there is the potted plant."

Potted plants, lamps, and other markers had been used by agents and handlers to signal each other. They could be used to notify the other party to check a dead drop for intelligence or supplies, like money, listening devices, or film. Or to notify a party for a meet at a predetermined location and time.

Franz glanced at me. "How do you know the anagram isn't a coincidence, or the potted plant, for that matter? Maybe it's the window with the green chair in front of it?"

"The red cloth hanging out of the potted plant on the second floor is the pocket square he was wearing a week ago," I explained. "It's a signal,"

I assumed Jake had an off-the-books safe house on

this side of the border, or he was simply squatting in an empty apartment. I tended to lean toward the former—Benji Dovecal was an anagram of Jacob Devlin. If it was a safe house, he'd probably squirreled away a weapon, canned food, and drinking water in there. Possibly medical supplies as well. At least, I prayed that he'd stocked those items. Otherwise, we'd be walking in on a dead man, not just an injured one.

A Soviet armored car roared down the road.

Lars started the van and pulled away from the curb. "We need to get off the street. This area is close to the border, and they increase patrols in the evening. The three of us will attract attention if we remain much longer." He drove us further into the city center of East Berlin, eventually turning in to a garage bay of a dilapidated, old canning warehouse. "Stay here," he told us and hopped out of the car to close the wooden bay doors.

A balding man wearing bedroom slippers, a dirty white T-shirt, and suspenders to hold up his baggy pants came through an exterior door. Using a spoon, he ate directly from a tin of beans. Beholding Franz and I, he stopped short, and his eyes widened.

"Uh-oh," I murmured under my breath.

Lars came around the passenger side of the van and spotted our interloper. He raised a hand in greeting and trotted over to chat with the bald man. Franz and I remained in place, and at one point, the pair turned our way. Lars held up his arm and pointed at us. I gave a small smile and waved. Bald man waved his spoon at me, nodded at whatever lies Lars fed him, and finally shuffled back through the door from whence he appeared.

"You can come out now," Lars told us.

"Friend of yours?" Franz asked, exiting the van.

"Neighbor. He's harmless. Took some shrapnel to the head during the war. It affected his brain," Lars said, tapping his noggin. "He hasn't been quite right since then."

Lars led us into a small work room, and we huddled around the coal stove to warm ourselves and create a plan of action.

I wasn't sure what directive Franz had been given, but when I suggested we plan a rescue mission, neither he nor Lars flinched. I wasn't ready to trot back to the office to report our findings. After all, we still didn't have confirmation Jake remained in that building, or even in apartment 2D. If we located Jake in the flat, there was no way I would leave without him—he'd be coming out with us . . . dead or alive. While I prayed it was the latter, should it turn out to be the former, I refused to allow his corpse to rot in some East German ghetto.

Franz agreed.

Chapter Thirty
The Retrieval

Franz unscrewed the lightbulb from the single wall sconce, dimming the hallway into darkness. We'd left the canning factory just after midnight. Beyond the creaking and pinging of the building and radiators, no noise came from the neighboring apartments. Franz held a mini flashlight for me while I made quick work of picking the lock. The door gave a low groan as it opened.

The smell hit me first. Instinctively, I covered my nose against the sour scent of body odor, urine, and something sickly sweet. The temperature had dropped, and the apartment was cold enough to see our breaths. Franz closed the door behind us, and we followed the smell into the main living room. The tiny torch only illuminated small pools of light as we went. The stink led us to socked feet, which led up to the covered body of Jacob Devlin. He sprawled beneath a wool army blanket on top of a worn-out mattress.

"Oh, dear lord," I choked out and fell to my knees. "Check the rest of the apartment."

Jake lay on his right side, and I put a finger to his neck. His jaw was prickly with the stubble of a growing beard. I found a pulse; it was sluggish and his breathing slow.

Franz made quick work of searching the tiny apartment. "He's alone."

I turned on my own light and swept it across his body

to discover a thick, dirty bandage wrapped around his forearm. Leaning forward, I sniffed and realized the sickly-sweet smell came from the bandages.

"The bag," I whispered.

Franz pulled a messenger bag off his shoulder and went down on one knee. With his help to hold Jake's arm up, I unwound the disgusting bandage, tossing it aside as it came off. The wound it unveiled had me gagging, and I turned aside for a moment to collect myself. It was swollen red, with a black center, and oozing with pus, clearly infected. With an angel's touch, my finger passed across the red area. Jake moaned. Though the room was cold, Jake's body was aflame with temperature. A nearby metal cup had been knocked over, empty of liquid.

Franz prepared a syringe of penicillin. "Help me roll him. I have to inject it into his backside."

Rolling Jake forward, Franz pulled down Jake's boxer shorts, only to find another bandage, this one not so dirty, and it didn't seem to give off that sickly odor. We took a moment to remove the bandage to see what was going on. Two sets of stitches, probably entry and exit wounds. Rosy skin puckered around the stitches, but nothing like the arm.

"Cover his mouth," Franz whispered.

I planted a hand over Jake's mouth and gave Franz a nod.

Franz gave him the shot of penicillin.

Jake jerked and moaned beneath my hand. He grunted, *"Was ist los?"*

I shushed him. However, we'd roused him out of a deep sleep, and he began fighting against me. His right hand flopped, and he smacked something that skittered across the hardwood floor. A sweep of my flashlight revealed a compact Walther PPK against the wall. Before I could retrieve it, Jake's good hand weakly latched onto my wrist. The left arm remained limp at his side. I grabbed the hand holding mine and tried to soothe him without hurting him further.

"*Sich beruhigen,* Greyhound," I murmured in his ear. "We're here to help!" The brass compass that I'd worn around my neck fell out of my blouse and dangled in front of his face.

He stopped fighting and tapped it with a finger. "Lily?"

I took his hand in mine and placed the flashlight beneath my chin to light my features. "*Nein,* it's me."

His face wrinkled with confusion.

"Your friend from childhood."

Recognition dawned. "Mir—"

I placed a hand over his mouth before he could say my real name. "Yes, that's right, Gerda. Gerda Scholtz." I prayed Jacob was coherent enough to realize I'd given him a cover identity.

Franz and I gently rolled him onto his back.

Jake winced and panted for a moment before croaking, "Who are you?"

"That is Franz," I supplied.

"We're going to put on fresh bandages. And I've got something for the pain," Franz said.

"I'm so very thirsty," Jake replied in a fadeaway voice.

While Franz gave Jake a shot of pain medicine, I took

the overturned cup to the kitchen sink to fill it. Half empty tin cans of rotting food and a dirty spoon littered the counter, which only added to the general stench of the room. I found a hand towel hanging off a cabinet door and soaked it in cold water.

The wound would need a professional to clean it out. In the meantime, we poured iodine on the injury, which stung Jake terribly. I had him bite down on the hand towel while we did it. His eyes scrunched shut, and he made pained grunting sounds as we rebandaged the wound. We did the same with the hip injuries, but he scarcely made a peep as we doctored up that area.

Afterward, he was so exhausted he would have fallen asleep again if I'd allowed it.

"Not time for a nap yet. Come on, big guy, I thought you were thirsty." Franz helped Jake sit up enough to drink the water.

After the first few gulps, he turned away, but I coaxed him to continue drinking. Once he finished, we allowed him to rest. I placed the cool, wet towel across his forehead to help with the burning temperature. The pain medication Franz had given Jake was only enough to knock the edge off. We were going to have to make a move soon, and we needed Jake coherent and mobile. Neither of which I was so sure we could accomplish.

Franz and I stepped into the kitchen to discuss the situation.

"He needs more fluids before we get him moving," I whispered. "He's been running a fever for days. His cheeks and eyes are sunken. I'm not sure how much he's been drinking."

"Enough to soak the bed," Franz commented.

"True, but it's dry now. Who knows when he did that? If we can get him up, he'll pass out before we make it past the door."

"I don't have an IV solution to give him."

I chewed my lip in thought. "Then we'll have to get him to drink more. Radio Lars and tell him we'll be a little longer."

Franz eyed me before he dug into the messenger bag and pulled out a two-way radio. "We've run into a problem. The package is damaged and needs repair work. Give us an hour," Franz said in low tones.

"Confirmed. One hour," Lars replied. "All is quiet."

Lars waited in the alleyway for us. We planned to exit out the back door of the apartment complex, the same way we'd entered it. Because it would draw attention, driving around East Berlin in the middle of the night, increasing the likelihood we'd be stopped, we'd return to the canning factory until dawn.

When the city came alive, Lars would drive the three of us to the Oberbaumbrucke Bridge, where we could cross easily into West Berlin. Only, nothing would be easy if we couldn't get Jake in an upright position. Franz had been smart enough to acquire a wheelchair which we could use to cross the bridge. However, we still needed Jake coherent and able to sit up without falling out of it.

During the next two excruciating hours, we both cajoled and hectored Jake into taking a pain pill and drinking more cups of water. Along the way, his fever broke, and we had to wrap him up in the dirty blanket to keep him warm. I held him to my chest as he shivered.

His hair was matted and greasy, but I could still smell the slightest hint of vanilla from his pomade. When the shivering finally ceased and he'd drunk more fluids, I laid him back down, allowing him to rest.

"What can he wear?" I whispered.

Franz prowled around the small living area. He held up Jake's pin-striped suit pants in the moonlight, only to drop them to the floor again when he saw they'd been cut and were stiff with dried blood. The jacket was the same. "We've got to clean him up and find clothes that don't stink."

"In the closet," Jake mumbled.

A tiny bedroom revealed a wardrobe and mini chest of drawers. I found underwear, socks, and a black sweater in the chest. Franz found a pair of blue serge pants and a collarless shirt hanging in the wardrobe. The mattress Jake lay upon had been pulled off the single bed and dragged out into the living area. A wad of soiled sheets lay in the corner, but the bed skirt seemed clean enough. I brought it out with the clean clothes. Franz and I dropped our bounty on the musty, velvet loveseat.

"See if you can find a bowl in the kitchen and fill it with warm water," I suggested to Franz. "I need to give him a sponge bath."

We moved Jake off the filthy mattress onto the relatively clean bed skirt and went to work sponging the stink off him. In deference of my feminine sensibilities, Franz cleaned the southern end of Jacob, while I did the upper parts. It wasn't as though Jake had things I hadn't seen before, but he was rather ripe down there, and I appreciated Franz's thoughtfulness.

Thankfully he slept through most of it, waking when we began dressing him. He tried to be helpful, but Franz and I ended up doing most of the work. The shirtsleeve wouldn't fit over the bandage, and Franz cut a slit up past his elbow. Luckily, the sweater was large enough to slide over the bulkiness. The pants were baggy, due to his ten-pound weight loss over the past week, and Franz removed his own belt to tighten the waist.

Clean and dressed, Jake smelled better. The apartment, on the other hand, still reeked. At some point, I'd begun breathing through my mouth. Before we could leave, there was another hurdle to conquer—getting Jake down the stairs and into the van.

Franz and I stood above Jake, who lay splayed out on the bed skirt, breathing heavily from the exertion of dressing.

"I've got a bottle of Dexedrine," Franz suggested.

Dexedrine was an amphetamine. The company had doled it out like candy through the war. I'd used it on missions, when I had to stay up all night or needed a boost of energy. We'd already pumped Jake with penicillin and pain meds. I didn't know what the impact of the Dexedrine would be on his system, but it was three in the morning, and we needed to get out of the apartment before the rest of the complex awoke.

The scratch of the radio sitting on the coffee table got our attention. "How much longer? VoPo circled the block twice." I could hear the concern in Lars's tone.

Franz plucked up the receiver and looked at me askance.

"Give him two pills and ten minutes. Then, come hell

or high water, we are getting out of here if I have to carry him myself."

Franz pushed the radio button. "Ten minutes."

The Dexedrine had the desired effect. Jake's eyes were wide, and he found the energy to get up. Between Franz and I, the two of us were able to help him down the stairs and out the back door. Loading him into the van, I heard the scuff of a shoe.

A man stood at the end of the alley, beneath a streetlight. He shifted, and the light illuminated the scar running down his face. Our gazes connected. I waited with bated breath for him to raise the alarm. He pulled the fedora lower and melted into the darkness. Franz closed the door as quietly as possible. It still sounded as loud as a gunshot to me, and I gave a jerk.

"Careful," Franz murmured.

Once seated, I told Franz and Lars that Wolfgang witnessed us loading Jake. Unfortunately, the three of us realized there wasn't much we could do. Five minutes later, with our package alert and sitting upright next to a toolbox, Lars drove us deeper into East Berlin.

"Where are we headed?" Jake asked in a chipper voice.

"A place to get out of sight," I replied.

"Oh, goody." Jake's good-humored countenance turned south when we hit a pothole, and he hissed, "Great Mother of Francis! For the love of Judas, slow it down."

Lars took greater care as he drove the van back to the canning warehouse.

"I'll get the doors." Franz hopped out and swung the

two wooden doors wide to allow the van inside.

Lars pulled into the bay. "The city will wake, and street and pedestrian traffic will be normal enough for me to drive you to the Oberbaumbrucke Bridge in a few hours."

"I don't like the idea of waiting that long to crossover," I commented. It would give Wolfgang more than enough time to notify the Stasi or KGB and allow them to set up checkpoints. While Franz and I could cross easily through a checkpoint with our West Berlin papers, the identification card Jake carried was the same one he'd brought into East Berlin—Heinrich Wagner. Thanks to our double agents, KGB would have notified East German intelligence.

"We haven't much choice. If we go now, we'll be the only ones on the bridge," Jake piped in. "It'll be too obvious."

Franz opened the van's side door and asked, "What's the problem?"

"We are determining the best course of action," I replied.

"The driver is right. We wait until the morning rush. More people. Easier to blend in," Jake said.

"We were seen leaving the apartment complex," I explained to Jake.

"By whom?" he asked.

"A man named Wolfgang Zollner," Franz supplied.

"Yes, of course." Jake's dark head bobbed. "Didn't you get my location from Wolfgang?"

Franz and I shared a look. "No, we did not," I answered.

"How did you find me?" Jake's voice rose with concern.

"The veterinarian followed you as far as the building."

"Damn. Sloppy. I wasn't thinking straight," Jake chastised himself and clenched his good hand into a frustrated fist.

"Not to worry. The veterinarian is one of us," Lars replied.

"I figured out the anagram," I continued, "and saw the red pocket square in the plant."

I couldn't see his face, but I could hear the smile in his next words. "Quite clever of you. The plant was akin to hollering into a deep well and seeing if there would be a response."

And here I'd thought Jake purposely laid out the clues for me to find. "Well, it worked."

"Tell us about Wolfgang," Franz said, leaning over the seat to better see Jake.

"I sent him to make contact with M—I mean, Gerda," he replied. "She was the one person on the team I knew I could fully trust."

The last sentence was a loaded response. At some point, Jake and I would have a conversation about how Operation Blackbird had been so thoroughly compromised, but that exchange would have to wait.

Returning to the topic of Wolfgang, I asked, "You believe we don't need to worry about Wolfgang going to the VoPo or Stasi?"

"Well, I wouldn't think so," Jake said with conviction.

I wasn't so readily able to believe in the goodness of

Wolfgang Zollner. "The man is a crook. He deals in black market goods and makes regular reports to district Stasi to gain favor. Don't you think letting them know you're on the run wouldn't cross his mind?"

"He brought me food and medicine," Jake defended.

I gave a snort of disbelief. "I don't think the medicine worked."

"The man owes me his life," Jake replied sternly. "He came at the beginning. I haven't seen him in . . . four or five days. I assumed he was still searching for you or felt unsafe visiting me."

Franz and I shared another look. He shrugged and said, "Well, if you trust him . . . we wait. Try to get some rest until we leave."

"Can't. The pills will keep me going for the next few hours," Jake explained. "If I start to wane before it's time, give me another."

"How's the pain?" I asked.

"Tolerable, as long as the injury doesn't get jostled, but I might need another pain pill before we leave."

"If your friend is mobile, let us go inside to warm up," Lars suggested.

We sat on hard ladder-back chairs, around the warm stove, smoking and drinking coffee. Considering I hadn't had a cigarette since we left for Jake's extraction, the first drag was like air to a drowning man.

Lars turned on the radio to listen for any concerning reports. We heard nothing but the constant barrage of Communist propaganda.

A commercial promoting the Free German Youth and the Young Pioneers went on for a solid ten minutes.

Styled after scouting, the groups taught kids arts, crafts, life skills, and healthy exercise, while repetitively pouring Communist ideals on their heads. The organizations encouraged children to inform on their friends, neighbors, even parents. They were akin to the Hitler Youth movement under Nazism. The Communists realized the strength they could build through the younger generation to increase acceptance and active support of its political idealism. The indoctrination got under my skin, and I breathed a sigh of relief when the music returned.

Chapter Thirty-One
The Bridge

Twenty minutes before we needed to leave, the wail of a siren and shouts drew our attention away from the radio reports.

"That sounds like my neighbor. Wait here." Lars scurried through the door toward the hubbub before Franz or I could restrain him.

When Lars didn't return in five minutes, the pair of us headed out to see for ourselves. The crack between the garage doors allowed us to view what was happening on the street. Lars's neighbor, wearing the same clothes he'd had on yesterday, was down on his knees, his hands cuffed behind his back. He sobbed with great, wracking heaves and rocked back and forth, while two men in VoPo uniforms stood above him.

Lars spoke calmly, but loud enough to be heard above his neighbor's distressed howls, to the police, trying to explain the man's situation. They accused the man of throwing rocks at their truck. The man shook his head and tried to say something, but he couldn't be understood through his own weeping. Lars laid a calming hand on the man's shoulder and crouched down, speaking in soothing tones.

The man's cries lessened, and the younger of the two police officers shifted uncomfortably.

Lars kept repeating, "The man is a wounded war

hero. Can't you understand, he has brain damage from the shrapnel?"

Finally, Lars's neighbor quieted. He explained that two young boys had thrown the rocks and run off.

"See here, this man has done nothing to you," Lars asserted.

The older officer pulled the younger one aside to have a brief conversation.

Time ticked by, and we needed to be leaving soon. There would be no way to exit without being seen by the VoPo. Their presence trapped our little trio.

The police officers returned. The younger man gave an unnecessary lecture to Lars and his neighbor about disobedience against the state. To everyone's relief, it looked as though the men would be let off with a warning. The younger officer removed the handcuffs and helped the man rise to his feet.

I think we all breathed a sigh of relief, and everything would have been fine . . . if it hadn't been for the military jeep. Seeing the flashing lights on the VoPo vehicle, an old Soviet GAZ-67 pulled to a halt. The driver, wearing a Stasi uniform, waved at the VoPo.

Franz placed a hand on my shoulder and squeezed. He didn't need to tell me the encounter had now become exceedingly dangerous. I glanced up and found him holding a gun at the ready. All the East German officers carried automatic weapons. I didn't like our chances. It would be a bloodbath like the shootout at the O.K. Corral.

Nervous glances were exchanged between the VoPo, and Lars's expression turned grim. The older officer walked over to the jeep and held a quiet conversation with the Stasi agent.

The Stasi agent frowned and made a sweeping motion toward Lars and his neighbor. The officer turned and explained that he'd be taking everyone to the precinct to make a statement.

"Which precinct?" Lars asked, glancing between the Stasi agent and the VoPo.

The police officer didn't answer Lars's question. "Get in the car," he snapped.

Lars put his arm around his neighbor's shoulders.

The younger VoPo officer held out his cuffs, but the older one, probably fearful the brain-damaged man would start sobbing again, pushed his hand away and simply guided the pair into the back of their vehicle. With everyone loaded up, the police car pulled away, its siren blaring through the quiet neighborhood.

I expected the Stasi officer to follow. To my dismay, he pulled the brake and got out of his vehicle. Franz and I both moved away from our peephole and flattened ourselves against the garage door. The Stasi officer pulled on one of the doors to no avail. Lars had chained and locked them shut while we'd gone inside to wait.

We held our breaths, listening to the crunch of his boots. The footsteps got further away. I crept over to the exterior door that Lars's neighbor had used the previous day and silently slid the bolt home. Mere seconds later, the officer rattled the doorknob, trying to get in. My heart hammered so hard, I thought the man would be able to hear it through the walls. I held a hand over my mouth to silence my breathing.

Finally, after what was probably only a minute or two

but seemed like an eternity, the jeep shifted into gear and drove away.

Franz and I made our way into the room where we'd left Jake. He'd turned off the radio and stood against a wall, at the ready, with a bread knife in his good hand. "Are they gone?"

"Yes. But we've lost our driver," Franz replied.

"Damn." Jake's arm went limp at his side, and he looked as though he'd fall over if the wall wasn't holding him up.

"It doesn't matter. We have to leave. It'll be ten times worse for Lars if we're found here. We'll take the van and park it near the bridge. I'll send a message through my contact, and they can retrieve it for Lars." I caught Jake's overwarm body as it started to slide sideways.

"Time for another pill." His eyes shut tight with fatigue and pain.

"The bag is in the van. I'll get it," Franz said.

"How bad is the pain?" I asked, helping Jake to a chair.

His head hung forward. "A grinding ache."

"Getting worse?"

"Yes," he grimaced.

I hollered out the open door, "Bring pain meds, too."

"Do we have the van keys?" Jake croaked out.

An excellent question I hadn't considered.

"If not, I can hot-wire it." Franz fell to his knees in front of Jake and dug into the messenger bag. He retrieved a little yellow pill and two white ones. "This should take the edge off the pain and give you some pep."

After Jake took the medicine, we helped him into the van. Sliding onto the bench seat, he jostled his arm and clamped his lips closed to muffle a scream.

The sooner we got him to a hospital, the better.

Franz didn't have to hot-wire the car. Lars had conveniently left the keys on the dash. I found the padlock key on the ring, and after checking the street to see if the coast was clear, I pushed open the garage doors.

The Oberbaumbrucke Bridge was twenty minutes from the canning factory, and Franz drove as fast as he dared. Car traffic seemed lighter than usual. Most East Germans couldn't afford or were placed on a long waitlist for a car. Bicycles, trains, and pedestrian traffic was heavy with workers heading to their jobs. Due to the personal car limitations, military trucks, official government vehicles, and work vans like the one we drove made up most of the traffic on the road.

While we'd waited for the right time to move, the skies had darkened to pewter, and clouds churned in the heavens. I surmised we had less than half an hour before they burst.

Franz took two wrong turns — one to circumvent an accident between a car and a bicyclist, the second to avoid a VoPo precinct. Unfortunately, we turned down a dead-end road sandwiched between two five-story buildings and a pile of rubble.

"Where the hell are we?" Franz mumbled.

"Just head west," Jake supplied helpfully as Franz spun the wheel, making a three-point turn.

Our driver slammed on the brakes in the middle of the road and glared at his passenger, who was now high as a kite. "Real helpful. Want to tell me which direction is west?"

In an effort to dispel the mounting tension, I said levelly, "Here, I've a compass." I drew the brass instrument above my head and passed it to Franz.

The needle bobbed as he held it flat on his palm.

"See" — Jake tapped the crystal and smiled — "west."

If looks could kill, Jake would have melted to the floor. In his current state, the death glare Franz delivered went straight over Jake's hopped-up head.

"Give me the compass." I held out my hand. "I'll navigate us out of here."

A few more turns, and we stumbled upon one of the main roads, which oriented Franz. Traffic slowed and came to a halt due to an overturned vegetable cart in the road. Fifteen minutes later, we found a parking space a block from the bridge. Franz got out the wheelchair and brought it around to the passenger side of the van.

Jake glanced at the wheelchair and chirped, "No need for that. I'm feeling better. I'll walk."

Franz's jaw clenched and his eyes turned squinty.

My head ached from the lack of sleep, and my body was tense from Lars's run-in with the Stasi and our detour through the city. I was ready to sock Jake in the nose. Instead, I hissed through gritted teeth, "Get. In. The. Goddamn. Wheelchair."

Either the language or the manner in which I delivered it must have filtered through Jake's high. He plopped down, and Franz draped a plaid blanket over his head and shoulders. The first fat drops of rain splattered onto the brick walkway.

Franz walked a few feet ahead of Jake and I. Random cars driving onto the bridge were being stopped and papers checked by military guards. A table had been set up in front of the covered pedestrian walkway. Silently, I cursed our bad luck. Ever since the installation of the East German interior border wall, the East German government would sporadically set up checkpoints on the East/West Berlin boundary roads in an effort to stem the tide of defectors. Occasionally, they'd shut down the East Berlin side entirely for days, and only West Berliners were allowed to cross back and forth. As we approached the bridge, the rain picked up and began to fall in a steady beat. Soot and ash from the coal burning stoves and factories gave the rain a gritty texture.

"This bloody weather!" I grumbled with irritation, until I realized the storm provided a silver lining.

The guards abandoned their posts and ran for shelter. Pedestrians alike put their heads down and quickly walked or jogged beneath the arched portico of the covered walkway. I pushed Jake's wheelchair at a fast clip directly past one of the guards jogging toward the refuge.

Unfortunately, two enterprising guards were already reconnoitering and began stopping the pedestrians. Not everyone paid attention to the guards. The cacophony of the train crossing above made it chaotic and difficult to hear. A man in a black plaid coat with a pot belly and fedora pulled low ignored the new set-up and sidestepped the table.

One of the young guards noticed this move and shouted, "*Halt!*"

Ignoring the command, the man strode onward.

"Halte dich auf!" the guard called again, swinging the weapon off his shoulder.

The culprit glanced back fearfully and then took off at a dead run, dodging between oncoming pedestrians. All the guards left their station and charged after him, causing even more pedestrians heading into West Berlin to begin running in a blind panic. The portly fellow had surprisingly fleet feet. Meanwhile, Franz and I fast-walked across the bridge uninterrupted.

The brick pavers made for a bumpy ride, and I heard Jake quietly cursing as he held his injured arm as steady as possible. Another train passed overhead, screeching and rattling above us.

The East German guards pulled up short as four American soldiers stepped into their line of sight on the opposite end of the bridge. I wheeled Jake between a pair of American soldiers, slap into a torrent of rain, which immediately soaked us to the bone.

I caught up to Franz, and as luck would have it, a vacant taxi trundled up the road. Giving a sharp whistle and wave, I flagged it down. A kind German gentleman helped Franz load the wheelchair into the trunk, while I helped Jake into the cab and directed the driver to take us to the Rudolf Steiner Hospital in Charlottenburg.

The pain pill must not have had enough oomph in it, or the jarring ride across the bridge was simply too much. Jake's face was a miasma of crumpled pain. He was wet and shivering, his teeth clamped tight, and his coloring took on a grayish hue. Franz removed his jacket and put it around Jake's legs, while I rubbed his frigid hands.

Chapter Thirty-Two
Prognosis

The nurses at the hospital whisked Jake into an examination room and bade Franz and me to sit in a waiting room, where there was a woman knitting and a young man who alternately paced and tried to read the newspaper. The walls were whitewashed and the chairs hard metal. A nurse came to tell us they were taking Jake in for surgery to clean and drain the wound.

I encouraged Franz to go home and rest, and then I located a pay phone and contacted Madden. "The package has been retrieved."

"I heard. That was not your directive."

"An opportunity presented itself."

He delivered a resigned sigh. "Where are you now?"

"At the hospital in Charlottenburg."

"What's the prognosis?"

"The doctor took him in for surgery. I'll know more in a few hours." I fiddled with the compass around my neck, hoping it would bring the luck Lily believed it held.

"Come in tomorrow afternoon to debrief." Madden rang off.

My next call was to Petrus at his office.

"It's good to hear from you," Petrus said. "I'm assuming you've returned safe with the package?"

"Yes, the package has been retrieved, but there were complications." I informed him about his friend who had been taken in by the VoPo and explained where we'd parked his van so that it could be retrieved.

"I'll pass the information through appropriate channels." Petrus rang off.

Before returning to the waiting room, I stepped outside to have a cigarette. The front portico provided shelter from the rain that continued to fall at a steady pace. A damp chill hung in the air, and I hugged myself to stay warm.

♠♠♠♠

I awoke to sunlight streaming through the blinds and a dark-haired nurse shaking my shoulder.

"Your fiancé is out of surgery," she said.

I might have lied when we checked Jacob into the hospital, because I figured I'd get more information from the staff. The metal chair creaked beneath me. I rubbed the sleep from my eyes, yawned, and stretched my stiff muscles. "Can I see him?"

She shook her head. "Today is not good. He needs rest."

"What about his arm?"

"The doctor is monitoring the situation. He tried to get all the infection out . . . we'll see." She raised a shoulder. "Come back tomorrow."

That wasn't the news I was hoping to hear, and I didn't like leaving without seeing Jake. "Just for a moment? I promise, I won't wake him."

"Tomorrow." Efficiently, she straightened, tucked her clipboard beneath her arm, and strode out of the room. The heels of her white nurse's shoes tapped against the tiles with a proficient, repetitive click as she marched down the hall.

It was past noon, and my body felt a thousand years old. I dragged myself out of the hospital and down the block to the U-Bahn station. The truncated nap only made my head fuzzy and my limbs heavy. It's the reason why I didn't notice I was being followed. He had the temerity to slide into the vacant seat next to me. I turned, and our gazes locked.

The scar rumpled as he grinned at me and doffed his hat. "*Wie gehts?*"

"Do I know you?" My handbag, where my knife currently resided, was jammed between my hip and the armrest, poorly accessible. The train jolted forward, and I took the liberty of moving the purse onto my lap.

"*Ich bin Wolfgang Zollner,*" he continued in German. "We have not formally met."

I remained mute.

"We have a mutual friend."

"Mm?" I didn't know where Zollner was going, or what the purpose of this meeting was, but I didn't want to tip my hand by letting *him* know that *I* knew his identity.

Undeterred by my non-answer, Zollner continued, "I am glad he reached safety."

"Mm-hm."

"I have been trying to locate you for days."

"Mm?"

"I would have helped you." When I didn't respond to this, he asked in English, "You speak German, do you not?"

"What is it you want from me, Herr Zollner?" I responded with a steely voice in his native tongue.

"Do not take offense. I merely wished to check on the welfare of our mutual friend."

Considering the squalor of the apartment and depth of infection, I questioned the sincerity of Mr. Zollner's concern. "The doctor believes our friend will be fine in a few days," I lied. I also began to wonder if he'd sent the Stasi agent that showed up at Lars's place.

The train slowed, and I grabbed the chairback in front of me to rise. "This is my stop. Thank you for your concern. I will let him know you asked about him."

Zollner got up to allow me to pass. The train jerked to a halt, and I grabbed the pole in time to keep from knocking into him.

"Careful." Zollner solicitously took my arm.

A shiver rippled through my body. "*Auf Wiedersehen, Herr Zollner.*"

I waited on the platform, watching the doors close, to make sure Zollner didn't follow me off the U-Bahn. Then I found a phone booth and contacted the office. Neither Madden nor Samuels were available to take my call. Franz was not at the furniture store, and I had no home contact information for him. I tried Petrus next.

He came on the line. "What's wrong?"

I told him about Wolfgang Zollner and the unnerving conversation we had on the train.

"And now you believe your friend is in danger?"

"I don't know what to think."

Petrus paused and I drummed my fingers against the glass, waiting for a response.

"If you had received a direct threat . . ." He let the sentence hang. I chewed my lip, unsure if I was making a mountain out of a molehill.

"I could come by later, after my shift," Petrus offered.

Perhaps I was mistaken. After all, Zollner had made no overt threats. "No. I haven't slept in thirty hours. I'm sorry I phoned. Chalk it up to exhaustion."

"I have the day off tomorrow. I'll meet you at the hospital," he replied in a reassuring tone.

"Very well." I hung up and hailed a cab to take me back to the *Gasthaus*.

Chapter Thirty-Three
Friends & Enemies

The following morning, Petrus met me at the hospital at nine sharp. He merely raised an eyebrow when I introduced myself as Heinrich's fiancée.

Jake had been given another sedative sometime in the night and was sleeping, but the nurse said we could sit quietly. A thick bandage was wrapped around his arm and held aloft in a contraption with straps and wires. He didn't look any better than when I'd dropped him off yesterday. A white sheet was drawn up beneath his armpits, and his face matched the pallor of the covers. Intravenous and drainage tubes snaked out of both of his arms.

I pulled up the metal chair to sit at his uninjured side and placed a gentle hand on his forearm. The nurse brought an additional chair for Petrus. After half an hour of silently watching Jake's chest rise and fall, I realized how ridiculous it was for Petrus to remain. Everything looked normal. With a good night's sleep under my belt, yesterday's fears about Wolfgang seemed overblown.

I turned to Petrus to tell him he could leave, when shouts from the hallway and the clanging of a metal tray interrupted me. Instinct had the pair of us bolting out the door to investigate.

We found Wolfgang Zollner with an elbow jammed beneath the chin of an orderly, while his other hand repetitively banged the orderly's wrist against the wall. The orderly, in turn, wildly punched Wolfgang in the side.

"*Hör jetzt auf!*" Petrus barked.

One last crack, and the orderly dropped the metal syringe he'd been holding. It rolled across the floor to rest against my toes. I crouched to pick it up. The commotion brought a nurse and a doctor into the hallway. Petrus pulled Zollner off the orderly, who slumped against the wall, placing a hand to his bruised throat.

"What is going on here?" the doctor asked.

"That man is a killer," Zollner accused, pointing at the orderly.

"What nonsense is this?" The doctor turned to the orderly, looking him up and down. "Who are you? I haven't seen you before."

The orderly shoved the doctor aside and bolted down the hall.

"Stop him!" Petrus and the doctor called at once.

A nurse exiting a room stepped into the orderly's path. He elbowed her out of his way, knocking her into the wall. She cried out in distress, but the perpetrator continued his headlong flight. Zollner hollered and made to give chase, but he didn't get far, because Petrus held him in a tight grip. The orderly turned a corner and out of our sight. The nurse and doctor jogged down the hall to check on their colleague who'd gone down to her hands and knees when she'd been thrust aside. Zollner stopped fighting Petrus's grip and went limp.

"Wolfgang Zollner." His hooded gaze turned to me, and I continued, "What are you doing here? And what" —I held up the needle—"is in this syringe?"

He surprised me by responding, "If I had to guess, ricin."

"Ricin?" My brows went up, and I was tempted to drop the syringe. Ricin was a poison favored by the KGB when they wished to eliminate a defector, spy, or other dissident. "Who was that man? KGB?"

"Most likely hired by the KGB," Wolfgang replied in an offhand manner. "Our friend has made a dangerous enemy."

I pinched my lips together. "And what about you? Have your actions just made an enemy?"

"Not for long." He gave a creepy grin but didn't condescend to explain further.

The doctor returned to our group. "The police have been called. I do not know what is going on here, but you have some explaining to do, sir," he said sharply to Wolfgang. "And who are you?" he asked Petrus in an imperious tone.

"I am the police." Petrus pulled identification from his pocket. "What is your name?"

"Doctor Holtz. I am the head of internal medicine." The man puffed up his chest.

"Doctor Holtz, this man"—Petrus pointed to Zollner—"believes that syringe"—he pointed to me—"is carrying poison in it."

Everyone's attention turned to me. I held the syringe away from my body, between my thumb and forefinger. Ricin was nasty stuff, and I didn't want to take any chances.

The doctor adjusted his glasses. "The orderly was

carrying that needle?"

I nodded and went on to explain, "Herr Zollner knocked it from his hand, and I picked it up off the floor."

"Doctor, can you have it tested for ricin?" Petrus asked.

"Yes, of course, but . . . did you say ricin?" The doctor's brows furrowed with confusion.

"Ricin," Petrus repeated.

"This seems a bit farfetched," Dr. Holtz protested. "Why would a man be carrying a syringe full of ricin?"

"Why did the man run?" I narrowed my gaze and held his.

"Well, I—I'm sure I don't know," he stuttered, adjusting his glasses again.

"Doctor." Petrus still had a firm grip on Zollner, and said in a no-nonsense tone, "How quickly can the lab run tests to determine if it is ricin?"

The doctor cleared his throat. "An hour, if I tell them to rush it."

Petrus pulled Wolfgang to face him. "Mr. Zollner, I can either take you down to the station and hold you for questioning, or if you cooperate, you may remain here until the tests are complete."

"I'll wait," Zollner said with an assuredness that made me believe he knew what the hospital would find.

Everyone looked to the doctor.

"Very well." Dr. Holtz picked up the small metal tray that had fallen to the floor during the contretemps and held it out for me to place the syringe on it. "I'll take it down personally and tell the laboratory director to get started immediately." He walked away, his head shaking as if he believed not a word of what he'd been told.

"If it's not ricin, tell them to test it for cyanide," Wolfgang called out.

The doctor's shoulders crawled up to his ears, but otherwise he didn't acknowledge the suggestion.

Wolfgang turned back to me. "How is our mutual friend?"

"Sleeping." I crossed my arms.

"May I see him?"

Petrus shook his head, while I scrutinized the scarred man for a moment. "Very well. But only for a moment, and Petrus is going to keep an eye on you."

Petrus gave me a hard look, but I wanted to test a theory. Preceding Zollner into the room, I halted a few feet from Jake. "Petrus, close the door, please." Zollner went to step beyond me, but I held out my arm to prevent him. "You can see him from here."

Zollner nodded. "You still don't trust me. If Heinrich was awake, he'd make you understand."

"He said you owe him your life."

"I owe him more than that." Zollner stared at Jake—now a pale shadow of the man who approached me a few weeks ago in Buenos Aires. "He doesn't look good."

I responded without inflection, "The infection was bad."

Zollner frowned. "I tried to obtain the penicillin for him. But it is not easy, and they watch me. I was afraid I'd lead them to him."

"How did you know where he was to begin with?" Petrus asked.

"He moved the plant into the window," Zollner

explained. "It's a signal. I brought food and bandages to him. That's when he told me to find you. I didn't want to risk returning to him until I'd made contact. You spotted me . . . that day in the street. I was too obvious. I continued to search for you at the airport and train stations."

My gaze narrowed, but otherwise, I didn't respond. Still unready to place my trust in Zollner, I wouldn't allow him closer to the patient.

Our little tableau watched Jake sleep for ten minutes before Petrus finally broke the silence. "Come, Zollner. We'll find a waiting room, where I can keep an eye on you."

An hour later, Jake's eyes fluttered open. "Where am I?" he croaked.

"Steiner Hospital, Berlin. The nurse left a glass of water. Would you like some?"

"Yes."

I adjusted the head of the bed upward, so Jake could drink comfortably, and held the straw steady. He drank half the glass and lay back with a wince.

"Pain?"

"Only when I move," he sighed, staring at the bandaged arm. "Glad it's still there. What are all the tubes?"

"Drainage. They're hoping to get rid of the infection."

A nurse bustled into the room. "Awake, I see. Time to take your vitals and check the bandage. The doctor is on his way." She turned to me and said, "Why don't you go get some coffee, honey? There's a lunchroom in the East wing."

Summarily dismissed, I wandered to the East wing and found Zollner and Petrus at a table in the cafeteria, reading the newspaper.

"Everything okay?" Petrus asked, folding the paper into a smaller rectangle.

"The doctor came in to check on him." I picked up the local section of *Die Welt* and perused the headlines but was not really focused on reading until Petrus pulled my paper down.

He passed the European news section under my nose and pointed to the top right corner. The headline read, "Former SS Officer Helmut von Schweiger Arrested!"

The article went on to explain that the French government claimed they'd found and arrested von Schweiger and would be prosecuting him for war crimes. The article debated where Helmut would be prosecuted. The French government insisted, due to the heinous and egregious acts Helmut had enacted on their soil, that his trial needed to be held in a French courtroom. The rest of the article speculated on how and where the French had located Helmut. I silently surmised French intelligence had breached Argentinian soil to capture him, or they hired someone in country to do it for them. The prison did not make Helmut available to the press, so there was no quote from him.

My gaze met Petrus's. He winked at me. There was no further acknowledgment of my involvement, and there never would be. I pushed the paper back to him, shook out the local section, and held it in front of my face to hide a smile. Helmut deserved everything that was coming to him. I hoped the French trial would eviscerate him.

"There you are!"

The three of us looked up from our newspapers to find Dr. Holtz bearing down on us. He slid into the seat next to me and lowered his voice. "You were right. The hypodermic was filled with ricin. Who would do such a thing?"

I jumped out of my chair so quickly it fell over with a clatter. I didn't look back as I raced out of there at a dead run. Dodging patients, nurses, and various equipment in the halls, I continued my headlong flight until I reached Jake's room and wrenched the door open. The nurse and doctor had left, and Jake was alone.

My abrupt arrival startled him. *"Was ist los?*

"Is he okay?" Petrus followed me into the room, along with Zollner.

"I'm fine. Someone want to tell me what's going on?" Jake made to sit up, but the tubes and hanging contraption prevented him, and he lay back with a groan.

"Stay with him. I need to make a phone call." I jogged my way to the nearest phone booth.

When Madden finally came on the line, I didn't mince words. "Greyhound's life is in danger. KGB tried to poison him."

"Whoa, slow down. Tell me from the beginning," Madden said in calming tones.

I drew in three deep breaths and started again. "Someone dressed as an orderly, probably KGB, was on the way to Greyhound's room to eliminate him. Poison of choice was ricin. The hospital has already tested it."

"Where is Greyhound now?" Madden asked in a

sharp tone.

"Still at the hospital. I've got a police officer guarding him."

"I'll make arrangements to get him out."

"When?"

"Today." The line went dead.

I replaced the handset and leaned my forehead against the glass wall of the phone booth. My breaths still came out in little pants, and I wasn't sure if it was from running around or the realization of how close we'd come to losing Jake. I'd been so suspicious of Zollner, I hadn't truly believed the hypodermic carried ricin.

Chapter Thirty-Four
Recovery & Reassignment

Jake was airlifted out of Berlin to the 97th General Hospital in Frankfurt, one of the busiest American military hospitals in Germany. Originally taken over during the war, the military had expanded it to hold over five hundred beds. I spent the afternoon debriefing Madden, then packed my bags and got myself on a duty train out of Berlin that night.

I sat vigil at Jake's bedside as his fever spiked and he suffered through bouts of delirium. My sinuses burned from the constant stink of hospital antiseptic. Forty-eight hours after his arrival, Jake took a turn for the worse. The infection began affecting his vital organs. The surgeons performed emergency surgery to amputate the rotting arm.

Doctors and nurses came and went. I remained the constant by his side. Arriving by eight in the morning, I'd stay until ten at night.

Sometime on day three or four—the days blended into one another—a pretty, redheaded nurse trotted into the room one evening and said, "Visiting hours are over. You'll have to leave. You can come back tomorrow at ten. You look like hell, honey. Go home. Get your beauty sleep. He wouldn't want to see you looking so drawn, dear." She had the temerity to pat my hand as if reassuring a child.

I marched out of the room, found an unoccupied office with a telephone, and made a long-distance call to a NATO general based in Bonn, with whom I'd once slept.

"How's your wife?" I asked. Did I mention he was married when we slept together?

"What do you want?" the general responded.

After that, no one bothered to tell Gerda Scholtz that she needed to leave.

On day five, I awoke late and didn't arrive until close to ten. I walked into Jake's room to find him sitting up, some color in his cheeks, looking less like the Grim Reaper hovered nearby. His hair was combed back, and someone had given him a shave. Doris, a nurse, with a mole the size of a pencil eraser on her chin, who wore her hair in a tight, steel-colored chignon, was helping him eat scrambled eggs. The first solid food he'd had in days.

"Oh, you are a silver-tongued charmer, Mr. Wagner." She gave a hearty laugh, and her jowls shook.

Jake saw me in the doorway and his eyes brightened with pleasure. A warm shiver ran down my spine.

"I wasn't sure if you were real or a dream," he murmured.

"Oh, your fiancée has been here every day since you arrived. We'd need a forklift to get her out," the nurse said.

Doris and I had come to a silent agreement. Whenever she'd come in to take care of Jake, I'd quietly step aside or exit until she finished. She'd given me updates, and when Jake's vitals began to slide downhill, it was Doris who I'd run to tell.

Jake didn't bat an eye when Doris called me his fiancée. I grinned at the pair. "Good morning, Doris. I see the patient is in his right mind today."

"A welcome relief for all of you, I'm sure," Jake replied.

"In just a few weeks, he'll be right as rain." Doris rose ponderously, wiped Jake's mouth, and removed the empty plate. "Would you like more tea?"

"I'll take a coffee," Jake said hopefully.

Doris shook her head. "Not until the doctor says so. In the meantime, I have a nice Earl Grey, if that would make it better."

"Maybe later."

Doris bustled out of the room, her rubber shoes squeaking as the door closed behind her.

We were alone, and the room remained silent as I removed my coat and hat to lay them on the foot of the bed. "You seem much improved." I crossed my legs and tilted my head.

His cheeks were less hollowed and the circles beneath his eyes were no longer deeply purpled. "They took the arm." He glanced at the fresh bandages on his stump. The surgeons had to amputate just above the elbow.

"Yes." I nodded solemnly. "It was either you or the arm."

"Can't believe I made it through the damn war with barely a scratch. One day in East Berlin and—this." He waved at the denuded stump.

"Bad luck."

"It was more than bloody bad luck. It was that bastard, Bernard." He stared angrily out the window.

"Eva, too."

His head spun back to me. "Eva?"

"I suppose you don't know. It goes deeper than Bernard and Eva. The Berlin station chief is being investigated, along with half a dozen of his lackeys." Turning away from his horror-struck expression, I brushed away a piece of lint. "You and me, we're lucky to be alive."

"Good God. I—I can't believe . . ." He stared at me. "Criminy. I apologize for dragging you into this mess."

"Why *did* you drag me into it? There were any number of operatives you could have tapped. Why me?"

He didn't answer immediately. His jaw flexed and he finally said, "I knew I could trust you."

It sounded too simple, but in the game of espionage, trust could be a slim commodity. "You knew Bernard was dirty?"

He shook his head. "I had nothing concrete. Only a comment made at a party, two years ago."

"Knowing our background, I'm surprised they allowed you to put me on the team," I commented.

His fingers fidgeted with the counterpane. "I think you were in more danger than I realized. Bernard had almost certainly planned to pin Ivanov's death on you. If you made it back alive, he could argue that your last mission left you mentally deranged."

"I don't suppose, I was meant to make it out alive," I replied faintly.

"No, I suppose not," he said baldly. "Is Eva . . . behind bars?"

"She's dead. Took her own life." I shrugged, closely

watching Jake's features. After all, they had been lovers. But I could not detect any sort of devastation or regret in his expression. "She knew it was the end."

His gaze shuttered. "The Ivanovs?"

"Safe."

His eyes popped open, and he watched me, unblinking. "How did you do it? If the station chief was a mole . . ."

Visions of Eva bleeding out on the kitchen floor and Katya crying in the back of the VW flashed through my mind. A siren wailed as an ambulance arrived at the hospital. I wandered over to the window and pulled it shut. Sighing, I replied, "I'll tell you about it one day . . . but not today."

"If you prefer, I can request the file and read about it."

I remained with my back to Jake, watching the medics carry their patient out on a stretcher. "Perhaps."

After a while, he said, "So . . . how long have we been affianced?"

A grin crossed my face, and I turned back to him. "Um, let me think . . . what is today—"Counting on my fingers, I came up with "—seven days. It was quite a whirlwind romance."

"And the reason we are affianced?"

"Access. The medical staff has seen fit to keep your *fiancée* informed of the situation. I doubt a female *'friend'* would receive the same courtesy. Your parents are gone, and I didn't know how to contact your sister. This seemed simpler. Apparently, the company doesn't know either," I gently scolded. "Who *did* you list for your emergency contact?"

"It's probably still my father. I never updated the paperwork."

I knew his father had passed away a year ago, and his mother six months prior to that. I'd been out of the country and didn't hear about it until I'd received a letter from my mother informing me.

I sat on the bed, on his uninjured side, and reached over to place my hand on his. "You can put my name down."

I went to draw my hand away, but Jake caught it and murmured in a serious tone, "Thank you."

"Of course." I said lightheartedly, "What good is a fake fiancée if you can't call on her for an emergency?"

"No. I mean it. *Thank you*," he replied in a serious tone. Those beautiful green eyes pierced my soul and sent a shiver down my spine. "I'd be dead if you hadn't come."

"Ah, well." Blushing, I glanced away from that penetrating gaze. "I couldn't leave you to rot under the dismal ministrations of Zollner. Whom, by the way, you also owe a great deal."

"That's what I understand." Jake's thumb brushed against my palm. "I suppose we're even now."

"Tell me about him." I pulled my hand away.

"Where are you going?" He stuck out his lip like a pouting little boy.

"To sit on the chair, silly."

Jake scooted to the side and patted the bed next to him. "Sit here, next to me."

"I wouldn't want to jostle your arm."

"You won't." He patted the bed again.

"It would be indecorous for me to climb onto your bed," I admonished.

"You're my fiancée. People will think it's sweet. Besides . . ."

I stood with my arms akimbo, chewing my lower lip.

"It'll be like that time I found you in your family's cellar during the thunderstorm. Only now, I'm the one who needs comforting."

The long-forgotten memory bubbled to the surface. I was ten. Gra-mere had gone to market. Fred and I were left alone at home. Jake and Hugh came over, and Fred sent me to the cellar to get a can of peaches. Fred must have forgotten about sending me to fetch the peaches. The jamb to the cellar needed repairs, the door closed behind me, and I couldn't reopen it. The storm that had been brewing all day charged in like an angry grizzly, and my cries couldn't be heard over the pounding rain on the tin roof. Then the thunder began.

Finally, Jake had wrenched open the door. He found me curled up at the bottom of the stairs, shaking and incoherently mewling. I remembered a comforting arm winding around my shoulders and being pulled into an embrace that smelled of Lifebuoy soap and talcum powder. He held me until the storm slackened.

"Miriam?"

The scent of disinfectant and the glare of the harsh lighting intruded on my thoughts, and the hospital room spun back into focus. "I'd forgotten about that incident. You were . . . kind to me."

"Fred . . ." He coughed. "Fred had a mean streak when it came to you. Less so when we got into high school, but when we were kids . . ."

"I thought it was just me," I mused and climbed onto the bed, sitting stiff and close to the edge. "Better?"

"Much. I can feel the healing happening as we speak."

I rolled my eyes. "Tell me about Wolfgang."

"Four years ago, I was following a Czech dissident on an op in East Germany. Zollner was crossing the street and got hit by a car."

"Were you working together?" My precarious position made me uncomfortable. I shifted my shoulders for better purchase.

"No, it was a freak accident. I acted on instinct. If I'd been thinking properly, I never would have drawn attention to myself. The driver of the car sped away, leaving Zollner in the street with his face sliced open, a couple of broken ribs, and a broken leg. Another Samaritan who witnessed the hit and run helped me load Wolfgang into my car." Jake took my left hand in his. "I drove him to the Charité Hospital. He credits me with saving his life. After that, it was easy to turn him into a source."

"Well, he saved your life, possibly at great risk to his own."

"As did you." He turned my hand over, running his thumb over the knuckles, and *tsked*. "People must think I'm a cheapskate or a slouch. I didn't give you a proper engagement ring. How did you explain that?"

"I didn't. Nobody asked, but I'll remember to tell anyone who does that you're a cheapskate." I bumped his shoulder in jest, but he didn't return my amusement. He continued to trace my knuckles with his thumb in contemplative thought.

♠♠♠♠

The following day, we reminisced with a play-by-play of the high school regional basketball finals in which Jake, Hugh, and Fred played. Talking about the good old days appeared to cheer him, and I did whatever I could to keep up his spirits.

"We won by nine points!" Jake told Doris.

She smiled, writing on her clipboard. "Were you two high school sweethearts?"

"Oh, no!" I exclaimed, then blanched at my stark response. "I mean . . . he didn't notice me until . . . later," I ended lamely, sipping my coffee to hide my discomfiture.

"That's not true," Jake denied. "My best friend stole the march over me."

My brows rose with incredulous disbelief. "What?"

"It wouldn't have mattered," Jake continued with regret. "You only had eyes for Hugh."

He wasn't wrong, and I didn't deny it. As a matter of fact, except for the crush I had on Jacob for about a year after the Charleston Chew incident, I hadn't thought much about him. He'd simply been a regular fixture in Fred's life, and by extension, mine.

Doris clicked her tongue. "Everything works out in the end. I'll be back in an hour, and we'll go for our afternoon walk. Get ready, Herr Werner!"

The day was bright, without a cloud in the sky, and Jake watched a robin land on the ledge outside his window.

I fidgeted with my earring and licked my lips. "Is it true?"

"Yes," he confessed, continuing to stare out the window. "While Hugh only took notice at your grandmother's funeral, I'd been watching you grow from a charming little girl into a beautiful young woman ever since the day I bought you a candy bar at the Five & Dime.

My mouth bobbed, and I fidgeted with the compass around my neck. "But . . . why didn't you say anything?"

His gaze speared me. "Because whenever Hugh walked into a room, every other boy disappeared."

I put my palms against my warm cheeks. "Was I that obvious?"

"I realized, once Hugh reciprocated your feelings, the schoolgirl crush turned into love." He gave a single-shoulder shrug, bowed his head, and smoothed the blanket.

The conversation was a revelation to me. Bits and pieces of my childhood refocused, as if I was seeing events for the first time. Jake picking up my books that some clod had knocked out of my arms on the first day of high school. Jake clapping energetically at my piano recital over top of my brother's booing. Jake watching me practice for cheerleader tryouts and giving pointers which got me on the team.

The ticking of my watch sounded loud in the stillness.

Though he wouldn't look at me, he finally broke the tension with a self-mocking tone. "Don't worry. I moved on."

"Oh, I remember," I teased. "What was the name of

that copper-haired girl you dated in college . . . Julia?"

Jake finally turned his gaze back to me with a brow-wiggling leer. "Ah, the fair Julia. She was *something*."

"What happened to her?"

"She married a pig farmer. I believe they have five children."

I choked, almost spilling my coffee. "A pig farmer! I can't imagine. I foresaw a Fifth Avenue New York lifestyle for the fair Julia."

"Julia wanted to marry money. Apparently, there are good profits to be made in pig farming."

I couldn't help the gale of laughter that overcame me, and it was a pleasure to see Jacob join me.

♠♠♠♠

Two days later, I received a directive to report to the London office. Greg wanted me to return as Brigitte Moreau and develop Sara as a source.

When I shared my reassignment with Jake, he grunted, "It's about time you got back to work and stopped mollycoddling me. You've got a job to do, and it's important."

I would have believed his gruff nonchalance had I not witnessed the dismay cross his features before he swiftly looked away to rearrange the newspapers lying in his lap.

"Jacob." I laid a hand on his to stop the paper rattling. "I don't have to do this."

"Of course, you do!" he snapped, turning an unexpectedly crystal-sharp gaze on me.

"No. I can stay here."

"What for?" he bit out nastily.

My head jerked at his unexpected attack. "Why, to—to . . . help you . . . recover."

His mouth flattened into a straight line. "There are a hundred doctors and nurses here to *help* me. Doris is more than up to the task. Your country needs your help. Not me."

On occasion, he'd been cantankerous and snappish with the staff, but I'd always been able to cajole him into better spirits. This was the first time he'd directed that ire at me.

"Jacob—" I murmured.

"Heinrich," he hissed, "and *I* am *not* the first man to lose an arm. I don't need your pity."

Shocked by his attitude, I drew in a shaky breath and calmly responded, "Yes, I realize that. I just thought . . ." What? What did I just think?

The past month, I'd woken to nightmares of Jake's death, and I'd moved heaven and earth to get both of us out of a dire situation. We'd shared memories. I'd helped him stumble around the room, his legs as weak as those of a newborn colt. We'd snuggled together in the bed, reading the newspaper. His caress. Did I no longer matter to him . . . as he'd come to matter to me? He'd confessed to a childhood crush. Was that it, a dead-and-gone crush?

I put a fist to my heart and whispered, "I thought we were . . . family? I—I thought you and I . . ."

His gaze narrowed and his mouth worked. He opened and closed it twice. He turned away to stare into the dark sky. "Miriam," he whispered my real name, "there is nothing for you here."

A pickax to the heart, that one was. I sucked in a breath and spoke in a deadened tone, "I see. I'll stop by tomorrow to say goodbye."

"What time is your flight?" He wouldn't look at me.

"Ten fifteen."

"Don't bother. You need time to prepare."

"It's not a bother." I gripped his hand, hard. "*You're* not a bother."

His gaze shifted to contemplate my hand. Eventually, he flipped his palm up to curl around mine as he'd done so many times this week. "I don't want you to think I'm ungrateful," he sighed. "I know I owe my life to you."

I muttered, "Don't—"

He cleared his throat, and those pain-filled, glassy eyes finally met mine. "You need to go. It's the job."

"My first free weekend, I'll come back to visit." I brushed aside the lock of hair that had fallen across his brow. I cleared my throat and said sternly, "I expect to see improvement."

He released my hand and, with the lightness of a feather, brushed my cheek, tickled my ear, and then, cupping his fingers at the base of my neck, pulled me forward. Our lips met. The kiss filled me with a warmth that spread outward from my belly, all the way up my spine.

We broke apart, and he leaned his forehead against mine. "Be careful."

"Always." I gathered my things and, on the way out the door, called, "See you tomorrow."

"No."

My feet halted in the doorway. "What? I thought--"

"Don't come back tomorrow. This is our goodbye."

"But—"

"The next time I see you, I want to be on my own two feet. Not in a bloody hospital gown."

I licked my lips and fidgeted with the handle of the handbag. "If that's what you want . . ."

"Goodbye, Gerda." He winked.

"Goodbye, Heinrich."

The whisper of my real name followed me down the hall. That whisper of my name upon his lips would haunt my dreams in the weeks to come.

My first chance to visit Jake happened in mid-November. When I arrived at the hospital, the first person I ran into was Doris. "What are you doing here, doll? Your sweetheart left last week. Didn't anyone tell you?"

My body went cold, and I dropped my handbag. "Nobody told me." I crouched to pick it up. "D-did he . . . leave me a message?"

She noticed my befuddlement and bereft expression. With pity in her eyes, she responded, "Why, no, honey, he didn't. I told him to send you a letter—even brought him stationary. Said he was looking forward to going home."

Recalling Doris believed we were engaged, I straightened and shook off the melancholy. "Yes, I—I see. I've been traveling for work. His letter must have . . . gone astray."

"Well, there you have it. A simple missed communication. That man talked about you every day."

She wished me luck and toddled off to her next patient.

I sent a telegram to his home in Pennsylvania, only to have it go unanswered. My query to Foggy Bottom led nowhere.

Even Greg couldn't get a location on Greyhound. Or, if he did, the information was above my security clearance. "He's a ghost, Little Girl. You know the business. New job, new name."

There was little else I could do to locate Jake if he didn't want to be found. The lack of communication let me know that he didn't want me to find him. Outwardly, I took the news with nonchalance, but I think Greg realized how hurt I'd been by Jake's disappearance.

Chapter Thirty-Five
Hannukah Miracles

Pennsylvania, December 12, 1952

"Miriam!" my mother hollered from the front door.

"In the kitchen," I called. "I'm finishing the latkes." The potato cakes popped and sizzled in the oil. Two dozen of them warmed in a casserole dish on the back burner. Fish baked in the oven, and sweet potatoes boiled on the stove.

"I hope you made plenty. We have two more guests joining us for Hannukah tonight." She entered the kitchen. "Friends of yours."

"Oh? Who?" I laid the last latke on the paper to drain and turned with the spatula still in my hand.

A beautiful, smiling woman trailed my mother into the kitchen.

"Lily?" I dropped the spatula and wrapped my arms around her, being careful of her protruding belly. We hadn't seen each other since the London Embassy. I stepped back to admire her. "You're absolutely glowing. When are you due?"

"End of March." She rubbed her belly lovingly.

"Where is Charlie?"

"Bringing in the luggage."

"We'll put them in the yellow room," Mom said.

My brow furrowed in confusion, and I shook my head in disbelief. "What are you doing here? Should you be traveling?" There'd been at least one miscarriage and years when Lily couldn't get pregnant. I thought they'd given up.

"The doctor said it's fine." Her smile lit up the room. "Besides, I've never celebrated Hannukah. When I got your letter about traveling stateside, we decided to come up."

"Did you know about this?" I asked Mother.

She gave a sly grin and winked. "I'll finish dinner. We only have forty minutes before sundown." Mother shooed me away from the stove. "Walter is on his way over with the *sufganiyot,* and Joseph and Clara should be arriving soon. Show your friends to their room so they can freshen up. Thank you, dear."

I removed my apron.

"My, don't you look pretty in that blue dress," she commented, making me wonder, once again, if an alien had taken over my mother's body while I'd been gone.

In reality, I knew it was no alien. A few weeks ago, one of her letters reached me. It had been simple and to the point.

Please come home for Hannukah, I have something of vital importance to tell you.

Love, Mom.

Mother had never summoned me in quite that fashion. Normally, she rudely hinted that I'd neglected her over the years, and she would die a withered, lonely woman. I generally ignored those missives, but the last letter had me envisioning the worst. I thought she had cancer or some other terminal disease, and I'd find her wasting away.

Instead, what I found was my fifty-seven-year-old mother looking younger than she had in years, with a bounce in her step and a kindness in her eyes that I'd only witnessed her bestow upon my brother. Not once had she delivered one of her cuttingly "helpful" lifestyle suggestions since I'd arrived home. Instead, she'd complimented me on my clothes, shoes, and hairstyle. On my second evening home, we ate dinner at a local Italian restaurant, and I discovered the reason for her transformation. He joined us for dinner that night.

Walter Hutchins, the owner of the local hardware store in town, had been a widower for the past five years. Apparently, after his wife died, my mother started taking meals to him, which turned into sharing meals every night, which eventually turned into a love affair. Walter had asked her to marry him. She said yes. Considering the change in my mother, I did not begrudge her this second chance at love. As a matter of fact, I envied her. The same way I envied Lily as I watched Charlie wrap his arm around her shoulders while they waited for me to make them cocktails.

Walter arrived with the *sufganiyot,* or jelly donuts, fresh from the local bakery. My Aunt Clara and Uncle Joseph came soon after. At sundown, we lit the first candle on the menorah before gathering around my mother's antique oak table. Not much had changed in the house since I'd left. The same green silk curtains hung in the windows, and we ate off my Gra-mere's Royal Doulton china with gold rims and a blue medallion in the center. The stained, blue tablecloth was the same one I'd grown up with. A pair of dreidels rested next to the flower centerpiece, and gold, foil-wrapped chocolate coins were scattered around the table. We'd just finished passing the serving dishes when the doorbell rang.

"I wonder who that could be." Mother made to rise.

"I believe it's for Miriam," Charlie said, wiping his mouth with a napkin.

All eyes turned to me. Charlie gave me a nod. With confusion, I went to answer the door.

He wore a grey topcoat over a black suit, black tie, and white dress shirt. The left arm of his coat was pinned at his shoulder. His eyes were no longer sunken, his cheeks were rosy from the cold air, and he'd put on some weight. The fedora he wore was perched jauntily over his brow, and the scent of his piney aftershave enveloped me.

My mouth dropped. "Jacob?"

"Hello, Miriam." He gave me a tentative smile, which reached those beautiful, soul-searching eyes.

My heartbeat sped up. A million thoughts, questions, and comments flooded my brain. I stood speechless, unsure which one to ask first.

The smile fell away, and he held out a candy bar toward me. "This is for you."

I took the gift from his hand. "A Charleston Chew?"

"Strawberry. Your favorite. Right?"

My eyes glanced from the candy bar, to Jacob, and back again.

"Miriam?" He whispered my name the same way I'd heard it floating down the hospital hall the last time we saw each other.

"Who is it, Miriam?" Mother called.

Her voice jolted me out of my fugue state, and

grabbing Jake's hand, I pulled him into the house, all the way to the dining room. Nobody spoke, but I watched a self-satisfied grin blossom on Lily's face.

My mother scrutinized our new guest, and then recognition spread across her features. "Why, Jacob Devlin, as I live and breathe! Is that really you?"

"Yes, ma'am." He nodded. "Sorry to interrupt your dinner like this, but I've something to discuss with Miriam. I can come back later, if you prefer."

"You do?" I asked.

"Nonsense, we've barely started." Mother brushed aside his apology. "You must join us. Joe, move down so Jacob can sit next to Miriam." Before he could protest further, Mother was pulling another plate from the china cabinet.

My aunt and uncle welcomed Jake, and questions pelted him from all sides. I supposed Jake was as close to the prodigal son as my mother could get.

"Miriam, fetch another napkin from the pantry," Mother directed over the din as our guests shifted their chairs to make room. "What's that in your hand?"

"It's a Charleston Chew. Strawberry." I hadn't let go of Jake's hand, nor moved to get the napkin. "Jake gave it to me."

Mother paused her table setting. "Oh, your favorite. Right?"

"Right." I nodded giddily.

"I always knew you were a thoughtful boy, Jacob. I recall that time he brought one back for you from the Five & Dime, after you'd fallen and torn your dress. Remember, Miriam?" Mother put the dish and a fork and knife on the table.

Jake and I shared a look, and I couldn't hold back the bright sunshine smile that blazed across my face. "I remember."

"Now let go of Jacob, so he can take off his coat and get settled. Would you like a glass of Manischewitz wine, dear boy?"

I finally released him, and he removed his hat. "Yes, ma'am, that would be nice."

The evening was like having an out-of-body experience. There were so many questions I wanted to ask Jake, but I couldn't with everyone around. Twice, I tried pulling him aside, only to be hailed by Mother, or my aunt, or my uncle.

The evening seemed interminable. After dinner we spun the dreidel and used the foil-wrapped chocolate coins as our gelt. Lily clapped her hands every time she won—which she did, often—ending up with a nice pile of chocolates. Then Aunt Clara sat at the piano and played the *Dreidel Song* before moving on to hits from the '40s, like *Chattanooga Choo Choo*, and *Boogie Woogie Bugle Boy*.

Finally, the night wound down. My aunt and uncle departed. Walter took his leave, and a yawning Lily said goodnight.

"Wait Lily, I have something for you." She followed me to the kitchen, where I'd left my purse. I removed a tiny velvet bag. "Hold out your hand."

The brass compass plopped onto her palm. "Are you sure you're finished with it?" She tilted her head.

I placed a hand on her belly. "You'll need its luck for

your new family."

A knowing smile crossed her face. "I told you it was lucky." She gave me a hug, fetched her husband, and retreated upstairs.

Finally, we were alone. I drew Jake into the parlor and invited him to sit. He remained standing. Now that we were alone, I didn't know where to start. Instead, I poked at the smoldering embers in the grate. He removed the poker from my hand and hung it on the rack. He caressed my shoulder, and I took a step backward.

I didn't know why he was here, and I wanted answers before things went any further. "What did you need to discuss with me?"

"It would seem, I've been remiss."

That was a loaded response. He'd basically disappeared on me. I crossed my arms and waited for him to continue.

Instead, he descended to one knee and drew a ruby-red velvet box from his pocket. "I forgot to give my fiancée a ring."

"Oh, Jacob," I whispered, taking the box from him. Inside lay an octagonal-cut diamond surrounded by white gold filigree, with a dozen tiny emeralds inlaid in the flowered filigree design.

"It was my mother's."

"I remember her wearing it. It's beautiful."

"Put it on, see if it fits."

Oh, I desperately wanted that ring on my finger, but there were too many unanswered questions. I shut the lid. "Why did you disappear without a word, Jacob? I thought you didn't care. You said you had nothing to give me."

With a deep sigh, he rose to his feet. "I know what I did was wrong, disappearing on you. But I needed time to get my head on straight. After I lost the arm"—he glanced at the stump—"I didn't think I could be of use to you. I thought I would be an anchor tied around your neck. Last week, I was in D.C. and ran into Lily." He stared at his shoes. "I didn't know what I could do as a cripple. After my rehabilitation, the agency released me."

"I-I didn't know."

"Lily found me sitting on a park bench alone and moping in self-pity. She dragged me to lunch and demanded to know what was going on. She made me realize what a fool I'd been at the hospital." He let out a low whistle. "She really ripped up at me. Told me, in no uncertain terms, I was a horse's ass for making the decision for you. For us."

"Yes," I agreed heartily.

"I know." He fidgeted with his suit pocket. "Everything she said was true. That last day in the hospital, the day you left—it was like watching my heart walk out the door."

"Oh, Jake." I caressed his cheek.

He slid my palm to his lips and kissed it. "The day after I met up with Lily, I received a summons to report to the State Department. Looks like I'm not so useless after all."

I put a finger to his lips. "I never thought you were useless."

"Do you think … you can put in for a transfer to D.C.? We could … give it a go?"

"Yes."

His face brightened. "Yes? You'll come to D.C.?"

My arms snaked around his neck. "Yes, Jacob Devlin, I'll do more than that. I'll marry you."

There were many more issues we needed to discuss, but not tonight. Tonight, was for celebrating miracles and light.

Author's Note

Operation Blackbird and the character Oleg Ivanov was inspired by Soviet defector Grigori Alexandrovich Tokaev. Born in Ossetia, Russia, in 1909, Tokaev grew to become a Soviet rocketry scientist and politician. Tokaev was initially an avid pro-Communist, however, he later became disillusioned and joined an opposition group that sought to remove Stalin from power. During World War II, Tokaev flew bombing raids over Stalingrad in American planes and rose to the rank of lieutenant colonel. Following the war, he was sent to Berlin as a ranking member of the Soviet Control Commission.

During his time in Berlin, Tokaev discovered a Soviet intelligence services plan to kidnap German rocket scientist Eugene Sänger, along with other leading Western scientists. Tokaev was not only concerned about the international political ramifications of the potential kidnapping plot, but he also began to fear his membership in the anti-Stalinist group had been discovered putting his life and those of his family in jeopardy. He reached out to British intelligence in East Berlin. Though under constant surveillance by the NKVD (the KGB precursor), in 1947, Tokaev and his family crossed into the British sector of West Berlin to seek asylum. Unfortunately, the full, detailed story of his escape is buried in a redacted British intelligence file.

After receiving asylum, Tokaev and his family were given false identifications and sent to live in the United Kingdom. In exchange for his Soviet military secrets, British intelligence protected the Tokaevs from potential assassination by the Soviets. After defecting Tokaev began to use the Ossetian version of his surname, Tokaty.

In 1953, Grigori Tokaty became a leading university lecturer on aeronautics and rocketry. During the 1960s, Tokaty was invited to consult on the Apollo Lunar mission. By 1967, Tokaty became a full professor at the City University in London, working in the Aeronautics and Space Technology Department. Grigori Tokaty died in Surrey, England, November 23, 2003, at the age of 94.

Acknowledgements

It's been five years since *The Brass Compass* was published, and, during that time, I had many calls and emails from readers begging for a sequel. Initially, I planned to create the story around Lily. However, to have continued Lily in this story, I would have had to kill off Charlie. After mulling it over, I decided I didn't want to unwind her happily-ever-after, which led to the development of Miriam's story. Once again, I couldn't have brought *Operation Blackbird* to you without help.

Thanks to Bill Rapp for answering all my oddball questions about Cold War Berlin, London clubs, and possible meeting places for clandestine and back-channel meetings. Your descriptions of the East Berlin architecture, automobiles and general atmosphere were invaluable. Historical memoirs such as *Forty Autumns*, by Nina Willner, and Brigitte Reimann's, *I Have No Regrets: Diaries 1955-1963* gave me insight into the lives of those forced to live beneath an authoritarian government.

Thanks to my father, Bill, who lived in Argentina in the 1950s. Your stories and photos of Buenos Aires allowed me to open Miriam's story at the Recoleta. To my editor Emily, you know I couldn't put out a decent product without you. Thanks for catching my plot holes and correcting those silly typos.

Finally, to my husband and family, I couldn't do it without your support.

About the Author

Ellen Butler is the award-winning author of *The Brass Compass* and bestselling author of the Karina Cardinal Mysteries. *The Brass Compass,* a prequel to *Operation Blackbird,* won multiple awards, including a Firebird Award an Indie Reader Discovery Award, and became an international Amazon bestseller in the US, Canada, Australia, and the United Kingdom. Ellen's grandfather was a cryptographer during WWII and sparked her interest in the OSS (the precursor to the CIA). She holds a Master's in Public Administration and Policy, and her experiences living and working in the Washington, D.C., area inspires her love of spy thrillers.

You can find Ellen at:
Website ~ www.EllenButler.net
Facebook ~ www.facebook.com/EllenButlerBooks
Twitter ~ @EButlerBooks
Instagram ~ @ebutlerbooks
Goodreads ~ www.goodreads.com/EllenButlerBooks

Novels by Ellen Butler

Suspense/Mystery
The Brass Compass
Poplar Place
Isabella's Painting (Karina Cardinal Mystery, Book 1)
Fatal Legislation (Karina Cardinal Mystery, Book 2)
Diamonds & Deception (Karina Cardinal Mystery, Book 3)
Pharaoh's Forgery (Karina Cardinal Mystery, Book 4)
Swindler's Revenge (Karina Cardinal Mystery, Book 5)

Contemporary Romance
Heart of Design
Planning for Love
Art of Affection
Second Chance Christmas

Made in the USA
Las Vegas, NV
21 December 2022

63842341R00199